the
wrong
Girl

CHAPTER 1
JAKE

A high-pitched voice carried down the hall. "Daaaad, where's my Spider-man book?"

I was elbows deep in a box full of loose tupperware, searching for something that resembled the dishes I still hadn't unpacked. "I don't know, Ethan; where did you leave it?"

"*I* didn't leave it anywhere. *You* packed it!" The reply was accusatory.

He sounded exactly like his mother, which immediately raised my hackles. I forced myself to draw in a slow breath and unclench my jaw before replying.

"Then check the boxes in your room, buddy. Anything that was yours went in there."

"There's like a hundred of them!" Oh man, here

we go. "I'll *never* find it." I could practically hear the tears already.

I glanced up to spot Olivia silently watching me with wide brown eyes. "Honey, can you please go help your brother find his comic books? There should be a box in his room labeled 'books.'"

"Sure Dad," she nodded seriously, then took off down the hallway with the determination of a soldier headed into battle.

"Thanks Livvie!" I called after her, but if she heard me, she didn't reply.

Giving up, I scooped an armload of plastic wear out of the box and directly onto the floor, and I could finally spot the multi-colored dishes the kids liked at the bottom of the carton.

Olivia would eat on whatever I gave her—I'd swear she was easier than half the Airmen I led—but Ethan insisted they have the same. And if he didn't have his particular green plate and special blue cup, the world would implode.

The doctor agreed with me that his behavior was a little immature for seven, but he *also* agreed with my ex wife that our home life was probably a contributing factor. He said Ethan would grow out of it when he was ready.

So, in the meantime, I had to placate my own tiny dictator.

And they say America doesn't negotiate with terrorists.

By the time the kids appeared, I had two bowls of cereal, twin glasses of orange juice, and two slices of toast with peanut butter—cut into triangles, naturally—set out on the dining table. The house was still an absolute wreck from the move, but I managed to clear a space for them to eat.

Ethan's splotchy face and glossy eyes were a dead giveaway: he had definitely been on the verge of another meltdown, even though the comic book was clenched in one hand.

I purposefully made my voice extra bright. "Oh great, you found it. Thank you, Olivia!" I hinted.

My eldest gave me a silent nod, then steered her younger brother to their seats and pushed him in. He muttered a thank you, then inspected his meal carefully and compared it to his sister's. Once he was satisfied, he picked up his spoon.

Olivia followed suit, and when my eggs were ready, I slid them onto a matching plastic plate and joined them at the table with my coffee.

"Daddy, you can't use that. It's *my* plate." Ethan glared at me with all the fire a seven-year-old could muster.

"I'm sorry buddy, but I couldn't find the norm—I mean, I couldn't find my plates in all the boxes. Do you mind if I use this one just for breakfast? I promise I'll unpack before you guys come back from Gramma and Grandpa's Sunday."

A sweat broke out on my back. If my troops could

3

only see me now, pouring sweat in fear of an angry second grader.

Ethan seemed to consider it, then nodded seriously. "Okay, but *only* for breakfast."

"Thanks buddy," I smiled, but he'd already turned his attention back to his lucky charms and was busily scooping out the marshmallows.

Breakfast was always a quiet affair for us. To be fair, all meals seemed rather quiet, as of late. The kids and I... were still getting used to each other. It was Cheryl who knew how to lighten Olivia up or calm Ethan down with just the right words.

Which made sense. She was their mother. And while I was either working all day or deployed for months, she had seen them through every skinned knee and tantrum.

Of course, she had also just decided she was over it and left—not even pretending to want our children. She stuck around to see the divorce through and made some vague promises about 'having the kids to visit' once she 'was settled' and then disappeared. Over a year later and she hadn't even called them. She'd answer if we called, but they'd pretty much stopped asking for her.

It fucking killed me, but I knew it was a good sign that they weren't relying on her for emotional support any more.

I just wished I was better at giving that to them.

I glanced at my watch and sighed, then finished

the last gulp of my coffee. "Okay guys, we have ten minutes before we have to be out the door. Just put your dishes in the sink when you're done, and make sure you've got everything you want for the weekend in your backpacks. Gramma and Grandpa have pajamas and everything already for you, but bring any toys you want."

"What about my toothbrush?" Ethan stared up at me stonily.

"Gramma bought you a *brand new* toothbrush to use just at her house." I grinned at him in encouragement.

"I don't want a *new* toothbrush. I want my raptor toothbrush."

"You know what? I told her how much you loved it, so she bought the *exact* same one. Now you have *two* raptor toothbrushes, one for each house. What do you think about that?"

"It's not the same," he shook his head. "It's not *my* raptor toothbrush."

"Okay, buddy, if you want to bring your toothbrush to Gramma's house, that's fine. Just put it in your backpack when you're done eating. I need to finish getting dressed."

Ethan scowled, then turned back to his food.

"Olivia, make sure you both wash your hands and that he doesn't forget his toothbrush, please." I kissed the top of her head as I passed.

"Sure, Dad." Even though I used my gentlest

tone and smiled widely, she replied with the stern expression of a hardened warrior taking orders.

Deflated, I placed my own dishes in the sink and headed for my room.

Experience had taught me not to wear my work clothes at the breakfast table, because accidents were bound to happen. I couldn't say how many times I ended up with jelly or coffee spilled on my pristine dress blues.

Since it was my first day at a new job in management civilian style, I figured it was a smart idea to dress to impress. I'd only worn the charcoal suit once—for divorce court—so it was still impeccably clean. Shirt bright white and starched, red silk tie spotless.

By the time I reemerged from my room, the kids were waiting silently by the door, faces clean and backpacks on. My heart pinched at their serious expressions—I hated they were so sullen all the time, but I had no idea how to change it.

Hopefully, this move to Aspen Ridge would be the fresh start we all needed. With my parents here to help and the beautiful mountain scenery, it was an ideal place to settle our family and put down some roots. It was a place the kids could make friends, settle in, and perhaps we'd all find some more joy in our lives.

I just prayed it worked.

Mom and Dad were waiting on the porch when we arrived, eager to spend time with their grandkids. The tightness in my chest loosened, confirming that I'd made the right choice, moving us here. Military bases provide a lot of support for families, but they don't compare to living a few blocks away from your parents.

As soon as we pulled into the driveway, the kids were unbuckled and tearing toward the house with eager smiles. I followed up the stairs to greet my parents, relieved to see my two serious children joyful about something.

"I don't know who's more excited, you guys or the kids," I teased. Ethan had jumped into my dad's arms and my mom was already telling Olivia the itinerary for their weekend.

"Well, we've got to make up for lost time, son." Dad greeted me with a hug and a firm pat on the back. "This is the first time we've all lived in the same state, let alone the same town."

"I just hope you don't get sick of us," I chuckled. "They're old enough to ride their bikes here once I get them unpacked. I have a feeling they'll be over a lot."

"You're always welcome, Jake," Mom replied with a warm smile. "You all can join us for dinner any time, too. The house has been quiet for too long, and I know you'll be working all day."

"Nah, we wouldn't want to put you out, Mom.

You should take more time to relax. Maybe you should come over to our house for dinner." Instinctively, I glanced down at my watch. "Speaking of working all day, I had better not be late. Love you guys. Call me if you need anything."

Dad waved me off. "We'll be fine. Tell JJ hello for me!"

"Will do. Thanks again, for everything."

"Nonsense." He shook his head. "You don't need to thank us for watching our grandchildren."

"All the same, they can be a handful, so call me if you need anything."

Dad just waved, so I climbed into the truck and took off. I used my GPS to get to the Aspen Ridge Lodging office, so I had no trouble navigating through the ski resort's downtown.

Of course, being the end of summer, there was no snow to be seen. The mountains were bald rock at the peaks, with bright grass-covered runs trickling downhill between swaths of evergreens. The town itself was an attractive cross between the charm of the old west and the sleek appeal of modern mountain style. It'd been a while, but I'd visited once on a ski trip and had always loved Aspen Ridge. When my parents retired here, I'd sworn we'd visit every season to ski.

That'd been four years ago, and this was the first time we'd come. But we were here to stay, hopefully, so I supposed that'd make up for it.

Despite the season, the small resort town was packed with visitors, thanks to warm weather activities like mountain biking, rafting, and horseback riding. I made a point to arrive at the tail end of summer. I wanted the kids settled before school started, and my boss wanted me on board before winter, their busiest season.

I navigated to the resort parking garage and inserted the card I'd received in the mail, granting me permission to park for free. Thankfully, since signs at the entrance proclaimed parking to be $35 a day.

After a final once-over, I grabbed my shiny new briefcase—which was empty apart from a few sheets of paper—and followed directions for the main offices.

My pulse raced, but I tried to focus on the important things.

One, I already had the job.

Two, training leaders was basically what I'd done for my entire career, culminating in a stint at the Air Force's prestigious Officer Training School. Turning one flighty woman into the successful CEO of a ski resort would be cake after whipping groups of sullen college grads into battle-ready lieutenants.

Three, this was the best opportunity I was likely to receive in Aspen Ridge, and for the kids' sake—and my own—I needed to be near my parents. JJ Tremont had promised that once his daughter was ready to take over, he'd make sure I had a position in upper management.

So first the daughter, then the cushy job with a view of the gorgeous terrain.

I made it to the elevator and mashed the button for the top floor, then closed my eyes and pictured the new dream I was chasing. Afternoons spent on the slopes, teaching the kids to ski. Finally being able to attend school events, holidays with my family, a community that didn't exist around a military life. I'd resigned myself to a long career of service, and Cheryl's decisions had ripped that right out of my grasp... but perhaps there was a better life waiting for me here.

The elevator slowed to a stop, and the doors opened.

Showtime.

Ellie

"Dad, I really have got to go. The preparation is going to take me all day," I made a show of tidying up my desk, hoping he'd take the hint.

"I know, Izzy. I just wanted to remind you about the golf tournament in a few weeks." He settled into my corner chair like he had no intention of leaving. I'd intentionally made it a cozy space with tall plants and a side table so I could curl up and feel like I'd escaped. I hadn't imagined my father would usurp it to hold me hostage when I was trying to leave.

The sigh poured from my lips like someone had punched me in the chest. "I really wish you'd listen when I ask you to call me Ellie. No one has called me Izzy for years."

"All the same, Zach said he hasn't heard from you in a while. Did you two have a falling out?"

My god, why was my dad discussing my love life with my ex?

"We broke up almost a year ago, Dad. You know that."

"Well, you two seemed pretty cozy at that fundraiser a few weeks ago."

"We're friends, Dad. We were friends long before we dated, and we're always going to be in the same circles. It doesn't pay for us to be enemies."

"Still, when I'm gone, you're going to need someone to help run this place. Zach knows all about how a place like this should be run."

My jaw clenched; sure, Zach knows all about it. Zach had huge plans for how he wanted to take over *my* family resort, which was the main reason we broke up. Not that I could tell my dad about it. He practically made Zach a member of the family ages ago, it would crush him to know what Zach's actual intentions were.

Instead, I just answered, "I have an MBA, Dad. I'm perfectly capable of running Lodging on my own."

"Still, I just don't want to worry about you struggling under all the pressure, Isabelle. It's a lot more than you think."

"I have a pretty good idea, seeing as how I've been here for the last few years as your 'Assistant CEO.'" I slammed my desk drawer a little harder than I meant to, but he was not getting the hint. At this rate he looked about ready to order a second breakfast and take a nap in my cushy chair.

"Well, it's a lot harder than it looks." His tone turned slightly defensive, as if I'd implied something about *his* ability to do the job instead of the other way around.

I closed my eyes and drew in a deep breath, letting it out before I settled my gaze directly on my father. His silvery hair and beard were perfectly neat, and the robin's egg-blue Aspen Ridge polo he wore matched his bright eyes. He was every bit the mountain executive: neat enough to be taken seriously, but casual enough to not to be too intimidating.

"I understand the responsibilities of the position, and I believe I am well-qualified to take over when you are ready to retire, Dad." I even managed a smile to go along with my patient-but-not-conde-scending tone.

Dad shifted in his seat. "Yes, about that, Izzy-"

I stood abruptly in frustration and snatched my purse. "Dad, I really have to go. I'll be at the reception hall all day. Call if you need me."

"Wait, honey, there's something I want to talk to you about-"

I was already on my way out the door. "I'm sure it can wait for tomorrow, Dad." I turned on my heel and crossed to the corner chair, bending to kiss his cheek before beelining again to the hallway.

With a final wave, I ducked through the doorway before he could call me back. "I'll see you tomorrow!"

Jake

I STRODE CONFIDENTLY UP to the reception desk, which was handsomely decorated with large polished letters spelling out 'Aspen Ridge Lodging & Hotels'. The young woman behind the desk eyed me curiously, but smiled in greeting all the same.

"Hello, how can I help you?"

I plastered on a smile. "Good morning. I'm

supposed to ask for James Tremont, Junior. He's expecting me." I winced at my stern voice, and the girl's eyes narrowed slightly as if I were acting suspiciously.

"You mean JJ? Not a problem. I'll ring him."

"Thank you."

While she made the call, I glanced at my surroundings. Directly behind the desk was a beautiful panoramic photo of the ski resort at peak winter season on a sunny day, taking up an entire wall. Banks of cubicles ran the length of a room tucked away to the left, and to the right appeared to be a row of larger offices disappearing down a hallway.

Sweat gathered at my collar, despite the air conditioning. I resisted the urge to tug at the fabric as my eyes roved the room and made a disturbing discovery: no one else was wearing a suit. Most people wore polo shirts with the resort logo embroidered on the chest, and the few who wore dress shirts had them casually rolled to their sleeves.

Compared to the crowd, I was way overdressed. Maybe it was a casual Friday. Don't people who work at billion-dollar companies wear suits?

"Jacob!" a deep, friendly voice called out from the direction of the offices, and I turned to see JJ approaching with a wide smile. He had on a polo and khakis like the front desk girl, and a full head of more salt than-pepper hair with a neat, matching beard. "So glad you finally made it. Quite a trip from Alabama! Did the kids enjoy the drive?"

"Jake, sir," I accepted his handshake. "They're troopers, they did alright. They're sort of used to moving. But it'll be nice to put down some roots."

"I can't imagine." JJ shook his head and patted my shoulder. "Thank you again for your service. We hope you like it here. Although it won't be quite as exciting as your former career, we get to have a bit of fun. Why don't we start with a tour? I'll show you your new office so you can leave your briefcase, and then I'll give you a rundown of our area of responsibility."

"Sounds good, sir." I followed him to a small, plain office. No expansive views of the ski hill, but it at least had a window. I could count on one hand the number of years I'd had one in my fifteen years of service.

"Okay, you've got to stop calling me sir, Jake. Never mind the white beard, you're making me feel old!" JJ chuckled at his own joke.

"Yes, si—I mean, sure thing, JJ. Sorry, habits." I clasped my hands behind my back to avoid fidgeting and squared my shoulders.

"Understandable. But you'll soon learn that things aren't that formal here. I'm sure you'll settle into it quickly."

"I'm sure I will." I set my briefcase on the chair and turned to him. "So, when are we starting?"

He gestured me down the hallway and we made our way back to the elevators. "I thought we'd start downstairs in the hotel, then I could take you to the condo registration, and if you like we could do a full lap of the resort, maybe grab lunch at the base of Peak 7. Our portion here only covers the lodging but the whole place is run by us and the Blackwells, so it's all sort of family business. Probably good for you to be familiar with the whole enchilada."

"Sounds great, sir, but I meant when we would start with your daughter?"

He chuckled. "So eager to get to work! No worries, Isabelle isn't here today, so you get a one-day reprieve. She's setting up for the employee party." We boarded the elevator, and he selected the button.

"Employee party?" I questioned. "Like a GI Party? That's what we called a weekly cleanup crew."

JJ laughed again. "No, son, like a *party* party. We like to treat the staff well, and employee satisfaction has sort of become Izzy's baby. Most of them are college kids. We want them to have a good time working for us. We always have an end of the season party for summer and winter, our two biggest seasons. Besides the parties, we organize a lot of mixers and events throughout the year. We work hard, but we play hard, too. Izzy likes to plan them. She is pretty much friends with all the kids... which I suppose is part of the problem."

"Is that what you are hoping I can fix, for her to be less friendly with the staff?" I really wanted to get a better understanding of what I was here to do, as it had all been rather vague up until now.

"Yes, and no. We want them to feel cared for, but I think sometimes Isabelle forgets that she's not one of them anymore. She can't be going to keggers in the dorms with the kids at night and then giving their bosses performance reviews the next day, you know what I mean? She's got to start pulling back, acting more like a manager and less like their buddy, before I can consider handing the reins over. Aspen Ridge employs nearly a thousand people in lodging alone, so she needs to get a wider view."

I nodded seriously. "I know exactly what you mean. It's like when we promote a Senior Airman to Staff Sergeant. Suddenly they're a non-commissioned officer and they can't get away with acting like Airmen fresh from basic training anymore. For some of them, it's a hard transition."

"Sounds like I hired just the man for the job." JJ grinned as the elevator doors opened. "This is our main hotel lobby, but there are seven in total that span the base of the ski resort."

For the rest of the day, I followed along as JJ gave me a thorough tour of the main resort highlights. It was daunting to realize how many teams he had, which started with a network of VPs, plus a manager for each site, then each building, of the extensive resort. JJ filled me in on the other family he shared ownership of the resort with, which included the events center, stables, and ski hills. He and Robert Blackwell had equal shares in the business and, as they came of age, passed management onto their children with the plan of eventually handing over the reins entirely.

"So, how many kids do you plan to hand this off to? It sounds like you've expanded quite a bit on what your parents built with the Blackwells."

"Indeed." JJ leaned back in his seat and stretched. We'd stopped for a late lunch at a restaurant on the resort, and the remains of a savoury meal cooled on the plates in front of us. "My sister, Lily, didn't want much to do with the place. She's on the books, but really in name only. I don't hold out much hope for her son, Blaise, either. Bit of a flake, that kid. But my eldest, James the third, is already managing mountain operations, and Robert's eldest, Reece, works with the events center. Robert's daughter, Estelle, seems to prefer riding the powder to working, but Robert's certain she'll step up, eventually."

"And Isabelle is primed to take over all of lodging?" I asked. "Based on what you've shown me, that seems like more than one person's work. Especially for someone who likes to be so hands on."

"I think we manage pretty well with our team of VPs, but that's where I need you to help her, Jake." He leaned in and slapped me on the shoulder. "She needs to be less hands on, and try as I might, I can't seem to get that into her head. She's almost never in her office. If she wants to take over for me, she's got to be in meetings with the VPs, approving payroll, signing off renovation projects. Instead, I'm far more likely to find her out with the landscaping crew planting flowers."

"Right," I nodded. "She needs to transition to a macro view of the business, and right now she's fully in the micro."

"You've got it." JJ checked his watch, then wiped his mouth with a cloth napkin. "Well, I've got some meetings to attend tonight. Why don't you take the rest of the afternoon off? Or even better, go to the employee party tonight. I'll have Larissa at the desk send you the address. It'll give you a chance to see how we run things here, maybe make a few friends. It's sort of a send-off for seasonal workers, but most of our full-time staff should be there as well."

"Okay, what time would you like me in tomorrow?" I followed him outside to the golf cart we'd used for the tour, and we zipped off toward the offices the second I claimed my seat.

"Tomorrow?" He guffawed. "Son, tomorrow's Saturday. I'm going to be working on my golf swing. We'll see you first thing Monday."

"Don't I need to sign forms with HR, or fill out a payslip?" I clung to the side of the cart to avoid spilling out. It didn't seem pertinent to mention that I assumed he wanted me to start on Friday because I'd be there through the weekend. Hence why I'd sent my kids to their grandparents.

"Nah, we already started your salary, and you can fill out paperwork on Monday. Go to the party and have a good time. Make some friends! We want everyone to feel like part of the family here."

"Yes, sir."

"I told you, stop making me feel old. JJ is fine."

"Yes, s—JJ."

"Better." He grinned and gave me a twinkly blue-eyed wink.

JJ dropped me directly at my truck, insisting there was no need for me to get my briefcase before I left.

I drove home in a daze, my mind churning on how I could make myself invaluable and earn a permanent place here. Aspen Ridge was a dream come true when it came to working environments. Everyone seemed genuinely happy, and JJ greeted everyone we passed, a lot of them by name. It was easy to see what he meant about it being a family business.

A text popped up on my phone just as I pulled into the drive, with a detailed message from Larissa about how to get to the employee party. Obviously the suit would not be appropriate, but I honestly didn't know what to wear for an end of season employee party at a billion-dollar resort. I concluded neat jeans and a button-down shirt were appropriate for the brand new five-million dollar events center.

It's always better to be a little overdressed as opposed to under dressed.

Even if it was a little uncomfortable.

THE DOUBTS STARTED AS SOON as I parked in the lot. All the crowd heading toward the fancy events center was young—like fresh out of high school young—and the dress code appeared to be flip-flops and backwards baseball caps. The sun had long since disappeared behind the mountains, and twilight shadows were verging on darkness, stars already appearing in the sky.

Although I wasn't sure what I was expected to do here, JJ had asked me to attend and make friends. Honestly, I had nothing better to do on a Friday night, and the kids were happy at their grandparents' house. I decided it was an opportunity to see more about this 'treating staff as family' thing JJ was so proud of. I steeled myself for the culture shock and followed the others from the parking lot toward the building.

Once I got through the main doors, I glanced around at the stunning facility. They had built a marvel—it was modern and clean in the lobby, but it still had a decidedly cozy mountain feel. The employees streamed through a second set of double doors with loud rhythmic music pouring out.

To the right, a woman who was decidedly older than the crowd and clearly pregnant struggled with a heavy cart laden with boxes and platters of food. She had a giant crystal bowl of punch, covered with saran wrap, balanced on top of a cardboard box, and was trying to keep it from tipping over while she pushed the cart.

"Ma'am, let me help you." I crossed the lobby and picked up the bowl.

"Oh, thank you." She smiled. "But please don't call me ma'am. That makes me feel old."

"That's not the first time I've heard that today," I laughed. "My apologies, it's a habit. I just left the Air Force, and everyone is 'sir' or 'ma'am', no matter their age. I didn't mean anything by it."

"Well, that makes me feel a little better." She resumed pushing her cart, and I followed her to the double doors. "I'm Alyssa. I manage the events center."

"Jake, nice to meet you. Today was my first day, and the boss said to come to the party, so... here I am. Do you normally handle the food, as the manager?"

She laughed breathlessly. "No, not usually. But we wanted the staff to have the night off, so I figured if they made all the food, I could get it inside for them. We try to let everyone have a chance for fun. I just underestimated how many trips it would take, and how tired I'd be." She gestured to her belly. "They really take it out of you. You have kids?"

My throat seized up, and I swallowed to clear it. "I do, actually. Two."

"This is my first. I'm already planning to stay home once I have the little one. I just didn't realize the last few months would be so much harder. I really appreciate your help."

"Not a problem at all. I'm happy to assist." I followed her through the open doors and to an enormous banquet table, already half full. Despite the loud music and flashing colorful lights, most of the crowd was standing around the bar set at the far side of the room, opposite the dance floor. There were small tables set up, but people were milling about, socializing.

Happy to have an excuse to avoid that exact scenario, I helped Alyssa unload the cart, and two more like it, until the buffet was filled. I escorted her back to the kitchen despite her assurances she was fine.

"Are you going to the party?" I asked, hopeful. She was closer to my age, and it was always nicer to know someone when you walked into a crowded room.

"Lord no," she laughed. "My ankles are two times their normal size and all I can think about is propping my feet up at home. But I can introduce you to some people before I leave, if you want?" She shifted her weight from one foot to the other, obviously uncomfortable.

"No, you're exhausted. You should get off your feet. I'll be fine. I'll just tell them I carried a watermelon or something."

She glanced around the kitchen in distress. "Oh shoot, did I forget something? My mind has been swiss cheese the last couple of months, I swear..."

My cheeks heated. "I'm sorry. It was an attempt at a joke."

Alyssa stared at me with a blank expression. "Why would a watermelon be funny?"

Cheryl always instructed me not to tell jokes because I sucked at it. I thought she just didn't have a sense of humor, but maybe I should have listened.

"You know, from the movie Dirty Dancing? Baby sees the guy juggling three watermelons, and she helps him bring them to the employee party, then when Johnny asks what she's doing there she says 'I carried a watermelon.' Because she didn't belong there, right?"

Alyssa's eyes narrowed, my only indication that she was trying to understand. "Yeah... I probably wouldn't open with that one. Or with the 'sir' or 'ma'am' thing. Just say 'Hi, I'm Jake.' It'll work about 100% better, promise." She gave me a wide smile. "It's nice to meet you, Jake. I'm sure I'll see you around. Thanks again!"

With that, she shooed me out of the kitchen and waddled to the exit door.

Squaring my shoulders, I lifted my chin and marched back into the party. I made a beeline for the bar, and ordered myself two shots of jack to soothe my nerves, and a long-neck beer to sip.

The party was sliding into full-swing mode now. People crowded the banquet tables, moving in groups through a set of doors leading outside that I had missed earlier. There was a large deck filled with tables and strung with Edison lights. I'd taken up residence at the furthest end of the bar, tucked into the corner, but most of the other drinkers were in a huddle closer to the dance floor.

A lot of them were dancing. Some in pairs, but most were in the awkward group circles that reminded me of high school prom. A fast-tempo song with a rhythmic beat pumped from the artfully concealed speakers, and the bass thrummed through the soles of my feet. My eyes traveled casually over the dancers while I sipped my beer, and instead of becoming more comfortable, I just grew more convinced this was a dead end. Everyone here had to be seasonal employees—they looked barely old enough to drive, let alone have a year-round job. A few slightly older people slipped out the doors with plates of food, and it occurred to me that people in management—or at least people closer to my age— might have hidden out there.

Just as I'd resolved to try my luck with the outdoor crowd, my eyes landed on a woman in a short red dress, and all thoughts of leaving immediately flew from my brain.

She was in a group of other people; although she was still young and beautiful, she was clearly older than her peers. Her long blonde hair was damp with sweat, sticking to her bare back and neck, but as she spun around, her wide smile betrayed zero discomfort.

My heart thumped in my chest—this woman was like a glimpse of life and freedom that seemed so far removed from the world I lived in. My eyes were glued to her form. I couldn't stop watching her. There was something so... *free* about her, and envy made my throat too thick to swallow. She didn't have a care in the world; she was just living her best life in this one moment.

What I'd give to feel that way. I couldn't remember a time where my life wasn't filled with duty, obligation, and responsibility.

And then, as if hearing my silent plea, she turned and locked eyes with me.

CHAPTER 2
ELLIE

I knew immediately I'd never seen him before. I never forget a face, and his was definitely worth remembering. Despite the dark hair and eyes, he had an unmistakable air of 'Captain America' I found intriguing. His hair was neatly cut, his jeans and shirt impeccable compared to the sea of rumpled band t-shirts around me, and even from here the broad shoulders and muscular fit of his pants clearly portrayed 'man' as opposed to 'boy'.

I felt his eyes on me long before I deigned to look back. These guys all know who I am, and even though I like to hang out, there's a definite line they don't cross with the boss's daughter.

This one clearly didn't know, judging from the way his eyes roved over my body.

Or didn't care, which was even more intriguing.

As the song ended, I decided refreshment was in order and excused myself to get a drink.

The man reclined against the bar with one muscular forearm, his other hand clutching a beer. When he realized I was heading his way, he froze completely, like prey attempting to avoid catching the eye of a predator.

Interesting.

"Hey Erik, a beer, please."

The bartender nodded and popped the cap on a brown long neck bottle before placing it on a napkin in front of me. I took a long pull from the frosty drink before I turned and looked directly at Captain America.

"Hi," I smiled, pulling damp hair from my neck and draping it over my shoulder. "Are you new?"

Seeming to come out of a trance, he straightened and offered me his hand. "Hi, yes I am, first day. I'm Jake, it's nice to meet you...?" he trailed off, holding my gaze as he waited.

"Ellie," I replied with a grin and shook his hand. "Nice to meet you as well. Did you have a good first day?"

"Yeah, I did actually. A bit strange, but I'll adapt."

"Strange? Strange how?" Oh yeah, he definitely had no clue who I was. The pleasure of anonymity widened my smile; I so rarely met someone completely unaware of who I was.

"I just got out of the military, so that in itself makes all of this strange." He gestured to the party.

"Ah, that makes sense."

"It does?"

"Yeah, I thought you had a whole 'Captain America' look about you. That's odd for Aspen Ridge. It's adding up now."

He glanced around, then dropped his gaze to his hands. "You're not wrong. Is it that bad?"

"No, it's not bad. Just... noticeable. We draw more of the earth-loving hippy types. Not that you don't love the earth," I corrected quickly. "Just... I mean, I'm sure you can see it."

Thankfully, he laughed. "Yeah, I get what you mean. Don't worry, I'm not insulted. I'm sure I'll adapt. I've already received some helpful tips." He snorted.

Suspicion rose in my chest. "Oh, no, what happened? If someone was rude to you, I'll-"

"No, no, nothing like that. Everyone has been very kind," he rushed to reassure me. "I met Alyssa, the events center manager. She was just tired and wasn't very amused by my attempt at humor. I'm pretty sure she didn't get the joke at all."

"Oh. I'm glad to hear you haven't had problems, at least. Yeah, I think her pregnancy has been harder on her than she expected. Honestly, I thought she went home hours ago, but I'm not surprised she stayed. I will say that her sense of humor has definitely tanked in the last couple of months. But you didn't make a joke about her being pregnant, did you? Because that never goes over well."

He raised both hands. "No, absolutely not. Trust me, I know better than to tease a pregnant woman."

"So what was it?"

"What was what?"

"What was the joke?"

"Oh, no," his cheeks colored. "She advised against repeating it. At the risk of betraying my age, I think I ought to listen to her."

I set my beer down. "Well, now I have to know, I'm too invested. Let me give you a second opinion, no judgement, I swear." I beamed at him, and his gaze darted to my mouth.

Jake licked his lips. "I'm not sure..."

"I insist," I pressed him. "I really don't feel you got a fair shot with Alyssa. Try me."

Heaving a sigh, he replied, "Okay. It's really not that funny and now I feel like an idiot. We've made too big of a deal about it already."

"I'll be the judge of that. Hit me with it. I'll buy you a drink if I hate it."

"It's open bar," he replied with a small curl of his lips.

"Then I'll buy you a drink either way. What have you got to lose?"

Finally cracking a smile, he chuckled. "It's seriously not that big a deal. I was helping her bring in the food, and she offered to introduce me to a few people before she left. I told her it wasn't necessary, that I'd just tell anyone who asked what I was doing here that I carried a watermelon." He tipped his beer back and finished it. "I'll take another of these, and a shot of jack, since you're buying."

The laughter rose in my throat and tumbled out. "Carried a watermelon, like from Dirty Dancing? No I get it, that's clever." I put in the order for two shots and another beer, then turned back to catch the pleased grin melt from his lips.

"But if you're Baby, then what does that make me?" I ducked my chin and smiled at him suggestively. "Am I Johnny?"

"Well, I'm glad you get it. Alyssa acted as if she'd never seen Dirty Dancing before. It made me feel old."

"Of course I do. It was one of my mom's favorite movies." As soon as the words came out, I realized what I'd said, but Jake just laughed.

"Well, I guess it's official: if you're comparing me to your mom, I *am* old. Where is that shot, anyway? It's past my elderly bedtime. I should head back to the old folk's home."

"Stop!" I laughed, pressing a palm to his muscular biceps. "There's no way you're that old. You can't be more than a couple of years older than me."

"Okay, I'm probably not as old as your mom. But

I don't know how old you are, so I can't comment on our age difference."

"Is that your roundabout way of asking my age? You know a lady never tells," I sniffed, pretending to be affronted. Erik arrived with our drinks and I pushed his shot over. "At least not first."

"I see, so I go, you go, is that it?" He eyed me with one brow raised. "Fine. I'm thirty-five. Your turn." He lifted the shot and waited, a playful gleam in his dark eyes.

"Fair enough." I lifted my own shot. "You're six years older than me, so definitely not mom-range." I clinked my glass to his, and we both downed the alcohol together. His eyes never left mine, and my hand shook slightly as I lowered the glass. The burning sensation ran down my throat, heating my body from the inside out.

He may not be in mom range, but he was definitely in the safe zone. Not one of the younger seasonal employees, and since I knew about all the hires in my department, definitely not someone I'd have to worry about being an issue at work. Dad frowned on me getting too close to our employees—particularly the younger ones—but Jake was an opportunity too delicious to pass up. He had that sexy 'older man who knows what he's doing' vibe that was hard to resist, and he clearly worked in another part of the business—totally fair game.

"Come on," I scooped my beer with one hand

and tugged on his hand with the other. "This bar can hold itself up without your help. Let's go dance."

His head shook back and forth vehemently. "Nah, I'm way past my dancing days. In fact, I should go find my walker. I think I left it somewhere next to my oxygen tank."

"Quit!" His self-deprecating humor was surprising, given the confident man-in-charge aura he presented. "If you keep insisting you're old, that means I'm basically old, and I believe you're only as old as you feel."

"Well then, according to my knees, I'm sixty-two."

That drew another chuckle from my lips, and I didn't miss his gratified expression. Despite his resistance, he was enjoying our banter.

"Fine, I know what's going on here," I sniffed, leaning across the bar to signal Erik yet again.

"Oh yeah? What's that?"

"You're too sober. A little more liquid courage will be just the thing." I ordered us another round of shots and turned back to catch his eyes raking over my body with his lip between his teeth.

Realizing I caught him staring, his gaze met mine with an expression I could only describe as 'guilty schoolboy', and somehow it was all the hotter on this grown man.

A slow smile spread across his lips. "I could be

mistaken, ma'am, but I believe you're trying to get me drunk."

"I wouldn't dream of it, good sir. I'm merely attempting to provide adequate social lubrication to make sure you enjoy yourself. It appears you need some help to separate you from the wall."

Our shots arrived, and I held mine up, waiting for him to clink his to it. He sighed, but lifted his glass all the same, and met my gaze with gleaming eyes. "Okay, but last one. I need to drive home tonight."

We tipped our shots back, and I resisted the urge to shudder—the second shot of liquor was much worse than the first.

Smiling instead, I tugged on his hand. "That's fine, because now it's time for our dance."

"Hey, I don't recall agreeing to dance."

"Didn't you read the contract? I bought you two shots and a beer. You owe me a dance."

"Pretty sure if I used that on a woman, I'd get charges filed against me." Despite the serious words, his expression remained playful. "Plus, it's an open bar, so you technically didn't buy me anything."

No sense in telling him I paid for the entire party, drinks included. It would just ruin the vibe.

"Quit stalling and get moving, soldier," I replied instead.

"Airman."

"What?"

"I was in the Air Force, not the Army. Therefore, Airman would be the most appropriate term of address."

"How about I stick with Captain America?"

"Captain would actually be correct, but my last name isn't America."

I rolled my eyes. "Then enlighten me, sir. How should I address you, exactly?"

"Captain Right."

The laughter tumbled from my lips. "Right? As opposed to Captain Wrong? That's a line I've not heard before."

Jake cracked a wide smile. "I've heard it once or twice. But no, my last name is Wright, with a W."

"Fine, Captain Wright, it's time for you to report for duty on the dance floor. No more stalling!" I added when he grumbled. "You can bring your beer. Just come on already."

I tugged harder on his hand and he finally started moving. Jake's fingers were warm and smooth against mine, and electric tingles spread up my arm from the contact. Hot blood raced through my body—I could feel my pulse in my neck, the flush of pleasure from my conquest combining with the heat from the liquor.

I dragged him out onto the dance floor where we were surrounded with small groups of people doing various interpretations of dancing. Jake's expression was placid, but it seemed frozen in place, like a studied impression of calm. Meanwhile, a vein throbbed in his temple, and his gaze remained distant while he swayed awkwardly.

"Hey, just relax. You're not getting graded on your dance skills, you know. This is supposed to be fun." I got his attention and smiled, moving my body to the pulsing music.

"Look, I never claimed to be an excellent dancer. This is what you get." He took a long pull of his beer and narrowed his eyes, doing a deliberate side-together step like he was performing some stiff approximation of a line dance.

A snort burst from my lips. "Anything can be awkward if you make it awkward. And anything can be cool if you own it." To demonstrate my point, I copied his steps but added my own flair, making the movement fluid and sexy.

"You got me," he admitted. "I make everything awkward. I'm ceding the point, you win. I'll go back and hold up the bar."

"Not so fast." I grabbed his hand, turning my back to him and placing his palm on my hip. "Just move along with me."

I knew the moment the alcohol kicked in. Or at least the moment he finally relaxed and went with it. His fingertips dug in to my flesh, squeezing my hip and drawing my body closer to his. I felt the heat of him behind me, his other arm wrapping around to press against my opposite hip bone. I had no idea what his expression looked like, but I imagined a face of pure concentration and it cracked me up.

Abruptly, the fast song ended and the next track was slower, more sensual. I disengaged his hand from my hip and turned in the circle of his arms, catching him biting that lip again. My pulse pounded, and I wrapped my arms around his neck, drawing closer to him while we switched to swaying back and forth in tune with the melody. His cologne was clean and woodsy, with a note of sweetness.

"Now this is more my speed," he admitted with a small curl of his lips. His gaze was soft, his breath warm on my cheek.

I batted my lashes at him. "What, you mean *slow*?"

"Ha ha, you know eventually you're going to run out of age jokes."

"That wasn't an age joke, that was a speed joke. Keep up. Unless you can't..."

"Oh man, the hits keep coming," he grumbled, but his expression was all smiles. "What did I do to deserve this abuse?"

"Hey, you showed up at my party. You should have prepared better."

"I thought this party was for all the employees. My apologies. I didn't mean to crash."

"Oh, it is, but it's also my party."

"That doesn't make much sense."

"It doesn't have to."

"I see." His arms tightened, drawing me closer, pressing my body lightly against his. The heat of him seeped through my dress, and I was electrically aware of how close his lips were to mine. "In that case, I suppose I'd better keep an eye on you, Ellie. Something tells me you're trouble."

I laughed, tossing my head back. He had no idea. "I've heard that before," I teased.

"I believe it." He didn't look put off at all, as if he rather liked the idea that I might be trouble.

The slow song ended and a faster one kicked off. Jake rolled his eyes and glanced to the side, as if he were considering escaping again.

Deciding to give him a break, I slipped my hand back into his. "Come with me." I tugged him toward the balcony doors, and he followed willingly.

I didn't realize how muggy the atmosphere had become inside until we passed through the doorway. Outside, the air was cool and refreshing, the moon huge and brilliant in the sky. It bathed the valley of trees and mountain peaks in the distance, leeching everything of color and setting a dreamy backdrop.

"Ah, so this is where everyone over the age of twenty-two went," he commented, glancing around the deck.

It was large enough to accommodate a wedding with seventy-five seats, the ski hill in the background. Right now, there were a dozen picnic tables spread around, with people sitting in small groups and chatting. The music was still audible, but much quieter than it'd been inside. I tugged Jake to the point of the balcony, shaped like the bow of a ship pointed over the forest below.

"This is quite the place," he admitted quietly, leaning against the railing. My eyes swept over the bulging muscles concealed beneath his shirt and a hot coal of desire burned in my stomach.

"Top of the line," I agreed. "It's already booked out for most of the weekends this winter, and half of next winter, too."

"Is that what you do here? Book the events?"

"I do a little of everything, I guess you could say." I switched the topic before I had to tell him too much. "What brought you here, out of the Air Force?"

Jake cleared his throat, as if he were uncomfortable with the question. "I was ready for a change," he answered after a pause.

"Fair enough," I replied. If neither of us was in the mood to go into details, there were other things to occupy us. "Come on, I want to show you something else."

I slipped my fingers between his again and he squeezed lightly, following me along the railing to the edge of the deck, where a set of stairs led down to the ground. I tossed our bottles in the trash on our way out, curious if anyone noticed us leaving, but no one was looking. We walked along a pine needle-covered trail for a short distance, catching glimpses of moonlight through the tall trees overhead.

"You're not dragging me off into the woods to kill me, are you?" He joked after a few minutes.

"Of course not, I'd never do something so cliché."

"And this isn't some kind of prank, like tie the new guy to a tree in his underwear?"

That made me chuckle. "Okay, who have you been hanging out with? You're very suspicious for a guy on a moonlit walk with a girl."

"Sorry, maybe I was in the military too long. My faith in humanity only goes as far as I can throw a person, and that isn't far."

"Well, rest assured I have no nasty surprises in store."

"No surprises?"

"I didn't say that," I answered with a grin. We followed the curve of the path and the gazebo came into view.

After we stepped up onto the wooden platform, he looked around warily. "Okay, I don't see any ninjas ready to ambush me, so that's good. But this is sort of an odd place to put a gazebo, isn't it? Like, there's no lake to look out at, no actual view. It's just forest."

I sidled up to him and pressed my body against his, sliding my hands up his chest. "It is quiet, but I wouldn't say there's no view." My gaze locked on his, and he swallowed awkwardly. "What I like best about this place is that there's no one around. It's a brilliant spot for *privacy*."

Even in the darkness, his eyes seemed to flash with comprehension. I waited, my breaths light past my lips and my heart pounding, to see how he'd respond to the invitation.

Jake's hand slid up into the tangle of my hair, cradling my head while his lips moved in to claim mine. He was firm, insistent, and I bent under the pressure, opening to welcome him. Heat built between my legs, a pleasurable throb of excitement when his mouth met mine. His tongue slid against my lips, followed by a gentle press of teeth, and a surge of heat shot up my spine as I pressed back against him. My fingers climbed his shoulders, tracing patterns over the soft hair at the nape of his neck.

Jake groaned deep in his throat, and his free hand pulled my body tight against his, then slid down my back, over the curve of my hips, to the place my dress split. In one move, he tugged my thigh up and clenched his fist in my hair, arching my back against the rail. My leg wrapped around his hip, tightening, and I had no problem balancing on one leg when I was pressed between him and the railing. His fingers massaged my thigh while his hips pushed between my legs, the pressure leaving me with little doubt that he was every bit as turned on now as I was. He tugged more firmly on my hair, trailing kisses along my exposed neck, followed by the gentle scrapes of his teeth that sent shivers coursing through my body. His lips tracked down further, painting a course over my chest, down to the indentation between my breasts.

My chest heaved, every nerve alive with sensation. Jake's hot breath on my chest; the sweet aftertaste of Jack Daniels on my tongue; his warm, firm fingers; the pleasurable sensation of the hand gripping my hair; the scent of his cologne mixed with the fresh scent of pine; the cool night air at odds with the heat between our bodies. I could imagine the steam coming off of us like a jacuzzi on a winter night.

And just like that, the spell was broken. A trio of voices reached us from the direction of the events building, coming down the path we'd just walked. We froze in place.

"Come on guys, we're almost there."

"Dude, we don't have to go this far out to smoke a bowl. No one cares."

"I dunno about you, but I'd like to be invited back next summer. Blazing up at the company party isn't exactly the best look, bro."

"I dunno if you've heard, *bro*, pot is legal in Colorado now."

"That doesn't make it fit for public consumption. We're almost there, man, just stop complaining."

Jake released me in a panic, pulling me upright, then stepping back two paces with a terrified look.

I almost felt bad for the guy. I approached and placed my hands on both of his cheeks, planting a soft kiss on his lips. "I guess it's not as private as I'd hoped. Let's head back."

He kissed me back more firmly, then claimed my hand and led the way out of the gazebo. Jake kept me slightly behind his body as if he were protecting me from oncoming threats.

"It's no big deal," I giggled quietly. "It's just some lift-runners coming down to smoke pot. They seriously won't care that we were down here making out."

"Yeah, well, I care. It's not a good look to be feeling a lady up in the dark woods alone."

"Hey," I tugged on his hand, forcing him to stop and turn around. "I happen to think it was a very good look." I reached up and tugged his face back to mine to emphasize my point. He kissed me back, but with less enthusiasm than before.

"Well, I still think I should take you on a proper date," he grumbled as he continued back up the path, my hand still in his.

"And what makes you think I want a date?"

That got his attention. "You don't?"

"I'm not sure. I'll guess we'll have to see what happens when you actually ask me."

Jake chuckled. "Fair enough."

We passed the trio of summer employees on their way to the gazebo, and I didn't miss their curious glances when they realized it was me. I gave them a wink but didn't say anything, and we finished our climb to the top in silence.

"So," I said finally, when we were back on the deck. I leaned against the railing and regarded him coyly. A light breeze ruffled my dress and drew goosebumps to my skin; the space was empty aside from us now, the sudden change in temperature having chased the other employees away.

That or the siren call of free booze inside.

"So, what?" At this point, I couldn't tell if he was confused or just teasing.

"So are you going to ask me out? Or was this all an elaborate ruse of some kind?"

He grinned, leaning against the railing next to me. "No, first I have to ask for your number. Then after several days of playing it cool, then awkward texting and random conversations about the weather, I might finally work up the courage to ask you on a date. Does that work for you?"

"I guess there's only one way to find out."

CHAPTER 3
JAKE

Somehow, I slept in to mid-morning. I couldn't recall sleeping that late on a Saturday since before Olivia was born. I could blame it on the booze, but some part of me knew it was because of Ellie.

I lounged in bed, letting my mind wander over every delicious detail of last night. The softness of her skin; the taste of her sweat when I kissed her neck; the sweet floral scent of her body and how all her soft curves fit against the hard planes of mine perfectly.

Even since Cheryl and I broke up, I hadn't gotten close to another woman. I went on a couple of Tinder dates—total nightmares—at the insistence of my friends. When I decided to get out of the Air

Force and move, it just didn't seem to make much sense to get involved with anyone. I needed to spend that time with my kids.

And here I was, my first week in a new town, getting drunk and making out at a party with the first beautiful woman I met.

Ellie was beautiful in a wild, completely irresistible way. The way the ocean was beautiful— untamed, unmanageable; free. Being around her last night was like unearthing a side of myself I didn't think still existed. She made me feel charming, funny, even interesting. My life had been about duty and family for so long I couldn't recall a time in the last decade that wasn't one or the other.

I checked my phone—no messages from Ellie, aside from the text sending me her number.

It took a good deal of willpower, but I resisted the urge to text her. Everyone knew a guy wasn't supposed to come across as too desperate. Three days minimum, according to my single friends in Alabama. That was long enough to let the air settle, but not so long it was weird. I'd text her on Monday —maybe around lunch time. Just a friendly message.

That decided, I stretched and clambered out of bed, immediately fluffing the pillows and smoothing the sheets and blankets. Best way to start the day was with the bed made.

The weekend went faster than I thought. My brain kept flitting back to Ellie the second it wasn't occupied with something more important. Because my weekend comprised mostly the manual labor of unpacking boxes, I found myself daydreaming a good deal.

I checked my phone far more often than I should have, just hoping she'd text me out of the blue. Obviously, if she messaged me first, it would be rude to delay responding. I didn't want her to think I was one of those guys who hooked up with a woman, then just ignored her. I almost gave in to the temptation to text, but then my mom called and asked me to dinner, so I accepted gratefully.

When I arrived, I didn't know what to expect. Some part of me assumed my parent's house would be completely trashed, the shutters hanging crooked, graffiti on the walls, my parents near tears. Even though I knew my kids were typically pretty good, I couldn't help the part of me that always expected the worst.

Instead, I was relieved to see their house was perfectly in order, and my kids were happy, with bright eyes and excited smiles as soon as I walked in the door. Joy bubbled in my chest immediately to see them this way.

"Dad!"

"Daddy!"

They both rushed me at once for hugs, then immediately began gabbing about their weekend.

"Gramma and I made like a *thousand* cookies,"

Olivia pointed to a stack of tupperware. "We get to bring some home."

"That sounds amazing. You know I love Gramma's cookies, and I bet they're even better because you helped."

She nodded proudly. "That's exactly what Grandpa said."

"Grandpa and I made a birdhouse. Look!" Ethan tugged my hand, pulling me to the window in the kitchen. Outside, a wooden bird house dangled from a tree branch, painted with the distinctive red-and-white web pattern of his favorite superhero.

"That's amazing buddy. It looks awesome. Did you have fun?"

He nodded. "Yeah! And Grandpa said next time we can build a tree house. Can we come back tomorrow?"

My heart stuttered, eyes stinging in the wake of their obvious excitement. "Well, tomorrow you guys start school, buddy. But maybe we can talk to Gramma and Grandpa and see if you can come over next weekend. How's that?" It was so much easier engaging them when they were already happy. I needed to compare notes with my parents and find out how I could replicate this joy at home.

"Hooray!" they cheered, then rushed into the kitchen where Mom was pulling a dish out of the oven.

"Daddy said we can come back next weekend!"

Olivia picked up a pitcher of iced tea and carried it to the table. "Can we make the lemon cake Saturday, Gramma?"

My mom laughed. "Alright, Livvie, one thing at a time. Why don't you go wash up? Ethan, will you go tell Grandpa dinner is ready? He's out in the garage."

"Kay!" Ethan raced off, and my eyes followed him in wonder.

Mom caught me watching him, and she smiled fondly. "He's just like you at his age. Did you know that? All he wants to do is whatever your dad is doing."

"I hope they haven't been too much trouble." I helped move bowls of mashed potatoes and beans to the table.

"Of course not. They were absolutely wonderful the entire time. Such happy, well-behaved children, like always."

"Are you sure we're talking about the same kids?" I raised an eyebrow, thinking how I couldn't get through a day without at least five total meltdowns from Ethan.

Mom just laughed. "Of course, dear. You and Cheryl have done an amazing job with them. I know you have some challenges, but I promise, they're doing just fine." She patted me on the cheek. "Now go wash up so we can eat."

Dinner was a whole new experience. Around my parents, my kids were... just kids. Goofy, playful, a little mischievous, but they mostly minded their manners. Not a hint of the serious little soldiers I had at home.

Of course, my parents spoiled them with too few vegetables and way too much dessert, but it was worth it to see them so happy. It'd been months, maybe a year, since I'd heard that much laughter.

My throat clenched as I realized the reason. I couldn't recall a time in the last several years that I made them laugh like that. They modeled their serious personas on me. Moving here was beneficial, and giving them access to my parents was a good move. They needed to be around family, and I still had a lot to do to create a similar atmosphere in our home.

And true to my revelation at dinner, they were quiet on the drive home. I tried to prompt them with some questions about their weekend and received short answers in response.

I thought they'd be excited to discover I'd unpacked most of the house—including their bedrooms—but their only response was a dutiful 'thank you' and they immediately started getting ready for bed.

We read a story, and I tucked them in like our usual routine, but the radiant glow from the weekend was already gone.

I got ready for bed, laying out my suit for the next day, and resolved to find a way out of the funk that our home life had become. Tomorrow they'd start school and hopefully it'd give us some opportunities to build a new life, a happier life, together.

***

Despite my best efforts at a 'happier' morning, it unfortunately went about the same as Friday had gone—without the comic book incident. The kids were polite and followed instruction, but they betrayed very little emotion to me. I got them to school and checked in, confirming they'd ride the bus beginning tomorrow, then headed in to work.

Even though I was nervous about meeting JJ's daughter Isabelle, I was confident I'd be able to help her grow into the leader her dad wanted. It's what I've been doing for years, in a slightly different context.

So I knew the nervous energy zipping through me wasn't about work at all—it was about my plan to text Ellie today.

For two excruciating days I'd thought over dozens of messages, ranging from flirty to playful, sarcastic to downright dirty. Even though I knew I wouldn't have the guts to send her a sext in a million years, it was still fun to imagine.

I left my briefcase in my office Friday, so I had nothing to carry up to the offices aside from a ziplock bag with two cookies in it. I'd included a cookie in the kids' lunches, which earned me a proud smile from Olivia, and a suggestion that I take cookies in my lunch, too.

How could I say no?

I had on a navy blue suit today, which felt familiar to the uniform I had worn for so many years. Friday had clearly been a casual day, but surely everyone would dress more formally, more like they worked in a billion-dollar company, for Monday.

When I got off the elevator, I knew immediately that I was wrong; Larissa was wearing a polo again, which meant Friday was probably an ordinary day, not a 'casual' one.

If she was surprised, Larissa didn't betray it. "JJ said to send you back to his office when you arrived, Mr. Wright. Just at the end of the hall," she pointed to the same hallway where my office was.

"Great, thanks Larissa," I smiled and marched in that direction.

I was only halfway down the hall when I heard the raised voices, and my steps slowed. The door at the end, with 'JJ Tremont - CEO' on the shiny gold plaque, was closed.

A feminine voice, obviously upset, carried through the door, although the words were muffled. A deeper male voice, clearly JJ, replied, his tone terse.

I hesitated in the hallway, then glanced at my watch. If I didn't knock on his door in the next minute, I was late. In my world, I'd already cut it close by only arriving five minutes early, but it took extra time to get the kids settled at school. Being on time was incredibly important to me, but there was clearly a heated discussion going on in the office.

Taking a few tentative steps closer, I positioned myself outside the door and glanced again at my watch. Unfortunately, this put me close enough to hear what they were saying.

I raised my hand to knock, then froze, unable to help overhearing.

"... Don't know what you're so upset about, Isabelle. This isn't a punishment! I just thought it would help you to bring someone on with leadership experience."

Oh shit, they were fighting about me. Now I definitely didn't want to knock on that door.

"You brought someone in to teach me how to do my job?" Her reply was shrill—this woman sounded like a real banshee. "How am I not supposed to be insulted by that? I've practically worked here since I could walk, and I've been doing this job since I got my MBA. I work with these people every day. How can you imply I don't know how to lead them?"

"Izzy, first off, I brought him in to help you take over *my* job, not to learn yours. I know you're very good at what you do, but I feel—and Robert agrees with me—that you need to start looking at things from a higher view. Right now you still like getting down in the weeds, and to be CEO you need to be at a thousand feet."

"I've told you a thousand times, don't call me Izzy," she snapped, irritated. "And just because I don't mind getting my hands dirty, it doesn't mean I can't have a broader perspective. I just think our employees respect me more when they see me working alongside them."

"And I know, from my time doing both, that they respect *me* more with the distance I've put between us."

"Dad, they don't even know you. How do you think that creates respect?"

"Honey, you can't be the CEO and have every hourly employee coming to you with their problems. There are too many important things that need your attention."

"Well, agree to disagree," she sniffed. "I had better go prepare myself to meet the stuffed shirt you brought in to ruin my life. When is he supposed to get here?"

The door clicked open and I jumped, hand still raised, when I came face to face with my worst nightmare turned into reality.

The funny, cool, irresistibly sexy woman I met on Friday, the one whose lips had been on my mind all weekend, stood before me with unmistakable fury in her blue eyes. Her gaze traveled up to my face, and anger melted from her features as they took on the appearance of complete shock.

JJ's voice was loud, clearly trying to gloss over their fight and knowing I'd heard at least part of it. "Ah, here he is now. Isabelle, this is Jake Wright. Jake, this is my daughter, Izzy—I'm sorry. Bad habit, she prefers to be called Ellie."

Ellie and I continued to stare at each other for seconds that seemed to drag on a lifetime. I remembered every detail of her face, every curved lash and striation in her eyes. Her hair was still a little wild, with the top hastily pinned back. She wore another dress, this one electric blue, with a boxy black blazer, as if she were trying to mask her curves. When the silence stretched on too long, JJ chuckled. "Is everyone okay, or did the Matrix just glitch?"

I cleared my throat and dropped my raised arm, reaching it forward for a handshake instead. "My apologies, nice to meet you," I stuttered out, heart racing.

As if reclaiming her anger from before, Ellie accepted the shake but narrowed her eyes. "Likewise. If you'll excuse me, I have somewhere to be."

"Oh, right, sorry," I stepped aside and allowed her to pass.

She marched into the office next door without a second glance in my direction.

"Ellie, let's plan for you to work with Jake after

lunch," JJ called after her, just finishing his sentence before her door shut loudly.

I stared after her, barely able to believe my terrible luck. The epic high of meeting a woman who made me feel flickers of the old me before life got in the way, followed by the incredible low of realizing that not only was she the boss's daughter, but she already hated me with every fiber of her being, thanks to my very reason for being here.

JJ chuckled again, this time with an affectionate but frustrated edge. "Kids, am I right?"

"Yeah," I replied vaguely, still staring at the door.

"Why don't you come have a seat, and we'll get down to some brass tacks."

I followed him and took my seat in a daze, still trying to make sense of everything that had just happened.

"So, she didn't know I was coming?" I asked carefully.

JJ had the grace to flush slightly. "No, she didn't. I suppose I convinced myself that she'd take it better this way, but perhaps I was putting off the inevitable. I should have known she wouldn't be pleased."

"It is definitely a complication," I agreed. "I'm used to working with people who volunteer for the training. While some may be hesitant, the chain of command is very clear, and they know they agreed to follow the plan."

"Oh, she'll go along with it, I promise you that. She knows getting the position as CEO depends on my say-so. She's not promised the job. We could always hire someone, or I could bring her brother over from the mountain ops side if necessary. So once she cools down, I'm sure she'll be on board to do whatever is necessary to convince me she's ready for it."

Unease swirled in my stomach, and I shifted in my seat. "So, how exactly do you imagine our training going?"

"Well, I sort of figured you'd know what needed to be done. You should shadow her for a while, give her time to show you how she operates, so you can see where the gaps lay in what I need and what she's doing. Then you'll set out an action plan to get her on board."

"I see. And what time frame are we operating with?"

"Ideally, I'd like her ready to take over by the end of the year. Then she and I can work together for a few months while I hand off more of my responsibilities to her, and get in one last season before I retire."

I nodded, mulling it over. "I'd say five months is reasonable. And after that, you'll be out completely?"

To my surprise, JJ laughed boisterously. "Not a chance. I'll no longer be CEO, but I'll stay on the board with Robert and our investors. So I'll still be around. Just not running the day-to-day."

"I see. And will you want me to stay on in this position after the new year, or do you have an idea where I would transition when you've determined she's ready?" I kept my voice neutral, but this was the vitally important question.

My job in the military always had a certain amount of guarantee attached, first my enlisted contract, then my commission, followed by the tour at OTS. As long as you didn't fuck up royally, they couldn't kick you out. Civilian jobs came with no such guarantee. He was essentially offering me a five-month contract, perhaps eight, with a promise to extend if he was pleased with the result.

Five months was terrifying—I had no back-up plan, and no chance of getting another job that paid enough to cover the expenses of my household in this town.

"We can make that determination at the end of the year. I have a few ideas in mind but I'm not ready to settle on them yet. But don't worry, we'll take care of you," he added with a wink. "If you can get my Isabelle ready to take over as CEO, that's all the proof I need that you'll be an excellent addition to our Aspen Ridge family."

I swallowed down the panic. "Excellent, I look forward to it, JJ."

CHAPTER 4
ELLIE

"No, you don't understand, it's an absolute nightmare," I protested, popping a ketchup-laden fry into my mouth and washing it down with a gulp of amber ale.

After that disaster of epic proportions, I had no choice but to run away to the other side of town—where my best friend Tessa's family owned the Aspen Ridge Brewery—for an emergency drink and comfort. I couldn't risk being overheard by employees at the resort. It was just too humiliating.

"So your dad hired some hunky Air Force guy to work with you, *closely*, a guy that you've been swooning over all weekend, and you're *upset* about it?" Tessa raised an eyebrow over her own pint. The bar was quiet for a Monday lunch rush, and we'd been able to chat undisturbed.

"I'm not upset he hired him, obviously. I'm upset he hired him to be my personal babysitter and tell me how to do my job. I don't need someone following me around and looking over my shoulder. I know my job, and I'm damn good at my job," I added vehemently, taking a giant bite of my burger so I could take a break from talking. Tessa had listened to me rant while my food cooled, and I'd now reached the point of repeating myself.

"You are good at your job," she soothed, flicking her chestnut ponytail over her shoulder. "But from the sounds of it, he's hoping this guy will help you transition into *his* job. That's not a bad thing, is it? Instead of just giving you the 'sink-or-swim' approach, he's trying to set you up for success?"

"It's insulting," I argued around my mouthful before swallowing. "Like he doesn't think I can do it on my own. I have an MBA, for chrissakes. What more does he want from me?"

"I don't know if you're looking at it the right way," Tessa disagreed. "I think all of this is just to help you be successful. He wants you to take over the biggest part of the family business—that's a huge vote of confidence! Even your older brother handles less, running the ski resort. So I think he just wants to verify that you're ready before he hands over the reins."

"Maybe," I grumbled saltily. "But I still don't get why he had to spring this guy on me."

"Well, maybe it will work in your favor. You can show Jake how you like to do things, and maybe he'll agree with you over your dad. He could become an asset to you if you win him to your side."

"Tess, he's military. He's come here to put me through boss boot camp or some shit. Plus, he works for my dad. He's definitely not on my side in this scenario."

"You never know," she disagreed. "Maybe your little hookup is in your favor. You should try to work that angle and see if it does you any good."

"I can't, Tessa." the whine in my voice was unmistakable. "Friday was an exception—I didn't know he worked in lodging, so there was no conflict. But now I'm going to be working directly with him. 100% off limits."

Tessa's cheerful smile melted. "I'm sorry, Ellie. After how excited you were about him, I know this is a double bummer."

"Exactly. I can't tell if I'm more upset that my dad hired me a babysitter, or that the babysitter turned out to be the guy I've been fantasizing about for the last two days. God, Tess, it was so hot. He just has this... intensity to him, but he's also, like, disarmingly sweet."

A shiver ran down my spine as I recalled Jake twining his fingers in my hair, pulling firmly to drag my head back so he could pepper fiery kisses down my neck.

Tessa sighed dreamily. "That sounds amazing. There is a disturbing lack of hot, fit, single guys in this town. They're either gay, taken, or only here for a week. Or they reek of patchouli or pot, sometimes both." Her eyes drifted to her fellow bartender, a skinny white guy with long, dirty blonde locs and a scraggly beard.

I stifled the giggle that rose in my throat. "No prospects, huh?"

She rolled her green eyes. "Please. I'm thinking about ordering one in from Russia. Is that a thing, like the opposite of mail-order brides? Can I get a mail-order hottie for a husband?"

"Girl, you own a brewery. If you can't find an eligible man, we're all doomed."

"My *family* owns a brewery." She tapped the side of her nose. "You know exactly why that distinction is important. And the only guys I meet here are tourists with their families, tourists looking to hook up, or locals coming in for the $9.99 lunch special." She glanced meaningfully at my plate.

"Hey, I came here to talk to you; food was just the bonus. I can pay full price if you want. Just because I like a cheap meal doesn't mean I can't buy you flowers, baby." I leaned in suggestively and waggled my eyebrows.

That drew a laugh from her. "I'm just teasing

you, but you know what I mean. At least you have Zach. I have no one."

"Tess, I don't have Zach. We broke up after college."

"Only because you went out of state for your MBA," she argued back. "And you guys were on-again, off again for ages when you both came back."

"That wasn't anything serious," I insisted. "We just go way back. It's comfortable. We've known each other forever and we're both in the same position. He's as stuck at Snowshoe as I am at Aspen Ridge, family drama and all."

"Yeah, well, methinks the lady doth protest too much," Tessa replied in a singsong.

"What is that supposed to mean?"

"All I'm saying is, he's exactly what you say you need: a peer who will never be an employee. He's super hot and also understands your position in the family business because his family has the *same* business."

"Yeah, well, that's part of the problem. Because he wants to take over our resort and form a network under Snowshoe."

"What did your dad think?"

I almost choked on my beer. "Are you kidding? You think I told him that? I didn't want to have to visit my dad in jail. There's no way in a million years my dad would be on board for a merger, let alone my brother or the Blackwells. I'm sure the Dubois kid would agree to whatever got him more money, but my dad and Robert? They bleed for this mountain. They'd never sell out."

"Are you so sure it'd be a sellout? I thought it was more like giving access for people staying at Snowshoe to ski here and vice versa."

"I'm sure. He laid out his whole scheme in complete detail. We'd be beholden to *their* board for all the ways they wanted us to run *our* business. No thanks. My dad and Robert made sure they collectively had sixty percent of the shares when they brought on investors. Even once James, Reece, Stella, Blaise, and I inherit, all of us will have larger shares than any of the board. They worked it out in advance, to make sure of it. If any of us decide to sell, we have to offer our shares to resort family to purchase first. So there's no way in hell my dad would even consider something like Zach proposed."

My blood boiled just to think of it. We'd been moving toward reconciling—Tessa wasn't wrong, we were a great match—and then he let slip his grand idea. A team of investors built Snowshoe Ridge Resort, and Zach's family had the largest single share, but the ruthless board outmatched them. They built a quaint resort town about twenty minutes from us, perfectly laid out, the way Napoleon III redesigned Paris—by plowing over the locals and rebuilding to suit their own needs. Oh, they paid the businesses in the small village a fair amount to pack up, and then razed the entire area. But while beautiful, Snowshoe had none of the historical charm that most of the other local resorts had. They literally tore it all down. It was like winter Disney World now, completely manu- factured.

Our resort was the lifeblood for the entire town of Aspen Ridge. I couldn't imagine what would happen if my family weren't at the helm, protecting the locals that supported us.

Anyway, after Zach told me what he was after, I couldn't trust that he was trying to get back together with me for the reasons he said. What if it was just a tactic to get Aspen Ridge? The doubts crept in until I just couldn't do it anymore and called it quits for good.

"I suppose you're right," Tessa sighed. "And I can't even date him, out of solidarity for my bestie. What a waste."

I knew she was joking, but it still sent a twinge through my heart. Even if I couldn't trust his motives, I still cared about him. The truth be told; he was a great boyfriend. Kind, attentive, and generous. Even though he technically owned the resort, I always saw him treat the staff with respect, and his management approach was much like my own. So while I didn't want him, I still wanted him to be happy.

I shrugged and rolled my eyes. "Hey if you want

my sloppy seconds, be my guest. But you should know he snores like a freight train."

"Snoring?" She feigned disgust. "Absolutely not. I'll settle for patchouli and pot."

We dissolved in a fit of giggles, and I felt the crush of anger in my chest loosen. This was why I came here—I knew Tessa would help put my mental train back on the tracks.

And she was right. In his own way, my dad was trying to help me out. He just didn't believe I could run Aspen Ridge Lodging my way—perhaps it was from his experience taking over the business. But in my world, today, we believed in different methods. I learned everything they taught me at business school, but I also had a lifetime of experience in our family business, and I knew it intimately. I knew which practices we could update, and so many ways we could make things better for our staff. Happy staff made happy customers, which was one reason I insisted on paying for the best at our end of season parties. When the staff felt appreciated, they kept coming back and passed that appreciation along to the customers. 'The way it's always been done' was a tired, dated excuse for not innovating.

So before I gave up and just did what Dad wanted to get him out of my way, I resolved to get Jake on my side. I could show him that my methods may be different, but that didn't mean they were wrong. If Jake, with all the military establishment/brainwashing, could see my side, then perhaps my dad could, too.

I just had to set the boundary now, because what happened Friday could never happen again. If my dad ever found out, he'd lose his mind—his one rule was to keep business and personal life separate.

Not that it was my fault I didn't know who *Jake* was, but it *was* sort of my fault that Jake didn't know who *I* was, and I'd done it on purpose.

So no matter how I felt about it, I had to keep things strictly professional with Jake.

From now on.

BY THE TIME I returned to the office, I had my plan well in place. I'd be cool, calm, and proficient going about my day, and let Jake see how well I could run things my way, with zero need for his leadership tips.

Having a plan didn't chase the butterflies from my stomach at the thought of spending so much time with him, but I'd just have to suck it up and get over it. Exposure therapy or something like that. It was a thing, right?

And of course, my extra stop at the restroom in the lobby had nothing to do with Jake. I just had a sudden, totally rational fear I had ketchup smeared on my cheek from that massive burger. Definitely didn't want to walk around, as Assistant CEO, with ketchup on my face.

I greeted Larissa when I left the elevator on the top floor and tried to ignore my rapidly elevating heart rate as I made my way down the hall to my office. My dad's door was open, and I could hear him laughing, then Jake responding with a chuckle and a comment.

Pulse pounding, I set my bag in my office, fluffed my hair, and strode into my father's office with all the appearance of absolute confidence.

Fake it 'til you make it was definitely my motto.

"Hi Dad, Jake. Did you guys have a good lunch?" I greeted them with a warm smile and friendly tone.

My dad beamed in response, but I didn't miss Jake's surprised jump when I spoke. He recovered quickly and turned around to smile as well.

"Yeah, your dad took me to the Peak 9 restaurant today. I think I'm going to have to start packing my lunches if I want to be in shape for ski season," he joked, and Dad chuckled appreciatively.

"A young buck like you? You'll be fine. You must work out pretty regularly."

Fine is right. My brain abandoned all reason and began this completely inappropriate commentary. My eyes roved over his wide shoulders, the fabric of his dress shirt clinging to the hard bulges of muscles. I could practically feel the ghost of his skin under my fingertips, and my thighs clenched involuntarily.

"Well, I normally work out, but I have yet to find a gym since we arrived. If you have any recommendations, I'm open to them."

"You're welcome to use the resort facilities for now, if you like," Dad offered graciously. "They're pretty quiet, even during winter, but completely dead the rest of the year. I'll have Larissa get you a key card."

"That sounds great. I'll take you up on that. At least for a couple of weeks while I get the lay of the land."

"Then it's settled. We'll go to Season's for lunch tomorrow. It's over on Peak 3."

Jake's head tipped back, and he laughed, a rich sound that sent tingles down my legs. "You win, no sack lunch tomorrow."

"I always win," Dad replied with a mischievous grin.

Time for me to interject. "I hate to break this up, but I'm about to go do my rounds and I thought Jake ought to tag along. You ready?"

He popped out of his seat immediately. "Sure thing. Let me grab my coat."

I stepped aside so he could pass to his office, and a waft of his cologne struck me by surprise, sending my eyelids fluttering as I breathed in deeply. *That scent...*

"Izzy, you okay?"

Shit, I have got to get myself under control. "Ellie, Dad, and I'm fine."

"I don't know when you decided you didn't like Izzy," he grumbled. "I'm an old man. Some habits are hard to break, you know. I've been calling you Izzy since you were born."

"Dad, you're not that old, and I've gone by Ellie for like twenty years. You're the only one that calls me Izzy, and I've asked you not to since I was a teenager."

"Exactly, it's special. Why can't you just let me have this one?"

"Bye, Dad," I replied with a sigh. "I'll see you later."

"Okay, bye Honey. Oh, and Izzy!" He shouted when I started to walk away.

Cringing, I turned. "Yes, Dad?"

"Take it easy on him, will you? It's his first day."

I bit back the sarcastic response that rose to my lips, suggesting that such a great military leader ought to be prepared for anything. Instead, I just smiled and replied, "Sure, Dad."

Jake was waiting for me by the door to my office, suit jacket already buttoned up.

Saliva pooled in my mouth, and my tongue froze in place. The man was too damned handsome. It just wasn't fair.

I unglued my tongue and said, "Why don't you step into my office for a minute?"

Jake's dark eyes reflected confusion, but nothing else in his expression gave him away. He stepped aside and allowed me to enter, then followed me in.

"Close the door, please." He dutifully followed the instruction.

"Take a seat." I gestured between the seat in front of my desk and my cozy corner nook, then claimed the chair behind my desk.

Jake's gaze followed, then returned to me with a slight curl to his lip. "In the jungle? Is that the time out jungle?"

A snort of laughter escaped me. "It's just a chair. I wanted it to feel like a retreat when I needed one." My eyes roved over the tall plants on either side of the over-sized chair that almost created a screen from the rest of the room. "Maybe it is a bit much," I admitted.

Jake sat on the edge of the chair with a serious expression, then leaned back so some of the foliage was now in front of his face. "I feel like I'm on 'Between Two Ferns'. Do I look like Zach Galifianakis?"

That drew a burst of laughter from my lips. "Okay, enough jokes about my décor, old man. We need to talk."

"Yeah," he sighed. "We do. Obviously, if I had known who you were Friday-"

"Exactly, if I'd known who you were..." I agreed.

"...nothing would have happened," Jake finished.

"Right."

"Because it's awkward as fuck now, isn't it?" His dark eyes held my gaze, his posture slightly slouched in defeat.

"Well, I dunno about awkward, but it definitely sucks."

"Yeah."

"It's too bad. I was looking forward to your cat-and-mouse texting game. I heard you were a champ."

"Whoever told you that was lying," he replied with a grin. "I have no game. At all."

"I'm not sure I agree with you," I answered with a smile of my own. "I'd say your game was pretty strong Friday."

"I think you just liked the mystery." His grin widened, and he leaned further behind the plant. "Does this do it for you? Should I carry around a giant plant to be more mysterious?"

Laughter bubbled up in my chest. He was just so disarming it was impossible not to like him.

"No, you'd better not. Now we both know who each other is, and what my dad has planned, we obviously can't be dating, or doing anything else."

Jake straightened up immediately. "Yes, of course." His voice took on a completely different tone, a serious, taking-orders-in-the-military sort of tone.

I already missed the warmth of his teasing.

"That doesn't mean we can't be friendly, but we have to keep it strictly business from here on out." Surprisingly, I managed to say that with a completely straight face. My brain kept pulling up delicious flashes of stripping that suit from his body and mounting him on that chair.

"Agreed. Strictly business. I certainly don't want anyone to think I slept my way to the top."

He said it with such conviction that I paused for a second, wondering if he was being sarcastic or not. When the corner of his lips twitched, I allowed myself to smile.

"Yeah, we'd better maintain your Captain America image. Don't want the boss's rebellious daughter to taint you."

"What if I want to be tainted?" His half-smile deepened.

"Jake!"

"Okay, sorry, I promise I'll stop."

"We have to. There is no intra-office romance allowed. Period. It wouldn't help either of us."

"Agreed."

"So, we're good?"

"We're good," he answered in that all-business voice again.

"Okay." I stood. "Let's head out."

Jake rose from his seat and followed me into the hallway. "Where are we going?"

"On my rounds," I answered vaguely, leading him to the elevator.

"And what exactly do you do on your rounds?" That sounded like less of a curiosity question, and more of an evaluative one.

"I try to spend most of my afternoons visiting different facilities in the portfolio, checking in on the employees, chatting with the managers."

"I see," he answered seriously. "And what do you do on these visits? What is their purpose?" Something about the question made me feel as if he were implying they *had* no purpose.

It was distracting how he switched from charming to all-business so quickly. Annoyance rose quickly in my chest—clearly we were already past the flirtation and straight into business—but I answered as genuinely as I could. "There are a few. Mostly, to make sure people know me, and I know them. I want them to feel like even though we've become a huge resort, their needs are not below my attention. I want to know that they're happy, or find out if there's something I can change to make their job better. I know this business inside and out. I know every job that every employee in lodging performs. So if they have an idea to make it better, I want to hear that too."

Jake listened with rapt attention, smiling widely at the end of my little speech. "That's definitely admirable. Have you had any employees that gave you valuable suggestions during your 'rounds'?"

"Well... not exactly. I think it's more about showing them I'm present, and that I care. Every job here is important, and every employee deserves to be recognized." My tone verged on defensive and I struggled to rein it in.

"No, absolutely, I agree with you one-hundred percent," Jake nodded. "For some reason, the population believes that everyone in the Air Force is a pilot. It's definitely the most flashy job, and most wing commanders are former pilots—it's just the nature of the force. We all revolve around the aircraft. But there are thousands of jobs that, while not glamorous, are essential to the mission. The runways have to be paved, for example. Pilots—not to mention everyone else—need to eat. We need properly functioning electricity and plumbing in base facilities. Each base has thousands of jobs, and only a handful of those are pilots. They don't get the media attention, but it's a huge policy in the military to recognize superior performers at every level, not just the top."

My chest warmed—maybe it wouldn't be as difficult as I thought to win him over to my side. "Yes, exactly! This resort is enormous. It started as a single ski hill, just one peak, and a tiny hotel. My grandparents, along with the Blackwells, slowly built it up. They added hotels, more runs, condos, restaurants, and when their kids took over, they expanded even more. We have stables, an events venue-" my words froze on my lips and heat rushed to my face immediately. I wet my lips and continued shakily, "Which, of course, you know. All I mean to say is, this business has grown so large it's important that we keep ourselves from forgetting all the people at the bottom who make it happen."

"No, you're absolutely right. So, where are we headed first?"

We began in the main lodge. I greeted the front desk employees and introduced them to Jake, pleased to show off that I knew them all by name. We continued down the hall to the service elevator, riding down to the garage level and chatting with a few of the maintenance employees before heading back up to the laundry.

Pride swelled in my chest as we continued. I knew every name, and each employee happily greeted Jake, assuring him Aspen Ridge was a great place to work and how well they were treated. He asked them a few questions about their job, or the company as a whole, or their families, genuinely interested in their stories.

When we finished with the main lodge, we crossed to the Birch Run condos, and repeated the process. Even though he didn't carry a notepad, I had the distinct impression Jake was filing all the information he received away for later. I couldn't have been happier there was nothing negative for him to note.

As usual, all we encountered were happy, satisfied Aspen Ridge employees, going about their day and performing their jobs admirably. By the time we made it back to the offices, I was pretty pleased with the results of our tour. Surely, he could only agree that my techniques of maintaining first-name relationships with the employees were beneficial to the business.

When we got off the elevator, he followed me straight to my office, settling into the corner seat when I sat behind my desk.

"Well, it certainly seems like you have a very happy group of employees," he complimented with a wide smile.

I tried to ignore the sparkle in his brown eyes when he said it. Damned Captain America charm. Heat rushed to my neck just thinking about the way those eyes devoured me on Friday night.

"Thank you. It's definitely one of my priorities."

"And what are the others?"

"I'm sorry?"

"What are your other priorities?"

"Oh," that took me by surprise. "I mean, whatever my father needs me to do, obviously, to help run things."

"I see. So what are you vice president of, exactly?"

"I'm not a VP, per se. Not in the way the other VPs are, like hospitality, lodging, food service. Technically, my position is Assistant CEO."

His head tilted back. "Ah, I see. So you're your father's assistant."

Indignation rose in my chest, straightening my back. "No, I'm not his *assistant*. He has an executive assistant. I'm more like his understudy—he didn't want to take a job away from one of our VPs to give it to me, so he created a comparable position that would allow me to see the top-down view of how the business is run."

"No, that makes sense. You can't take over as CEO if you haven't seen how the job works. So, how long have you been in this position?"

"Three years," I answered, chin high. "I have made employee satisfaction my top priority for the last two years and it's had a dramatic effect on our retention rates of hourly employees."

"That's really impressive," he smiled indulgently. "I'm sure it's gratifying to see that your policies have a direct effect on your employees' lives. So what did you do before this position?"

"I was mid-level manager for a year, working directly for the VP of Lodging. Before that I managed the hotel downstairs for two years, directly after I finished my MBA. Summers during college I managed the housekeeping team, and while I was in highschool, I worked the reception desk downstairs."

"Even more impressive," he complimented. "Not a lot of kids would take a low-level job when their parents own the company."

"Oh, my dad insisted on it. He said that if we wanted to be the boss some day, we had to start from the bottom like everyone else."

Jake's head tilted slightly at that statement, and I rushed to explain. "I mean, I know it wasn't *exactly* like everyone else, but I had to do the same high school job as most of my friends. So I wasn't scrubbing toilets, but I learned firsthand how to deal with rude customers and what the rest of the staff hated about their jobs. I've taken those lessons with me as I've gone up the ranks."

"It certainly seems like you have a good understanding of all those positions. So, what do you know about your father's job?"

A snort pushed from my lips. "You mean besides long lunches and golf with the VPs?"

Jake's eyebrows lowered, his expression immediately becoming serious. "Yeah, what does he do when he's working in his office? What are his primary concerns? What are the things only the CEO manages?"

"Honestly, I think the VPs do most of the work. They bring my dad things to sign off on. They present their quarterly budgets and costs, profits, needs, and anything that he can't decide on himself he takes to the board. Other than that, it's meetings... I think more of his days are spent on duties related to his position as board chair than they are on things relating to being the CEO of Aspen Ridge Lodging."

"So, how would you change that?"

That took me by surprise. "Come again?"

"When you take over as CEO, and your father steps back to merely serving as the chair of the board? You said his days are filled with board duties. So what would you do differently, as CEO, than your father does now?"

Pleasure swelled in my chest, and I settled further into my seat. He was definitely interested in my approach, already talking about the changes I'd make when Dad retired. "Frankly, I don't think my days will differ greatly from what they are now. I'd have reports to look over, things to coordinate for the VPs to make sure they have what they need to run their portions of the business. In the afternoons, I'll continue my rounds. I might have occasional meetings that take me away, but I don't see why I can't mostly stick to how things are now."

"So your father told me I'm as likely to find you outside working with the landscaping crew as I am to find you in your office. Would you consider that an exaggeration? Are your rounds pretty much what we did today?"

A worm of unease wriggled in my belly. "Well, I have pitched in and helped if I saw someone who needed it."

"Like how? Give me an example."

Suddenly, it felt like an inquisition again. I spent the entire day Friday decorating and helping prepare food for the employee party, but I certainly didn't want to bring that up. It would renew the awkwardness as I forced him to remember getting drunk and making out. "One time we had a long-time client wanting to check in early, and the housekeeping staff was short-handed, so I stepped in to help get the rooms ready."

"Okay. And did the staff appreciate the help?"

"Absolutely. They thanked me a lot. I mean, they kept insisting they didn't need the help, but I don't want anyone to feel overwhelmed and I was there. It was no problem."

Jake's expression turned thoughtful. "Did you consider they might not think it was helpful?"

"What? Why not?"

"Well, they could have interpreted you jumping in to help as a sign that you don't think them capable of doing their jobs. Or they could have seen it as posturing: either showing that they're replaceable, or that you simply wanted to 'step down to their level' in a condescending way. Did you think about them possibly taking it that way?"

Heat flooded my cheeks. "Of course not, because

that isn't what happened. They were short two team members, and I just wanted to help them out. They knew that. There was no underlying intent aside from helping."

Jake nodded, raised his hands defensively. "Okay, I'm just asking. You should always remember that intent and interpretation aren't always the same. You can intend to be helpful—like that shoe company who gives a free pair of shoes to a kid in Africa for every pair sold. They obviously had altruistic intent. However, what happened was they put a lot of local shoemakers out of business, and the people who needed that income didn't feel as gratified by the reality."

The indignation broke like a wave over me, this criticism all the more frustrating coming from the lips I kept wanting to kiss. "You're being ridiculous. I helped to make a few beds so our staff could get home on time. That's it."

"Fair enough," he replied mildly. "Speaking of getting home to our families, it's about time for me to head out and pick up my kids."

A wave of shock rippled through me. "You have kids?"

"Yep, two. Olivia is nine and Ethan is seven."

"Wow, I didn't realize...." I trailed off, not really sure where to go from there. We hadn't exactly had the type of conversation that led to a discussion about kids and wives.

My eyes darted to his hand, but there was still no ring.

"Yeah," he chuckled awkwardly. "Not really something that comes up when I first meet someone. But they're why I got out of the Air Force. I was missing too much."

"That makes sense," I nodded, rubbing my sweaty palms on my skirt. "By all means, if you need to go..."

"Great. I'll see you tomorrow, Ellie." He stood and turned, pausing at the door for just a second before continuing.

I wondered if he was going to say something, then changed his mind. There was a charge on the air, a moment, and then he thought better of it and was gone.

A waft of his cologne trailed behind him, and I sighed, dropping my head to my hands.

Despite our agreement to keep our relationship strictly business, I had no idea how to pack up and tuck away my desire for Jake.

Stuffed shirt and all.

CHAPTER 5
JAKE

Tuesday the kids caught their bus without a hitch, and I got to work in plenty of time. My mind had been buzzing all night with thoughts on Ellie's tour the previous day, and where I could implement some changes.

I could see what JJ meant—Ellie was intent on projecting a sort of 'I'm one of you' persona to the staff. While there wasn't necessarily anything wrong with that, I wasn't ready to conclude it was completely harmless. Clearly, she didn't have a very good idea of what her duties would be as CEO. JJ and I had discussed at length what occupied his days, and it was far more than lunches and golfing. Ellie seemed to believe the meetings he was in from dawn til the end of day were not important to the position of CEO, which was likely the first thing we had to fix.

However, I still wanted to get a true feeling for how Ellie spent her days. So I went into the office intending to observe her morning schedule to see how much she handled as the Assistant CEO.

And just like yesterday, heat grew under my collar the closer I got to her office. Knowing I'd be in her presence all day was equal parts pleasure and torture. After her initial upset, we'd fallen into a comfortably flirtatious tone. Which she stamped out with the insistence that we keep everything professional.

Which was fair. There was no way around that. But it seemed that every time I so much as asked a question, her attitude toward me was like I'd betrayed her somehow through no fault of my own. I still got flashes of her sultry fire from time to time when she forgot her annoyance in the heat of something she was passionate about.

Then she quickly returned to the present and pulled back those tantalizing threads of sparkle. I had no idea how to return to a friendly tone, work together, and keep my attraction to Ellie firmly in control.

But somehow, I had to do it.

After dropping my briefcase in my office, I pulled in a deep breath, then followed the sweet, warm fragrance of her perfume down the hall and into Ellie's office.

"Morning," I knocked twice on the open door and waited to be invited in—military habit.

"Morning," she replied, glancing up at me with a cautious smile. "Did you need something?"

"Erm, just checking in to see what's on our agenda today." I was still standing in the doorway, trying not to be awkward and failing miserably. Ellie had on a yellow flowered sundress that displayed a tantalising glimpse of cleavage and reminded me far too much of the red dress from Friday. The warm vanilla and musk of her perfume filled the room—I might as well have been standing right next to her, for all the good keeping my distance did me.

"Did we have an appointment?" She asked, confused.

"Well, I'm supposed to be here to help see how I can develop your leadership style into what Aspen Ridge Lodging needs from a CEO. I'd say in order to do that, I need to do more than follow you around for a few hours, wouldn't you?"

A grimace crossed her face briefly, telling me exactly how she felt about that idea, before she recovered herself and smiled. "Sure, take a seat. But I'm not doing anything interesting this morning. Just answering some email at the moment."

I slid into the chair facing her desk, as opposed to the jungle chair in the corner. "Well, that's inevitable," I replied with a grin. "I think everyone has to deal with the occasional email."

"Nature of the beast," she agreed, her eyes darting back to her computer screen.

"So, I have a question for you: Did JJ give you any sort of list of responsibilities? Or an evaluation of any sort, to update you on your progress or his thoughts on your responsibilities?"

She snorted. "Hardly. The first year I was here, he had me sit in on his meetings and just follow him around everywhere. It was a total waste of time, and that's how I figured out how little he actually does that pertains to this job. In fact, it was my idea to take on employee satisfaction as my focus. I never had an agenda or goals. It's like he expected me to glean his priorities and just materialize the job for myself out of thin air. I found where I thought I could have the most impact."

The holes in this chain of command were becoming abundantly clear. "So, would you say you feel as though your father has given you very little direction in terms of what he expects?"

"Absolutely," she nodded, relief clear in her expression. "So I figured out a path for myself, and now I feel as if I'm being punished for not doing it his way. If he'd told me he had certain expectations, I would have met them. I thought the point was to allow me to find my way, and now that I finally have, he's brought in the calvary to fix me," she gestured in my direction. "Which, no offense, is pretty messed up."

I drew in a deep breath to force down my annoyance. I understood her frustration, but that didn't mean she was 100% right, either.

"I think it's reasonable to state that his expectations may have been unreasonable. You can't tell someone they failed to accomplish something when you never told them what you wanted."

"Exactly, thank you."

"So I will ask him to provide us with a list of expectations to work on. That'll help us figure out where the gaps lay between what you're doing and what he wants."

Anger flashed across her stunning features. "Now wait a second—what do you mean, a list of expectations?"

"Well, if your commanding officer believes you aren't meeting expectations, he has to first set forth a list of expectations and provide them to you. It's setting you up for failure to just expect you to glean what he wants without clear directives. No wonder you two are at odds."

"We're not at odds." Her body stiffened and her voice became sharp. "Just because we have different management styles, that doesn't mean I'm failing."

I straightened in my seat. "No, absolutely not. I didn't mean to imply there was some sort of failure on your part. Just a miscommunication that we can certainly clear up."

"I'm not following." Her tone was flat, and the slight downturn to her lips did nothing to make them less appealing.

"Look at it this way: Imagine you're back in school, and the professor gave you a test. Except the questions are all blank, and you're still supposed to choose the right answer. It's not fair for him to have some sort of expectations that he doesn't tell you. There's no way you could live up to them."

"Well, yes, but that's not the point. The point is, I don't *want* to live up to his criteria. I want him to trust me to lead the way I want to. *My* way."

I tried to think of an example to use, but unfortunately the military didn't really set a precedent for 'willful daughter wants to do her own thing with the family business.'

"I hear what you're saying. But before we can try to spin him over to your way of thinking, we have to first understand what he wants, right? At least then we can meet in the middle and see where the differences lay."

Her eyes narrowed as she thought it over, but eventually she sighed. "Okay, you have a point."

"Thank you. That has been known to happen once or twice."

A half smile curled her lips. "Don't get cocky. You could just as easily lose it."

"Okay, I'll be careful." I waited for a moment, but she had nothing else to add. "So... is this entire morning devoted to email?"

"No, actually Tuesday morning is my office hours."

"Office hours?"

"Yeah, I make sure I don't have any appointments and just am in my office, available, for anything that may come up."

"What sort of thing comes up on Tuesday mornings?"

"This is when employees know I'm available to take their suggestions, or address an issue they have."

This employee hand-holding thing went much deeper than even I realized, although I had my suspicions about why. "And how often do employees take advantage of your office hours?"

"I mean, I can't say it's every week, but I have been able to help someone out of a tight spot before," Ellie replied with an edge to her tone. She was shockingly defensive to even the simplest question.

"Okay," I replied, appeasing. Even though I understood why, her defensiveness was quickly becoming frustrating. "Just so I'm following, you devote this morning to checking your email and waiting for someone to need your help? And that's at any level, right? Not just VPs and managers?"

"It's not for the managers, actually. If they need something, they go to the VPs. This is only for my hourly employees." She answered flippantly, eyes on her computer screen as if to show how little importance I held.

I swallowed down my surprise. "So, you have separate office hours for the managers?"

"No, why would I?" She tapped at her keyboard, obviously replying to an email. "I try to do things in blocks, so every day I tend to the urgent email, then I leave the rest for Tuesday office hours. If it can wait, it waits."

"And how do your managers and VPs feel about this practice?"

She shrugged. "If they need me to take care of something sooner, they mark it as urgent. Otherwise, they seem fine with waiting."

"No, I meant the office hours thing. How does the rest of your management team feel about it?"

Her eyes flashed with annoyance when she redirected her gaze in my direction. "Is there a point you're trying to get at? Because you're asking a lot of vague questions, but I feel you have a point somewhere."

"It's just unusual to me, so I'm trying to understand."

"What's there to understand? I want to be available if the employees need me. End of story."

I kept my tone light, attempting not to flare up

her anger. "Yeah, that's the part that doesn't make sense to me. You have an entire management network whose job it is to make sure the employees are taken care of. There's a chain of command. And you're encouraging your employees to bypass the system that's designed to help them and take their issues straight to the top."

"Well, sometimes there are things that the manager can't handle. Maybe their problem is *with* their manager." She stated this as if it made perfect sense, but was seemingly oblivious to the obvious.

"So, there's no system in place to deal with that?"

"There is, but I wanted to offer an alternative."

I couldn't help the head shake. "I'm sorry, it just seems like something from the good idea fairy."

"What is that supposed to mean?" Ellie's tone was sharp, the crack of a whip in an otherwise quiet room.

"Sorry, the lingo is so ingrained in me I don't really know what civilians say instead. When a higher up comes up with something they think will be a great new program—something they want people to move on immediately but haven't thoroughly vetted—we call it the good idea fairy. Like a fairy flew by and dropped this magic idea in their head without any sort of practicality to back it up."

"Well, I'm sorry I don't know the lingo," she snapped, her cheeks going red as she turned in her seat to face me fully. "But I happen to think taking care of our employees is important."

"I don't disagree with you," I hurried to agree, gesturing with open hands. "It is. But—and correct me if I'm wrong—instead of working with your management to come up with an actionable plan at all levels, you made it your particular responsibility."

"So?"

"So, you've taken agency away from your lower-level managers to provide that care and connection." I crossed my legs, trying to assume a more relaxed posture.

"I know you did it because you were bored and needed to feel you were doing something of value, and that's on JJ for not giving you enough duties to keep you busy. But did you consider your managers may feel stuck or overruled by these policies? It undermines their authority, for you to allow employees to come sit in your office and complain whenever they get the urge. It undermines yours as well."

Ellie's hands splayed on the surface of her desk, the color on her face continued to darken. "You have a lot of nerve to make any sort of assumption about how any of my employees feel. You've been here all of a *day*. You know nothing about how I relate to my teams, my managers, or even the VPs. And yet you sit here telling me everything I've worked on for the last three years is a dumb idea from some fairy."

I backpedaled, raising my hands to show contrition. "Look, I'm not saying your ideas are bad—far from it. The whole point of the good idea fairy is the ideas *are* good—the issue is that most ideas have to be massaged and vetted before we can turn them into something actionable. I think you took a good idea and ran with it, which is admirable. I just don't think you took the time to work out all the kinks."

I could practically see the steam coming out of her ears. "Well, thanks for your opinion," she snapped. "I will take it under advisement. If you don't mind, I have a meeting that's just come up and I think it would be better if you didn't tag along. But I'll see you after lunch so we can do some more rounds and perhaps help you get a better perspective."

There was clearly no cooling her down—I thought being direct was the best approach, but I'd obviously ruffled her feathers. Perhaps I showed my cards too early. "Okay, I think that's a great idea. I'll reconnect with JJ and see if we can put together a list of expectations in the meantime. I look forward to this afternoon."

Ellie flashed me a hard, sarcastic smile, waiting for me to depart.

I stood and turned my back, feeling once again as if the conversation hadn't gone the way I intended.

"Jake?" When she spoke, her tone was softer, and I turned eagerly to find some sort of silver lining.

"Yes?"

But she wasn't looking at me, her focus completely on her email. "Will you close the door, please? Thanks."

"No problem," I replied, pulling it gently behind me before I breathed a deep sigh.

That did not go how I wanted at all.

I HAD some success getting a list of appointments and regularly scheduled events from JJ's executive assistant, but getting a list of expectations out of JJ for Ellie was much harder.

I thought we'd talk it out over lunch and I'd be able to discuss it with Ellie this afternoon, but it was soon clear that even JJ didn't know what he wanted.

"She just needs to be more... authoritative," he threw out, leaning back in his chair. "She's too wishy-washy."

"How would you like her to show you more authority?" I probed. "She took it upon herself to create this employee satisfaction program, right? I'd say that shows a fair amount of authority."

"It's hard to explain," he sighed, scrubbing at his beard. "She's so intent on making the employees like her, she's not spending any time running the actual business."

"Well, if you have a list of duties you'd like her to

take over, I'm happy to bring that to her so we can get started."

"It's not as simple as a list of tasks," he huffed. "It's more about *how* she acts. She doesn't act like a CEO."

It was only my second day working with Ellie, and the lack of clear expectations was even frustrating to me. How was I supposed to help Ellie meet JJ's criteria for taking over as CEO when he didn't even know what he wanted? How was I supposed to be successful at this job, and earn my place, if I couldn't glean what he wanted, either?

I need this job, I reminded myself with a slow breath. "And how should she act as a CEO?"

"Authoritative. Confident. Dutiful." JJ listed these attributes without hesitation... or further explanation.

I copied them down, then probed further. "Can you give me an example of a time when you thought she should have acted more authoritative? It'll help me illustrate it to her."

JJ was looking seriously annoyed at my continued questioning. His brows furrowed, and he ran a hand over his short beard thoughtfully. "I don't have a specific example. It's just a feeling. She doesn't feel ready to take over."

The more I talked with JJ, the more I squirmed with the realization that I may have taken an impossible job. It seemed to me as if the real problem was that *he* wasn't ready to let his daughter take over... but obviously, I couldn't tell him that.

Instead, I tried another tack. "JJ, can I be straight with you?" My heart rate sped up, heat rising under my collar. This could go one of two ways, and I didn't know JJ well enough to guess.

"Of course, always."

"I've developed a lot of leaders, both the enlisted and officers. And one thing I know—it's imperative to have a clear set of goals for them to meet. I can't tell someone they need to be more confident, because it's impossible to measure. What if they believe they are confident? What exactly is 'confident *enough*'? Where do we draw that line? I think Ellie has a lot of great attributes, and I'm not capable of declaring her 'suitably confident' because it's not a measurable metric. Without measurable goals, we'd just be setting ourselves up for frustration all around."

JJ's mouth formed a hard line while he mulled over my words. It was a risk, calling him out for being vague versus placating him, but we needed to agree if we were ever going to reach a solution where everyone was happy. My heart pounded, wondering if I'd just shot myself in the foot.

Finally, he nodded. "I see what you're saying. But how do we come up with these goals? What do you propose?"

My racing pulse slowed, and I laid out my

thoughts on how we could find some middle ground.

Finally, we had a plan, and hopefully one that Ellie would agree to as well.

I'D SCARCELY MADE it back into the office, the plan in place, when Ellie shot it straight to hell.

"Jake, you ready?" She stuck her head through my open doorway. "We've gotta get a move on."

"Sure thing. More rounds?" I stood and slipped my suit jacket back on.

"Something like that," she replied with a dark smile.

I couldn't be sure, but there was something alarming about the way she said it that set my teeth on edge. It felt like a challenge, somehow, even though I couldn't quite explain why.

However, I had been the one arguing that I needed to observe how she spent her day to help me could find the disconnect between her and her father, so I swallowed down my trepidation and followed her to the elevator and downstairs. I should have been curious about the wide sun hat she had materialized during the morning, or noticed the unmistakable fragrance of coconut sunscreen.

However, I didn't know what I was in for until she led me outside. It was a surprisingly hot day for the mountains—apparently that thinner atmosphere made up for the high elevation—and the sun beat down mercilessly on the stone court-yard between towering buildings.

Ahead, smack in the middle, a stand was erected with a sign bearing the words 'Employee Apprecia-tion Day' draped across the top. Several coolers were arranged behind the stand, and large jugs of yellow liquid, surrounded by stacks of paper cups, filled the surface. Already a small line had formed, people wearing Aspen Ridge Lodging polos chatting while they waited. A small cheer rose from the crowd when they spotted Ellie, who waved and beamed back at them.

I followed Ellie to the stand, taking it all in. "A lemonade stand?"

"You're a quick one," she teased, pouring a cup and handing it to the first person in line. "What are you waiting for? Get to work." She gestured to the jug and cups before me.

We got busy drawing cups of lemonade and handing them out. Ellie greeted most of the employees by name, mentioning some personal detail about them to show she knew who they were. She had light-hearted conversations with each employee while I waited dutifully to hand her the next cup.

The sun roasted me from behind, sweat sticking my dress shirt to my back under my suit coat. Eventually I slipped it off and rolled my sleeves up—taking off the layer helped, but it was too late to wish I'd put on sunblock. The skin on the back of my neck was painfully hot, but more people kept joining the line and so we kept serving, pausing only to refill the pitchers from gallon jugs in the coolers.

Eventually, the flood of employees slowed, and I could slake my thirst with a cup of lemonade. My shirt was thoroughly damp, and my socks were squishy with sweat inside my highly polished dress shoes. My feet ached from standing on the hard brick for so long, and I desperately needed a shower.

The lemonade was light and refreshing, not too sweet or sour. I put away three cups before I glanced up to see Ellie watching me with a self-satisfied smirk on her perfect lips.

I couldn't help but smile back. "Did we become enemies at some point in the past 24 hours?" I asked. "I feel like I was just punished, but I have no idea why." I gestured to my over-heated body.

"I mean, punishing you is not why I had a lemonade stand, but I'd definitely say it's a perk," she replied.

Despite my elevated temperature, I couldn't help but grin. Something about Ellie just disarmed my defenses. "Did you put this together this morning?"

"No, of course not. We have something every Tuesday. I send out the email Tuesday morning letting them know what it will be, but the employees already know to expect some kind of treat."

"Doesn't that take away from their attention to their work?"

She shrugged. "They're entitled to a break, and this way I can give them a little something to look forward to. Sometimes I deliver baskets of treats from a local bakery to each building. Maybe in the winter it's hot cocoa and coffee set out in the individual break rooms when we're too busy, so people don't have to step away from their work centers."

"And this is all part of your employee appreciation campaign." I swiped a hand across my sweaty forehead and downed another cup.

"Of course. There are companies in silicon valley that have free food, video games, fancy gyms and spas for their employees as perks. Car washes, for chrissakes. We can't do all of that, but we can do something small like this. It's not much, but it makes a difference."

Her passion for caring for her employees brought a smile to my lips. It was admirable how much she truly cared about their happiness... so much so that she was out here in the baking heat of the midday sun to provide them some refreshment.

"Well, I think it's a great idea," I commented. "The employees definitely seem to appreciate it."

Her answering smile was brilliant, and my heart

thudded in response. "Thank you. I guess not all visits from the good idea fairy are bad."

"Hey, I never said that," I protested. "Just that sometimes people try to act on them before thoroughly working out all the kinks. But I'd say that this one seems to be pretty smooth."

"I'll take that compliment." The smile she graced me with in that moment was all warmth and happiness, and my heart lurched.

This gorgeous woman was the picture of summer freedom with sun-kissed skin and long shapely legs that I had to actively restrain myself from stroking. They were too well-featured in a sundress that ended several inches above her knees. The dress perfectly accented her curves, and my gaze roved over her body for a few moments too long before I drew my eyes back to her face. To her credit, she pretended as if she hadn't just caught me leering.

"Um, you're welcome," I replied awkwardly, acutely aware that I was drenched from head to toe in sweat and probably looked like a half-drowned, sunburned rat next to the elegant creature beside me.

If we kept this up, I'd probably die of humiliation long before JJ fired me for lusting after his daughter.

MY CLOTHES HAD MOSTLY DRIED when I brought the kids over to my parents' for dinner. My mom offered and I could hardly pass up the opportunity to enjoy a home-cooked meal I didn't have to prepare—that was truly a rare occasion these days.

However, I didn't take into account how Ethan and Olivia would feel about it.

As soon as they clambered into my truck and buckled up, I told them.

"Guess what guys? We're going to Gramma and Grandpa's for dinner!" I assumed they'd be excited, given that they'd been asking to go back since I picked them up Sunday night.

I one-hundred percent did not expect the shit storm that I stirred up.

Olivia stared out the window, complete disengaged. Ethan, however, lost his mind.

"No! I don't want to go to Grandpa's. You said we were going to have grilled cheese for dinner. I want grilled cheese!" His face was already tomato-red when I glanced in my rear-view mirror.

'What's wrong, buddy? I thought you wanted to go back? You love Gramma's cooking, and I bet she still has some cookies." The ones we had taken home were already long-gone.

"I don't WANT cookies, I want GRILLED CHEESE." The shriek was ear-splitting, and I had no idea how he managed to make that sound.

I took a deep breath to control the tide of anger

rising in my chest. I was the adult here. I needed to practice patience. "Well, I'm sorry bud, I already told Gramma we're coming. So she's cooking dinner for us. We can do grilled cheese tomorrow?"

"You PROMISED we'd have grilled cheese TONIGHT. You promised me FIRST!" Tears were streaming down his little cheeks, already leaving damp spots on his shirt.

My patience dwindled. Instead of appeasing, I went for the firm 'dad-voice shut it down' approach. "I'm the parent here, okay? I say we're going to Gramma and Grandpa's and that's it. We'll have grilled cheese another night."

"I WANT-"

"I DON'T CARE what you want!" I shouted back, slamming my hand on the steering wheel. "I'm your dad. You listen to me. End of story. Screaming about it doesn't get your way. It's about time you learned that."

Ethan devolved into hysterical crying, kicking the back of the seat in an all-out tantrum. Olivia ducked her head, covering her ears.

Shit. So much for dad of the year.

We were only a few blocks from my parents' house, but I pulled over and got out of the truck, closing the door and taking a moment to breathe.

He was only seven. I knew he didn't handle change well. I was supposed to be the adult here. I should know better.

Drawing in a deep, fortifying breath, I walked around to the passenger side and opened Ethan's door. He was still wailing.

I put my hand on his shoulder. "Ethan, I'm really sorry. I shouldn't have yelled at you. Can we talk for a minute?"

His eyes grew wide, and he gulped down air, wiping his cheeks with the back of his hand. His sobs quieted somewhat, but his little face was still angry.

Progress.

"I'm sorry, I should have remembered that I promised you grilled cheese tonight. I know you don't like it when we change plans, and that's my fault, okay?"

He nodded, although his expression remained resentful.

"I just thought you'd be excited to go see Grandpa again, so when Gramma called to invite us over, I didn't even think about it. I bet you know how that happens, sometimes? When you just say yes to something that sounds good without thinking too hard about it? I'm a grown-up but I still make mistakes. I know I'm not perfect, but I'm trying my best."

"I know, Daddy," he hiccuped. "It's okay."

"Thank you, Ethan. Do you think, just for tonight, we could go to Gramma's and be happy to be there? I already promised we were coming and I know she and Grandpa would be sad if we didn't go now."

He thought about this seriously for a moment. "Okay, but can we still have grilled cheese another time?"

The tension in my chest loosened. "You got it, buddy. And I promise I won't change plans on you like that again. Can I have a hug?"

He threw his arms wide, and I leaned into the truck to embrace him, still in his booster seat. I felt his little hand patting my back, like he was comforting me, and tears pricked at the back of my eyes.

When I pulled back he smiled, his face already returning to a normal color.

"Thanks buddy. Now let's go see what kind of goodies Gramma made for us!"

I closed his door and climbed back into the driver's seat, then finished the trip to my parents. Ethan raced up the walkway and into the house, and I climbed out, surprised to find Olivia still in the truck.

"You okay, honey?" I opened the door for her. "I'm sorry for yelling. That wasn't very good daddy behavior."

She unbuckled her seat and gave me a half smile. "No, it wasn't. But you did good after."

"I did?" I asked, surprised at her speaking up at all.

"Yeah, it's what mommy would have done."

My throat clenched. "It is, huh?" I hoped this would not be a conversation that led to more tears.

"Yeah. Mommy wasn't always nice, you know. She lost her temper sometimes. But she always apologized. She said she wasn't perfect, but she tried to be better."

"Well, that sounds pretty smart. Maybe I should try that."

Olivia smiled. "You should."

"When did you get so smart and grown up, Livvie?" I teased, pulling her in for a hug and lifting her from the truck.

She clung to me until I set her feet on the ground. "I've always been smart, Daddy."

"That's true," I agreed, straightening up.

"Daddy?"

"Yeah, honey?" I reached for her hand and we started up the walkway.

"You need a shower."

"Hey!" I laughed. "That's not nice."

"But it's true, Daddy."

"Fair enough."

AFTER DINNER, mom was watching a movie with the kids while Dad and I cleaned up.

"So... hows work going?" He was scraping

mashed potatoes into a clean Country Crock container. It made me smile and shake my head; I'd bought my parents a full set of fancy Tupperware so they didn't have to use old food containers, and it was still sitting in a box in the pantry. Apparently, it was more about habits than necessity.

"Work is good," I replied, carrying dishes from the table.

My dad and I were not brilliant conversationalists together. We worked in silence for a few moments before he spoke again.

"How are the kids adjusting?"

"They're doing alright, I think."

"You think?" He set the serving dish in the sink and reached for another.

I continued transferring dishes to the island. "Olivia doesn't tell me much of anything, and Ethan is just as likely to scream at me as he is to talk. So, I don't actually know."

"Well, perhaps you need to talk to them more."

I snorted and grabbed the dishrag to wipe the table. That was pretty rich, coming from him.

Apparently, Dad didn't need to hear my inner monologue to pick up on my reaction. "I know I wasn't around as much as I should have been when you were a kid, Jake. Trust me, your mother and I had plenty of discussions about it."

Dad never used the word 'fought'. It was always discussions or talks.

"But I'm telling you now not to use me as an example for how to father."

That pulled me up short, and I turned to face him. "Dad, I don't resent you. I know you were busy with your career. You were still a great dad." It was uncomfortable talking to him about this. He never discussed anything emotional when I was growing up, or in the long years since I left the house.

His tone grew gruff. "I could have been a lot better, I know that now. And I regret it. I can't get that time back, and I'd much rather have spent it playing baseball and building bird houses than at the club, carrying on with a group of guys I don't even talk to anymore."

"Dad..." my voice was soft. I had no idea he'd been harboring these feelings.

"No, don't look at me like that," he waved me off. "I've made peace with it. Just take my advice and be better than I was. Your kids need you, and I bet if you open up to them, they'll do the same for you."

"I dunno. I think they need a mother."

"Well, Cheryl certainly isn't coming back, so I wouldn't start barking up that tree," he snorted, pressing the lid on a sour cream container filled with corn and stowing it in the fridge.

"I don't mean Cheryl, Dad. But I'm a poor substitute for the complete family they deserve. I'm not in a hurry, but I hope to meet someone who genuinely wants to be their mother and take care of our home."

"Bah, that's a load, and you know it. This is your chance to really have a relationship with Ethan and Olivia, Jacob. Don't blow it waiting for another woman to make your home complete. There are millions of people in the world who raise children on their own, a lot of them much less capable than you."

"I'm not sure if that's a compliment or an insult."

"Maybe it's both. Focus on being their father, Jake. That's all they need right now."

CHAPTER 6
ELLIE

"Well, that sounds positive?" Tessa's long sweatpants-clad legs draped over the side of my swivel chair, and she swirled the glass of wine in her hand. "I mean, from where I'm sitting, it sure sounds like he's on your side." She spun in the chair like it was a theme park ride, and I knew better than to comment about it. She'd just go faster.

"Then I'm doing a poor job of explaining it," I sighed. "It doesn't *feel* like he's on my side. Just when I think he's seeing things my way, he brings up asking my dad for a freaking list of goals." I rolled my eyes, certain Tessa couldn't see it where I lay sprawled on the couch.

"That... also seems reasonable," Tessa replied. "How are you and your dad ever going to see eye-to-eye if you don't know what he wants in the first place? It has frustrated you since day one because he didn't give you a specific job. And now you've got Jake here saying the same thing. You can't be mad at him for it."

"It's not that simple, Tess. Sure, it was frustrating at first, but I made it work. I created my own programs, really took ownership of something, you know? And now he's brought in this guy to tell me all the stuff I've done is pointless."

She paused in her spinning and regarded me skeptically. "Is that really what he said?"

"No, it's not." I sat up and retrieved my wineglass from the table. "But that's how it feels. It would have been great to have him here three years ago, but now? I feel like I've got a handle on things. I know what I need to do, and my dad should trust me to do it. It honestly feels like a slap in the face for him to bring this guy in now and try to tell me what to do."

"I know it sucks, and I'm sorry. Now, do you want to whine some more, or do you want to hear about my latest catch?"

I glared at her, then took another sip. "No, you're right, I'm whining. Sorry. Tell me."

"Okay, so this guy came into the brewery and started hitting on me straight off. He was with his buddies, all obviously here for biking, and obviously married."

"How do you know he's married?"

She leveled a stare at me. "Please, I'm no amateur. He had a freaking tan line from his wedding ring."

"Okay, fair enough. Continue." I gestured and leaned back into the couch.

Tessa sat up in her seat to refill her glass and leaned forward with excitement. "So, he started asking what I did for fun around here."

Realization set in, and I straightened. "Tessa, you didn't."

"You bet your ass I did." Her grin was incredibly evil.

"How many poor saps have you done that to now?"

She snorted, leaning back in her chair. "Listen, if they're up here looking to cheat on their wives, they deserve it."

"I know, but getting tourists to skinny dip with you in a leech-infested lake, then stealing their clothes and ditching them is kind of high school, don't you think?"

"I don't actually steal their clothes, Ellie," her condescending tone was heavily sarcastic. "I leave them one piece every quarter mile or so for the walk back. By the time they get to their car, they're fully dressed."

"Yeah, but I bet they don't realize they've brought back hitchhikers until they get into the shower." The laughter bubbled up in my throat, but I tried to stifle it. "It's really..." I pursed my lips, trying to keep the giggles in. "It's really... cruel," a laugh slipped out, and Tessa started snorting. "What kind of impression are you giving our guests about Aspen Ridge?" Tears were forming at the corners of my eyes as I tried to hold back the peals of laughter that wanted to escape.

"I'm giving them an excellent lesson in karma for being cheating assholes," Tessa declared triumphantly. "And don't worry, I send them a text letting them know to check for leeches. And how to remove them. In the morning." At this point she couldn't hold in her own laughter, and once she started, I couldn't help it. We shared a solid thirty seconds of belly laughs before it finally died down.

When we regained control of our senses, I shook my head. "You're diabolical. What if you meet a truly good guy and you have no idea because you're too focused on getting revenge against those losers?"

Tessa just shrugged. "I'll know when I meet a good one. But I might just die from shock."

"Maybe I should have you meet Jake. I'm pretty sure he's a good one. Perhaps you two would hit it off." I said it as a throwaway statement, but she saw right through me.

"Hell no, I wouldn't touch that guy with a ten-foot pole. I don't care how good of a guy he is."

"Why not?" I asked, immediately offended on Jake's behalf for the rejection.

"Because whether you want to admit it, you like him. And even if things are complicated now, that doesn't mean they'll always be. There's no way I could even attempt something when I know how you feel."

Sometimes, having a friend who knew you almost too well was annoying.

"Fine. You're right, I do like him."

"See? There's a chance it could work out. You just need to avoid jumping his bones until your dad's out of the way."

"If only it were that easy," I sighed, reaching for the nearly empty wine bottle and pouring the dregs into my glass.

Tessa spun in the chair again. "Is he really that hot, El? I mean, Zach's pretty good looking and you were never really hot under the collar for him."

"I know. I know! Yes, he's hot, but there's more to it than that. He's got this whole vibe that's hard to explain. It's like two parts Captain America, one part naughty schoolboy, and one part take-charge boss man. It's a confusing mix. I keep imagining what he'd be like in bed."

"There's only one way to find out..." Tessa's

suggestive tone sent immediate warning bells through my head.

"No, no, no. We agreed, no messing around while we're working together. Period."

"I'm curious now, I have to admit. Is he going to be at the Fall Fest?"

"I don't know, honestly. I haven't really discussed it with him."

"I think it's high time your bestie met this complex puzzle of a man. I can help you sort it out. Just bring him by my booth."

"Sure, because that won't look obvious," I snorted into my glass.

"It doesn't have to be. Just think of it as a chance for me to evaluate if he's worth all this angst."

"It's not angst! It's... it's..." I searched for something that sounded more mature than angst.

"Hormones?"

"Fuck off, it's not hormones. I just like him, and I can't do anything about it, and it's frustrating."

"I can tell you're very frustrated. You should take out some of that frustration on Captain America. Maybe you can just get it out of your system."

"God, will you stop already? I thought you were supposed to be my friend."

"I am, and that's why I'm giving you permission to jump his bones." Tessa lifted her wineglass and made the sign of the cross in front of her chest with it. "Go forth and bone."

I couldn't help chuckling. "You're impossible. I can't."

"El, your dad doesn't need to know. Maybe once you scratch that itch, you'll be over it."

"Yeah, or maybe I'll just be even more *into* it. Did you consider that possibility?"

"Why is that a bad thing?"

"I don't have space to deal with this right now. I need to be focused on getting my dad to let go of the reins."

Tessa blew out a breath. "Fine. Want to go tourist trapping with me? I find it an excellent way to get out my frustrations."

"Look, I don't judge you for it, but that's just not my cup of tea. You enjoy, though."

"Suit yourself! But if you ever change your mind, just know that a lot of these sleazebags would love the idea of a threesome. It'd be easy kills."

AFTER TESSA LEFT, I thought about what she said for a long time. I already knew what frustrated me about my dad. I found my own way, figured out where I could be of value to the business, and made things happen.

And in two days, Jake had ripped it all to shreds.

Perhaps that wasn't fair. He didn't exactly rip it to shreds. But he accused me of not thinking through or vetting my changes thoroughly before implementing them, which was a punch to the gut. I saw a lack, and I stepped up to make changes. As CEO, I'd have to be decisive. That's how it worked. If I was constantly second-guessing myself, I'd never get anything done, and my father would accuse me of being weak-willed.

Jake's gentle criticism was frustrating. He wasn't being a dick, just telling me what he thought directly. I hated that he made sense, even more than I hated that he was so damn attractive while telling me how I'm doing everything wrong.

Even today, when I knowingly set him up to be sweaty and miserable at the lemonade stand, he was still handsome and impossibly attractive. Even his sweat smelled good. That was weird, right? That I thought his sweat smelled good?

There was something about him that appealed to me in a way I couldn't deny. And he seemed to genuinely want to help.

So maybe we couldn't be lovers right now, but perhaps it didn't mean we had to be enemies either. Maybe I could tone down my attraction to the man and meet in the middle... as friends?

Vowing to give it more consideration, I went to bed planning to focus more on what Jake had to say, and not so much on how his lips moved when he said it.

THE NEXT MORNING, I wasn't even surprised when Jake tapped at my door a minute after nine.

"Come on in, Jake. You really don't have to stand in the hallway like that." I smiled to show I meant it in a friendly way, and my smile naturally widened when my gaze landed on him. Once again, he wore a full suit and tie, not a hair out of place, and he treated me to a rare smile in return. It was entirely unfair for him to look that good and expect me to keep my hands to myself. My tongue swept over my lower lip instinctively and heat pooled in my belly.

"Sorry," he stepped inside and sat down. "Military habit."

"Is the suit part of that habit?" I gestured. "Surely no one told you that was required? I think my dad only wears a suit about three times a year, aside from board meetings."

He shifted, obviously uncomfortable. "To be honest, no one really told me anything about a dress code, so I erred on the side of caution. I'm pretty sure I saw one of the VPs in jeans yesterday." He leaned forward to transmit this information in a low voice, as if he were telling a dangerous secret.

I couldn't help the laugh that followed. "We encourage the VPs to dress appropriately for their duties, so it's possible. Whenever Jen is going out to the stables, I know she feels more comfortable in jeans when she's around the horses."

"You oversee the stables, too?" He flipped through a sheaf of papers in his hands as if checking for a bullet point he missed.

"Not exactly. She just likes to ride, so sometimes she takes her lunch break on horseback."

"Oh. Well, I suppose that's a perk."

"Yes, one of many. Speaking of, are you enjoying the gym?"

"I haven't gotten in there yet, I'm afraid. Still adjusting to the schedule and altitude." He looked almost embarrassed by this admission, like going a week without hitting the gym was shameful.

"That's fair. It can take a while. But regardless— you don't have to wear a suit, if you don't want to. Pretty much anything you see others wearing is okay. I wouldn't recommend the jeans for office work, though, just a tip." I smiled, and he beamed back at me.

"Duly noted."

"So, I assume you have an agenda today?" I gestured to the folder in his hands.

"Well, first I wanted to ask what was on your schedule for the day."

"How kind of you."

"It seemed smart, given the circumstances."

"Absolutely. I appreciate your consideration."

"I'm glad to hear it," he grinned, and the flirtatious gleam was back in his eye. "Always nice to be appreciated."

"Of course. But truthfully, I don't have much. It's a rather quiet morning for me, I'm afraid."

"Excellent. Then perhaps we have some time to talk?"

"I was planning on getting to work on my next employee appreciation event, but I suppose we can do both."

"Perfect. Let's devote half the morning to my notes, and the other half to working on your event. Does that work?" His sparkling eyes and wide smile were captivating, like a snake-charmer's flute. I might agree to anything when he looked at me that way.

Somehow, I managed a reasonable response. "Seems fair to me, although I'm not sure I want to know what's in your notes."

He chuckled. "It's not like that, I promise. It might surprise you to hear it, but your dad is a hard man to pin down."

"Shocking."

"I know, right? Well, he was tricky, but I think I got a list of things you and I can work on."

My back stiffened, and the smile froze on my face. "A list?" I asked, my voice strained.

Jake picked up on it immediately. "I asked your dad for some criteria he considers important for you to take over as CEO. I told him it's not fair to say you aren't ready when he has given you zero guidance on his expectations."

Something warm and gooey settled in my stomach at those words. It almost sounded like he was on my side...

"It wasn't easy. He didn't really know how to verbalize what he was looking for at first. But we talked for a while and I feel I at least have a start."

The annoyance about the entire situation welled in my chest, dampening the warmth from a second ago. "Well, that's a relief." The sarcasm in my tone was clear.

"Hey, Ellie, this isn't personal, okay?" Sincerity radiated through Jake's warm brown eyes, his tone gentle. "Your dad has to adjust his attitude about this, even more so than you feel you need to adjust. The issue isn't that there is a right and wrong way to manage this company. The issue is that you two need to meet in the middle and work together. Getting a list of expectations from him gives us a starting point."

"So what, I check off all the items on his list and he sails off into the sunset? Somehow, I don't think it'll be that easy." I leaned back in my seat, arms crossed over my chest.

Jake's eyes darted between me and my open door, then he abruptly stood and closed it before returning to his seat. "Look, can I be frank with you?"

"Always."

"I don't think your dad has a solid grasp on why he thinks you aren't ready to take over."

"Tell me something I don't know."

"I think he's not sure what he's going to do with himself when this isn't his life anymore. I think he knows he needs to bow out but is looking for excuses not to. Which is why getting a straight answer from him about what expectations you're *not* meeting was like pulling teeth—there aren't any. He's just going off of some general 'feeling' and I told him that's not good enough. So our goal should be to steer him."

"Steer him how?" I knew my dad was a tough man to dictate to, but I had a growing flower of hope in my chest. Perhaps Jake had a plan that would form a bridge between me and my dad, and I just needed to hear him out.

"To put it bluntly, steer him into a corner. I'll keep working on getting specifics from him about what you need in order to be 'ready' by his standard. We'll work together on showing him how you meet those criteria. Trust me, it'll reach a point where he won't have another place to turn, and he'll just have to accept. That's our goal."

This was sounding an awful lot like Jake was on my side. I didn't want to let my hopes get up too high, but it was definitely a start.

"Okay," I said with a small smile. "Hit me with the list."

CHAPTER 7
JAKE

Once Ellie agreed to work with me, things got a lot smoother.

We mapped out a game plan for the list JJ gave me, and then, true to my word, we started working on her next event together. Besides the end of season parties, Ellie liked to throw a few smaller events per season. During the slower fall and spring seasons, she welcomed employees and their families to use the resort amenities.

She laid out her idea for me, and I had to admit, it was solid. Since it involved resources that already existed and were underutilized during the season, it didn't cost the company much aside from time. All employees who wanted to take part would work a half day so they could participate in the festivities the other half of the day. The few guests on the resort would be steered to another part of the property. Ellie had blocked out the horseback rides for the entire day, as well as one pool area and the ski hill nearby.

Employees and their families could go on trail rides, downhill mountain bike using the chair lifts, swim, or enjoy a variety of lawn games that we'd set out on the grassy field that housed the base of Peak 9 during the winter. Aside from the price of food for the lunch barbeque, the only cost to this event was our time planning and coordinating it. The employees working volunteered their hour shift at the event, which allowed everyone to have a good time.

"This is... outstanding," I commented after looking everything over. Ellie flushed prettily under my praise and allowed her gaze to drop for a moment. "Have you done this before? It looks like a pretty solid plan. I'm not sure what needs to be worked out."

"Thank you, yes this is my third year hosting this particular Fall Fest. It's by far the most popular one we put on. We try to hold it before the season really kicks into fall—we get busy with leaf peepers when the colors are near peak—so I've done most of the planning already. But we need to coordinate our volunteers, get people signed up for the trail rides since those have limited slots, and get our list of participants so we know who needs a half day off for the event. Would you prefer morning or afternoon?"

She glanced up at me abruptly, her pen poised over paper to take down my answer.

"I'm sorry, what?" I stuttered out a response, not quite following.

"Would you prefer to bring your kids up in the morning or the afternoon? It's on a Sunday, so it doesn't interfere with school."

"Oh." I scratched the back of my neck. "Should I? I mean, this seems like something more for the hourly employees. I don't want to take anything away from them."

"Nonsense. It's for all employees. Besides, Dad particularly likes management to show up to these things and mingle with the other employees. I recommend the morning. It's usually nicer." She glanced at me with sly blue eyes. "If it makes you feel better, you can volunteer for an hour or two in the afternoon. Most of the VPs and managers help with the barbeque."

"I see what you did there," I replied with a laugh. "Alright, you got me. Sign me up for a trail ride for three in the morning. I'm assuming seven is old enough to ride? That's my youngest."

"We'll put you down for two horses. The youngest can ride with you. And I'll sign you up for an hour at the grill at noon? That way, you'll be able to sit your kids down to eat while you work, and they can run off and play when they're done. You'll be able to see them from the patio."

"Sounds like you've got it all figured out."

"It's what James, my brother, does. In fact, I'll sign you guys up to work together. That way, your kids can hang out and maybe make some new friends. You two should meet."

"That's great, thank you. Does their mom come too?"

Ellie's gaze dropped again. "My sister-in-law died a couple of years ago."

"I'm sorry, I had no idea."

"Don't worry about it. There's no way you'd know. It was big news in town, of course, local resort owner's wife driving off the mountain in a snowstorm. But you didn't live around here then."

My stomach dropped. "That's awful. How are they handling it?" It was one thing for children to be without a parent because of a divorce. It was another completely to have their mother ripped from them because of a terrible accident.

My brain made a startling realization: that's exactly what some of my friend's families went through, when the Airman got killed in battle and it left the family without them. It was a reality we all accepted, but I'd never stopped to consider what it was like for the family. Only from the perspective of the one who could be gone. A sick feeling swirled in my gut; that was the reality

Cheryl lived with, and I'd never taken her concerns about it seriously.

"They're doing pretty well, all things considered. James works a lot in the winter, since he runs the ski resort. He keeps the kids busy with skiing and his nanny then, but he's able to spend a lot of time with them the rest of the year."

I forced myself back to the present. "One benefit to a seasonal job," I agreed.

"Yeah, if only we could all be that lucky," Ellie snorted.

That note of derision surprised me. "You don't like your position?"

She glanced again at the door, as if to confirm it was still closed. "It's not that—it's that I didn't even get a choice. Dad decided what rolls we'd fill far in advance, along with the Blackwells and their kids. They didn't give us any say in the matter."

"What would you have chosen, if given the chance?"

She backpedaled quickly. "I don't mean to say I'd do anything else. I've just never felt like I had a choice in the matter, you know what I mean? It would have just been nice to be asked. But I'm happy enough with my lot, and now that I've found a place where I can really make a difference—our employee satisfaction—it's a lot more meaningful for me."

"I understand," I replied, swallowing down the stab of guilt that hit my chest. She had agreed to work with me on JJ's list, but she wouldn't like the other item on my agenda... it would be an issue when we had to face it. Luckily for now, I could set it aside.

———

ELLIE and I continued to work together closely. I got better at ignoring the urge to wrap my hands around her waist or run my fingers through her hair. She got me a stack of Aspen Ridge branded polos to spare me from my suits, although I still wore dress shirts a few days a week out of a sense of duty.

And while I wouldn't say I'd grown immune to her charms, I was definitely doing a better job of acting like it. After our tentative truce was established, she threw herself into mastering the list her father provided to prove her readiness to take over his position.

Or rather, the list I had filtered out of his rambling. He wanted her to 'act more professionally' and 'be present.' We agreed to cut down on the sundresses (as much as it killed me—I certainly had no complaints about being able to gaze at her legs all day) and she cut back her walk-abouts. Ellie agreed to attend a host of meetings she'd been ignoring because they were 'boring'.

The result was that Ellie was far more clued in to the things her father was working on—which I

suspected was the first issue that bothered him—
and that she appeared more professional at work,
which also made him happy.

Meanwhile, Ellie helped me learn about their
preparations for the winter season. It officially began
the week of Thanksgiving, but they always had a
burst of activity at peak leaf season for a couple of
weeks—she called it their dress rehearsal. The entire
resort was busily onboarding new staff, setting up
interviews and training, coordinating lodging—not
to mention preparing for the Fall Fest.

And the way Ellie ran from one thing to the next,
I couldn't help being impressed. She always knew
what needed to be done. The staff greeted her
warmly everywhere, and she left the employees
smiling in her wake. Even in long skirts or pant suits
instead of the floaty sundresses that revealed far too
much of her toned thighs, she was still Ellie. And
yards of extra fabric did nothing to dampen my
desire to touch her.

The employees were genuinely excited about
the Fall Fest, always commenting on how much
their kids were looking forward to it, or how fun it
was last year. The signup list was full, and Ellie
had dutifully dispatched the data to each work
center so the employees would receive their time
off to enjoy. Even the VPs—on the rare occasion I
spotted one walking around the office—were
buzzing with excitement about the festival. There

was a magic here that Ellie tapped into, or something she created all on her own, that was truly special.

So I kept my hands to myself and did my best to keep my mind out of the gutter, despite my increasing desire to do the opposite. I thought working with Ellie would cool the heat of that first night—typically knowing a woman was off limits was enough to shut me down completely. Trysts happened in the military, but I knew better than to get involved in one, and I'd been married for my entire career. Passing flirtations aside, I'd never been unfaithful. But the more time I spent with Ellie, the more I admired her. I thought I could find things about her, working so closely, to dislike.

The problem was, there was nothing about Ellie to dislike. She accepted my criticism and my suggestions, adapted to fit better in the mold her father was looking for, and did it all with grace. She was beautiful and smart, sophisticated and down to earth, and I'd never met a woman like her.

Cheryl was the only romance I'd known, and we were kids when we got together. It was never really great, but I cared about her and we'd been happy enough for a while.

But this—this was different. There was nothing about Ellie for me to point at and say, 'absolutely not, I can't live with that'.

I found myself having tiny flashes of daydreams,

imagining a tryst in the office, her coming over to my place after work...

And then I'd be hit with the cold reality that my kids needed all of my focus right now.

They were settling in and being near my parents definitely helped. But I'd already had a note from Ethan's teacher that he was struggling to make friends and his temper made it difficult for him to focus on school. I had no such notes from Olivia's teacher—she was always an exceptional student—but she remained quiet and helpful at home, not much else.

If I was going to make this a proper home for us, I needed to make sure my kids felt like they belonged here. I was absolutely certain that was the key to opening them up, and I had a feeling that the Fall Fest would be a great opportunity. They always enjoyed the family events on base, and I knew that Ellie's care and attention to the event would make it even more special for them.

Even her promise to introduce Ethan and Olivia to her niece and nephew was an exciting prospect— with any chance they were in the same school and could actually become friends. How many schools could a town this size have, really?

So I kept pushing down my increasing attraction to Ellie, hoping the light at the end of the tunnel would come soon. Once her father signed off on her promotion and I got offered a regular job as thanks for my help, it'd be an opportunity either way: To work somewhere else and not have the daily torture of being so close to Ellie... or to finally make a move.

I KEPT the Fall Fest a surprise for Ethan and Olivia right until the day of the event. As I'd hoped, they were incredibly excited to see the place I'd been working and to ride the horses. We bolted down a quick breakfast and hurried out the door to make our trail ride reservation.

Thanks to JJ's tours, I had a pretty good idea of where the stables were located. It was shaping up to be a nice, sunny but cool day, and there were already several families milling around when we arrived.

One person I hadn't expected to see, however, was Ellie.

She wore faded jeans that hugged her hips, a white t-shirt, and a wide-brimmed hat, with cowboy boots to finish the outfit. Ellie was standing with a slightly older man sporting a greying beard, and two kids that looked about Ethan and Olivia's ages. If I had to wager, I'd guess this was her brother.

My suspicions were confirmed when we parked and she waved us over.

"Jake, this is my brother James and his children, Liam and Ava. Guys, this is Jake."

James offered me a firm handshake with a small smile. "Nice to meet you."

"Likewise," I shook back, then addressed his kids. "Guys, this is Olivia and Ethan. This is our first time going horseback riding. Have you gone a lot?"

"We go all the time," Ava announced proudly. "Buttercup is my favorite. She's really smart."

"She's really slow," Liam snorted. "I like to ride Duke. He's way bigger."

"Well, for this ride we'll all be going the same pace," Ellie interjected. "Olivia, do you want to try on your own? Liam and Ava do, but they have ridden quite a bit."

Olivia glanced at Liam, then returned her determined gaze to Ellie. "If *he* can do it, I can do it."

An abrupt laugh escaped Ellie's perfect lips, and she glanced up at me over Olivia's head with a twinkle in her eye. "Well, that sounds pretty confident to me. I like your spirit. You know, Buttercup's best friend is Rosy. They like to walk together. Maybe you and Ava can ride together, and me and your dad will be right behind?"

Olivia nodded again, then turned to me. "What about Ethan?"

"He's going to ride with me, honey. That way, he's got some help if he needs it."

Ethan's eyes darted between Ava, obviously younger than him, and the smug expression Liam wore. "I don't *need* help. I can do it myself." Hot color rose in his cheeks and I could practically see the steam building inside his ears.

Dammit. It hadn't occurred to me there would be kids his age here riding on their own. I met Ellie's eyes for just a second before she turned her focus to Ethan, crouching down to his level and lowering her voice.

"Ethan, can I ask you a favor?"

Completely enamored with her already, he nodded with wide eyes.

"Would you ride with me? Just in case I need someone to help me? I'm going to be on Buckhouse. He's even bigger than *Duke*, and sometimes he scares me a little."

"I'll keep you safe," Ethan replied seriously.

"Thank you, I mean it," Ellie replied with equal weight. "Let's go this way and see if our horses are ready."

When she stood back up, her gaze drifted to me once more, and I mouthed 'thank you'. Her answering smile was nearly blinding. I thought my heart would melt into a puddle and pour out the bottom of my jeans when Ethan slipped his tiny hand into hers and tugged her toward the stables. Ava snaked Olivia's hand, and Liam followed them.

James and I shared a glance and followed, bringing up the rear on the wooded path to the stables.

"So," he began casually. "How are you liking it at Aspen Ridge?"

"So far, so good," I answered honestly. "It's still a bit of an adjustment for the kids, but I definitely think getting to spend time with them like this will help. I didn't have much time for them in my previous career."

"Which was?"

"I was in the military for quite a while. Air Force. My last assignment was training new officers."

To my surprise, James laughed loudly in response. "So she wasn't exaggerating."

"Sorry?"

"My sister, Ellie. A few weeks back, she was ranting and raving about Dad bringing in a drill sergeant to get her in line. I thought she was exaggerating, but you actually are. Unreal."

"Well, not exactly." I scratched the back of my neck, chuckling. "I left as a captain, so not a sergeant. And I taught officer candidates, not enlisted. So we were actually called Military Training Officers... Drill Sergeant is kind of an Army thing."

He threw his hands up, still chuckling. "I'm sorry, didn't mean to cause offense."

"None taken at all," I assured him. "It's just habit, correcting nomenclature. Trust me, at this point, I don't expect civilians to know all the lingo, but I'm always happy to clear things up."

"So, how long were you in?"

A knot stuck in my throat. "Fifteen years."

James let out a low whistle. "Fifteen years, huh? Why didn't you stay, if you don't mind me asking? Can't you retire at twenty?"

"It wasn't a good choice for the kids. Life in the military is hard, especially for a single parent. And after their mom left, I thought they would benefit from having a stable home with family nearby. My parents retired here a few years back, so it seemed like a good choice to get all of us back on track."

"I'm sorry to hear that," James replied, his tone somber. "Ava and Liam, their mom is... not with us anymore, either."

"Ellie told me, I'm sorry. A different circumstance, to be sure, but I doubt my kids will see much of their mother in the future. I don't know which one is worse, if I'm honest. Losing a mother who loved them and wanted to be with them, or having a mother that doesn't want them."

James shook his head. "Now that I can't understand at all."

"Same. I don't claim to be a perfect man—lord knows I have my share of blame about why our relationship went south—but I'd never just walk away from my kids. It was like—one day she just decided this wasn't the life she wanted, and she'd had enough of all of us."

"Well, you picked a solid place to land and pick up the pieces. I grew up here, but there are lots of people who fall in love with Aspen Ridge and just never leave."

"Yeah, I've visited a few times, and it always seemed like a great place to raise a family. Small town, but big enough to feel you're not missing anything. Not to mention a world-class ski resort in your backyard. My kids have never been skiing, but they're already looking forward to learning."

James smiled widely at that. "Well, you couldn't pick a better place. We have great instructors here—of course my kids have been on skis practically since they could walk. Liam actually switched to snow-boarding last season, and now Ava wants to switch as well. But if you need a hookup for an instructor, just let me know. We're all family here. We take care of each other."

A cinder of warmth spread through my chest. "Thanks, man, I appreciate it." I offered my hand for another shake and he gripped it firmly, his expression far more open than a few minutes ago.

"Of course, anytime. Not that she has a lot of enemies, but if Ellie likes you, you're good people in my book."

I tried not to read too much into the statement 'Ellie likes you' and followed silently while he led me into the barn.

The phrase 'back in the saddle' felt rather ironic, in more than a few ways. I rode a horse a few times, long before I joined the Air Force and definitely before I had kids. The handler walked us through some basic horse info and made sure everyone had a good seat before we took off up the trail. Olivia attacked horseback riding the same way she approached everything in life: with single-minded, fierce determination. Ava rode beside her and gave her friendly pointers like only one kid could teach another.

Ellie rode beside me, and I was extremely grateful she offered to take Ethan on her horse. There wasn't a ton of room in my saddle and my horse seemed a little skittish, while hers plodded dutifully along. Ethan had a firm hold of the reins and was one-hundred percent convinced he was all that stood between them and certain death. Ellie kept him from over compensating and we enjoyed a pleasant ride along the wide, smooth trails that wove through the mountains.

When our tour was over, the kids asked to visit the other events together. James and Ellie agreed to meet us at the festival entrance. During the short ride between locations, I enjoyed listening to Ethan and Olivia chat excitedly about the horses.

When we arrived, James immediately offered to take all four kids around to play lawn games while Ellie gave me a tour of the festival. I could hardly say no, so while the kids ran off to start a game of corn hole, Ellie led me up a wide aisle of booths.

When she said the town participated, I didn't really understand what she meant. But now I was quickly grasping the importance of Aspen Ridge Resort to the community. There were dozens of booths, each with a sign proclaiming their business, but all hosting some sort of carnival game. Some were simple games for kids–like Go Fish, where the child could cast a line over a wall and someone behind would attach a small prize to their 'hook'. Others were more games of skill or chance, and all free to play. A local coffee shop, Bear Paw Brew, offered fresh coffee and tea. Crowds of employees shuffled between the booths, visiting friends and enjoying the festival atmosphere.

"This is pretty epic," I commented, and Ellie grinned.

"Thank you. I think it gets better every year."

"It's like..." I searched for the right words to describe my feelings. "It's like an eighties movie."

Ellie barked a laugh. "I can't say that's what I was going for."

Heat rushed to my cheeks. "I just mean there's this warm, 'welcome home' feeling to it. It reminds me of watching an eighties movie." When I saw her one-eyebrow raised side-eye, I gave up. "Ignore me. I'm not making sense."

"It's an interesting description for our little Fall

Fest, but I think I understand where you're coming from. I love eighties movies too, and this certainly evokes a feeling of nostalgia."

"Yes, nostalgia, thank you. There's something very nostalgic about it."

"I agree."

We walked in silence for a moment while I struggled for something to say. Ellie didn't seem bothered. She beamed around at the people enjoying the celebration she had put together, seemingly just appreciating the results of her work. A few people passed and offered their thanks, and Ellie accepted graciously.

"The ride went well," she commented eventually.

"Oh, yes, the trail ride. It did! It's been awhile since I've been on a horse, but I think I did okay."

"I meant for the kids, but yes, you did a great job, too." Her voice turned indulgent with a hint of sarcasm, and I flushed deeper.

"Of course. I hope Ethan behaved for you. Thanks, by the way, for redirecting him when he got upset. I'm still learning how to manage it, but you seem to be a pro."

"Liam was like that, at his age. Super quick to blow his top over the littlest things. I think it helps to have an outsider redirect, since I seemed better at it than James, now that I think about it."

"Or maybe you're just great with kids," I

suggested, bumping her shoulder with mine. "It's okay to own it. I'm not offended that you might be better at handling my kids than I am. I'm working on it, but let's just say it's not something I consider myself naturally gifted at."

Ellie's smile widened. "I do like kids, but I'm not sure I'd say 'gifted'. Sometimes it's just easier to go with the flow, try to bolster their little egos instead of crush them."

"You think I was crushing his ego?"

"Well, yeah. You said he's seven, right? And Ava is six, she's obviously younger, but she sits a horse herself. So with her older brother watching—Liam being a giant nine year-old, you know–Ethan couldn't be caught dead needing help."

"But he needs help. He's never ridden a horse before. It's nothing to be ashamed of."

"That's easy for you to admit now, and to have that grown-up perspective on. But for him? It's a lot harder to own. So when you said he needed help, it was a challenge to his ego, since his sister didn't need help. And giving him an out–saying that *I* needed help–allowed him to ride with assistance without feeling like he lost cool points in front of an older boy. Win-win."

I shook my head in wonder. "You really are a marvel. I would have just insisted he ride with me and not really understood why he was so upset."

"Well, logic is helpful, but kids are mostly emotional creatures."

"Not my eldest," I chuckled. "That girl rivals my battle-hardened commander for stoicism. Is being born middle-aged a thing?"

This time Ellie laughed loudly. "You mean that girl?"

She pointed, and I followed her finger. Clearly the festival had some sort of arts and crafts booth— my daughter had two blotches of bright pink paint on her cheeks, and was racing madly after Ava, whose hands were coated in the same color. The girls emitted peals of laughter as they darted around festival goers, whose eyes trailed after them in delight. The two radiated joy outward, like ripples in a pond.

A smile spread across my cheeks and tears prickled my eyes. I couldn't remember the last time I heard Olivia laugh like that—full, high-pitched belly laughs that were pure joy.

"Alright, point taken, she actually *is* a nine-year-old girl. So it must just be me who makes her devoid of all happiness."

The very thought confirmed every fear I had harbored deep in my chest: my kids were miserable with me. It was my fault Ethan was so moody and Olivia so joyless. Always my fault.

My expression must have changed to reflect my thoughts, because Ellie stopped me with a hand on my shoulder. "Hey, don't be so hard on yourself. I'm sure things were hard when your wife left, and now they're just getting used to a new routine. But as you can see," the girls raced past us laughing, Ava circling in a loop and Olivia hot on her heels, which made Ellie smile fondly, "they're adapting well." Her eyes trailed the girls then settled on mine, and her smile widened. "You're doing a great job. I promise."

A thick lump formed in my throat, so large I couldn't swallow. I didn't know until that moment how much I'd needed someone, *anyone*, to say those words to me.

I held her gaze for much longer than I should have, and when I spoke, my voice was unexpectedly rough. "I'm not sure you're right, but thank you all the same."

"Oh, I'm right. I wouldn't lie about something like that."

"Well, thank you again." Somehow things had gotten more awkward, and I was entirely at a loss as to what to say next. We reached the end of the row and turned around, heading back toward the lawn games and my suddenly mischievous children.

As we passed a booth sponsored by Aspen Ridge Brewery, a leggy brunette in jeans and a flannel shirt immediately approached us.

Ellie cleared her throat. "Jake, I'd like you to meet my friend Tessa. Tessa, this is Jake."

I held out my hand for a shake, and Tessa shook

it vigorously, her green eyes rolling over my body speculatively. "Nice to meet you, *Jake*," she said at last with a wide grin. There was a hint of meaning in the way she said it that was clearly not meant for me.

"You too, Tessa. Have you known Ellie long?"

Her eyes darted to Ellie, and she answered with a mischievous glint in her eyes. "We've been friends since elementary school, actually. Ellie's parents didn't really approve of their princess being friends with a townie, but somehow they couldn't get rid of me."

"Now that's not true," Ellie protested. "Aspen Ridge is our home, so technically I'm a townie, too. And they just didn't like that you were constantly getting me in trouble."

"Not fair. We got in trouble together. It was 50-50."

"Well, I never got in trouble before I met you, so draw whatever conclusions you like."

The pair of them bantered like siblings, and I couldn't help chuckling. "Well, Tessa, I look forward to a long chat with you soon. I'm sure you can give me all sorts of dirt on Isabelle Tremont."

A wicked smile took up residence on her face. "You bet your ass I can. Did Ellie tell you about our junior prom? She-"

"THAT'S enough," Ellie said loudly, stepping between us. "We'd better be moving along."

"I'll find you later," Tessa said with a wink before returning to her booth.

"She seems nice," I commented as we walked away.

"She's... Tessa," Ellie answered with a laugh. "Watch out for that one. She can strike like a cobra if you're not paying attention."

We continued making our way back toward the games, but a bear of a man with an auburn beard and a young athletic woman with platinum blonde hair stopped us.

"Ellie!" the girl squealed, bouncing forward and squeezing Ellie in a tight hug.

She stepped back to allow the man to embrace Ellie, and I waited for some sort of introduction.

Unsurprisingly, Ellie was on it. "Guys, this is Jake Wright. He's working for my dad at the moment. Jake, this is Stella and Reece Blackwell. They're the kids of my dad's partners. Reece supervises the events part of the business, and Stella-"

"Wastes all her time snowboarding instead of taking over her duties for the family," the younger woman intoned in what was clearly a mockery of some sort of authority figure.

"Nice to meet you both." I shook Reece's hand but Stella just gave me an odd little wave and whipped out her cellphone to take a selfie with Ellie.

"Have you been here long?" Reece's tone was pleasant despite his burly appearance.

"Just a few weeks, actually. Pretty sure I'm already in love, though."

His eyes drifted to Ellie, and I suddenly found myself choking on nothing.

"With Aspen Ridge, that is. I love it here."

"Ah, yeah, that makes sense. What's not to love?" But his gaze returned to Ellie, who was dutifully snapping photos with the younger woman. When he looked back to me, his meaning was clear.

I rushed to find a different topic of conversation. "Indeed. So how long have you managed the events? Are you the one behind building that new center? It's really beautiful."

"Yeah, I'm the one that pushed for it. I see a lot of opportunities here to grow and expand the business. Honestly, I'd like to get out of the events management and start a distillery. We have quite a lot of property and there's so much we could do with it. The more value we can bring to the town, the better for everyone."

I chuckled. "You sound a lot like Ellie. She seems very passionate about the community."

"Yeah, we have a lot of similarities. We both grew up here and want to make sure the resort is doing everything in its power to benefit the locals."

"I think it's in excellent hands," I replied, and the larger man grinned.

"Come on Reece, Jess's insta story says she's working the Bear Paw booth and I have to talk to her right *now!*" Stella appeared between us and grabbed Reece's arm, towing him back the way Ellie and I had just come.

"Nice to meet you!" he called over his shoulder.

Ellie watched them go with a fond smile before we continued.

"That was... interesting," I commented.

"Yeah, that's a good word for them. But they're basically family, so it doesn't bother me."

"What was Stella's comment on snowboarding about?"

"So Stella is 22, and her life is snowboarding. She was actually on her way to the olympics in her teens, before she took a nasty fall and ended up with a broken leg. She missed out on that year, plus a year of training while she went through physical therapy. She was still not at the top of her game for the last olympics qualifications, so she's spent the last few years really working hard. This year she's going to all the qualification events to hopefully secure a spot for the games in two years."

"Wow, that's sad, but also exciting. I hope she gets it." I didn't want to think about how many things I gave up to dedicate my life to the military. I made my choice, and I didn't regret it. But the idea of having the freedom to chase a dream...

"Well, her parents aren't thrilled. They worry about her getting hurt—it can be a dangerous sport —and they want her to think about the business.

But she's just 22, you know? It's not on her radar yet."

I cast a skeptical expression at Ellie. "From the sounds of it, running the business has been on *your* plan for most of your life."

Ellie flushed. "Yeah, well, I'm not a gifted snowboarder. Maybe if there was something else I was really good at, dedicating my life to Aspen Ridge would have been a more difficult choice."

"I think you know this is your calling," I replied in a low voice, and Ellie glanced up at me in surprise. "Caring about people, improving things for them through your family's business. That's a gift, Ellie. Few people can do that."

Her sky-blue eyes locked on mine, and suddenly the world around us was a blur. Sound dampened in my ears, and all I could hear was the rush of blood through my veins and the soft breaths Ellie took. Her lips were parted, an invitation so tempting I leaned in to take it without thinking. My hand rose to cup her cheek, and Ellie's breath hitched as she waited for my lips to meet hers.

A shrill scream brought me back to reality, and I jumped away from Ellie as if her skin had burned me. My eyes darted around us for the source of the scream, finding a pair of children racing through the crowd, the girl holding a toy truck above her head and the boy in hot pursuit. The girl screamed in delight again, and they disappeared between two booths.

I turned back to Ellie, my face hot. "I'm sorry," I said, shoving my hands in my pockets. "I shouldn't have-"

"It's okay," she replied quickly, folding her arms across her chest. "Let's go back and find my brother."

When we located James, we found Liam patiently coaching Ethan at corn hole, and following their impromptu race the girls had returned to the craft booth and were working diligently at painting birdhouses a lurid shade of pink. James stood between the two spaces, monitoring both pairs.

"If you like, I can take over," I offered. "So you can go enjoy some of the festival?"

"Don't worry about it," James waved me off. "The kids are entertaining themselves. It's really no problem at all."

"I just feel bad, leaving you to watch my kids like this."

James smiled. "Pro tip? When someone offers to help with your kids, always accept."

"Unless they're a creeper," Ellie interjected.

"Yes, obviously, that is the exception," James agreed.

"Duly noted: Always accept help except from creeps. Got it."

"Come on, I'll show you the rest." Ellie tugged

my arm, and we waved goodbye to James as she steered me up the hill.

By the time we finished the full tour, it was nearly time for my shift at the grill. James and I got to work slinging hot dogs and hamburgers by the dozens, and Ellie entertained the kids for the rest of the afternoon.

And it finally hit me: that sense of community, of belonging, that I'd missed ever since leaving the Air Force. There was an intangible quality about it, something difficult to explain to someone who never sought it out, never craved that feeling of being part of something bigger.

But here I was, a million miles from my life in the military, and I found it all the same.

I couldn't help but wonder if that was more to do with Aspen Ridge or Ellie Tremont.

CHAPTER 8
ELLIE

Monday following the Fall Fest, I was on edge as I settled into my office, and it took me a few minutes to realize that I was nervous to see Jake. Something changed yesterday; perhaps it was in the works for a while and I just didn't realize it. Or maybe we just connected in a way we hadn't before. He was far more relaxed, more open with me, than he'd been since we met. I could easily say being around his kids humanized him. There was no Captain Stuffed Shirt in sight when his kids were around, just a dad who clearly wanted the best for his children.

But even I knew it was more than that.

I'd done my best to keep him out of my head and at arm's length since he started, but now I questioned if that was really what I wanted. He clearly didn't have it out for me the way I'd first thought. He'd made that abundantly clear by trying to find middle ground between me and my dad instead of just barking orders like I'd expected. Granted, I'd kept my distance mainly because I knew Dad would disapprove of me being involved with someone that I worked closely with.

And when he almost kissed me yesterday... heat rushed to my cheeks just remembering it. The intensity that made my breath catch in my throat was back. Even though it would have been a disaster if my dad got wind I was making out with Jake in the middle of the festival. In that moment I sincerely didn't care.

I wanted him.

On the plus side, we wouldn't be working closely for too long. Dad already told me he intended to place Jake under James in the Mountain Ops side of the house after he was done 'coaching' me. I was happy the plan to introduce Jake to James at Fall Fest had worked out so smoothly. It never hurts to know more people, and with the two of them being single dads, it couldn't hurt to have each other to lean on.

And that gamble had swiftly paid off—I caught them exchanging numbers before the party broke up yesterday. Hopefully sooner rather than later Jake would work in a different building, and us being involved would no longer be a problem. So, fair to say the potential conflict of us being the same part of the business and in a relationship was moot.

As if summoned by my thoughts alone, Jake ducked his head into my office. He had finally dispensed with his habit of knocking and standing in the hallway, waiting for permission to enter. Instead, he grinned and walked in after only a slight hesitation. I couldn't help but notice how well the Aspen Ridge polo hugged his wide shoulders and clung just slightly to his muscular chest. Honestly, he put everyone but a few of the groundskeepers to shame in terms of physique, and those guys worked outside all day.

I shoved down the flutter of heat that tickled my chest and smiled in greeting. "Long time no see. Did you have a good night?"

"Oh yeah," Jake laughed, taking his seat. "Ethan passed out before we even got off the property, and they were both asleep by the time we reached my parents' for dinner. They scarfed down some food, and then it was all I could do to keep them awake long enough for a shower. Slept like the dead."

Jake's cologne wafted its way over to my seat, and I resisted the urge to close my eyes and breathe him in deeply.

"I'm no expert, but I'd consider that a successful day."

"Definitely. Thanks again for suggesting we go. I probably would have skipped it otherwise. And thanks for introducing me to James. Olivia has basically adopted Ava, and I'm pretty sure Liam has taken my place as Ethan's hero."

"Nah, no one can replace a boy's dad as his hero, I'm sure."

"You'd be surprised. Liam knows way more about Spiderman than I do, so that's probably the basis of it. Regardless, James and I plan to get the kids together again soon, and I have you to thank for it."

"Not a problem at all, but you're welcome all the same. It's hard for kids with single parents. They always think they're missing out on something. So knowing other kids who are in the same boat helps them to feel more normal."

"Ellie Tremont with the kid wisdom strikes again," he grinned, and a flush of pleasure spread across my cheeks.

Jake continued. "Did everything go as expected?"

"No issues. We know what we're doing now, so it's a pretty smooth process." I shuffled a few papers on my desk to tear my gaze away from his face.

He settled further back into his chair, throwing one arm across the high back and crossing a leg over his knee. "Okay. So, when's the next event?"

I gave him a mock-appraising look to avoid ogling. "Already looking forward to the next one, huh? I thought my little projects were all 'good idea fairy' nonsense."

He seemed genuinely upset. "Hey, I didn't say that. It's more-"

"Jake, I'm just teasing you."

A knowing grin curled his lips, and his tone turned flirtatious again. "Oh, I see how it is. Alright then, I see you Ellie Tremont. So, what's next?"

I clicked on the calendar on my computer. "Well, now we prepare for the fall leaf-peepers. We're already booked over 60% for the two weekends in October we expect to hit peak color, and it'll be closer to ninety by the time we get there. After that, it's a quick break before the season starts Thanksgiving weekend."

"And that's like, the super bowl around here, right?"

"If the super bowl lasted for five months."

"Okay, so perhaps not the super bowl."

I tried to join in his sports analogy. "I'd say it's like March Madness for a month, and then the super bowl for the two weeks around Christmas and New Year. Then every three-day or holiday weekend is another mini super bowl after that, with just mid-season craziness in-between."

Jake ducked his chin and regarded me with warm brown eyes. "So, a five month-long super bowl."

It wasn't far from the truth. "I guess, yeah."

"So how can I help?"

"Help with what?"

He shrugged. "Whatever you need help with. We're already working on JJ's requirements, and I still check in with him to see if there's anything he wants to add. But to be honest, he seems pretty happy with how things are going so far. So, if there are things you need help with, there's no time like the present for me to learn."

"Okay." I thought about it for a moment. "We're going to be doing an eighties movie trivia night Friday, if you want to help with that?"

He raised an eyebrow. "Wait a minute. Did you bring that up because you think I'm old?"

The laugh burst from my lips. "You're really sensitive about the age thing, huh? It's nothing personal. We've talked about eighties movies a couple times and I thought it would be something you'd have fun with."

Jake grinned, clearly not offended. "Fair enough. I do like eighties movies."

"Me too."

"Aren't you a little young? I barely remember the eighties and you're like a decade younger than me."

"Six years," I reminded him with a sniff. "I watched them with my mom a lot when I was younger. She loved them, showed me all the classics. Whenever I had a sick day from school, or the weather was crappy, we'd hole up on the couch and watch her favorites."

Jake's eyes were wide, a smile curling his lips. "Me too."

"Really?"

"Yeah, my mom was obsessed. I think it comes from being a military wife. She was alone a lot while my dad was working—she was a stay-at-home mom —so she watched a lot of movies. And when I came along, we watched them together. Dirty Dancing was one of her favorites. That's why I thought of it... you know, that night." Color spread over his cheeks, and his gaze dropped to the floor.

My heart picked up speed, heat rushing to my face at the reminder of the night we met. I spoke quickly to get past the pregnant moment. "My mom's favorite was Dirty Dancing, too. She always admired Baby, how she was such a rebel. An independent woman."

Jake's head tilted to the side, and his eyes narrowed in thought. Unfortunately, there was no angle where he didn't look absolutely delicious. "Mmm, would we call Baby a rebel? I think she was more of a hormonal teenager."

"Hey now, watch yourself. Baby was definitely a rebel. First she was planning to join the Peace Corps, which, let's be honest—that's already rebel territory for a woman in the fifties. Then she started hooking up with the biggest hunk on campus, who was from the other side of the tracks. It's like Romeo and Juliet, with less death and whining."

Jake chuckled. "Fair enough. I suppose for the era it was pretty rebellious. What other movies did your mom like?"

"Big Business, Baby Boom, Nine to Five... she loved how they portrayed career women in the eighties."

"That's... oddly specific. Any reason why?"

The familiar ache that clutched my heart when I thought of Mom pushed all of my attraction to Jake aside. "Well, my mom gave up her own career goals to stay here and marry my dad. She went to school, planning to move to New York and live in a penthouse overlooking Central Park. She studied finance, wanted to work for a big bank and live a fancy city life. But she fell in love with my dad at college and moved here to help him run his family business instead. She worked for the resort for a while, but once she had my brother, she stayed home to be a full-time mom. Which was awesome, and she said she loved it..."

After waiting a moment, Jake interjected gently, "But?"

"She died of cancer a few years back. And one night when she was feeling particularly poorly, she had a fit of remorse-fueled-honesty, I guess you could call it. I was the only one home, and we were watching her movies, just hanging out. She started telling me all these things she needed to get off her chest. One of them was that she wished she'd still pursued her dream and gone to New York."

Jake's voice dropped an octave. "Wow, that must have been hard to hear. I'm sorry, by the way. That she's passed."

I waved him off. "It's okay. We knew it was coming. She insisted she loved Dad and wouldn't trade her life for the world, but she said she believed that she could have had both—had her career, and the love of her life. She regretted choosing just one."

"How did you feel, hearing that?"

The pain clenched again, and I answered honestly instead of giving him a trite answer. "I mean, I kind of blew it off at the time—she was on a lot of medication. But those words stuck with me. It's hard to explain; she didn't say it in such a way like she regretted being a mother or any of the choices she made. She just kind of made it sound like... she thought she could have had her big city life and then come here when she was ready to settle down. My parents didn't have James until their late thirties, so they had over a decade after college with just work and being young. I guess she thought she could have done something else with that time."

"She wanted to have it all, huh?" Jake's expression darkened even though his tone was light. His eyes focused off to the side, as if lost in thought.

"Yeah, something like that, I guess. Anyway," I added more loudly, and his focus snapped back to me, "the trivia night isn't a monumental event, but it's a good time. We host it in the bar at Seasons, and mainly what needs to be done is making the questions I pulled off the internet into slides."

"I think I can handle that. You should know, I earned a specialty badge as a PowerPoint Ranger."

Now I regarded him skeptically. "That's not actually a thing, is it?" I never knew when he was talking about actual military stuff or their inside jokes.

Jake's head rocked back, and he released the warm, genuine laugh that made my insides gooey. "No, it's not. But you know how it is: we're in the military, we have to make everything sound cool."

"I dunno, Mister Ranger Sir, that sounds like an old person thing. I don't think anyone under sixty-five calls it PowerPoint. But do it your way. I'll email you the questions, just put the answers on the slide immediately following. The trivia night is next Friday, if you want to come."

"Sweet, I have a feeling I'm going to win." He stood from the chair and locked me in that gaze that stole my breath away.

My stomach fluttered, and I struggled to keep up the flirtatious tone. "Funny... but you know you don't get to play, right? You're already disqualified for being so old, let alone already having the answers."

"Ouch, you wound me!" He turned and headed

out the door with a wink. When he reached the hall, he spun and stuck his head back inside. "But just so you know, I would have won without all the answers."

With one final wink he left, and it took me the rest of the morning to drag my thoughts away from how his eyes twinkled when he did that.

CHAPTER 9
JAKE

It seemed as if the weather in Aspen Ridge turned to autumn over night. Leaves began turning colors and dropping, much like the temperature outside. Now when I bundled the kids up to catch the bus, we could see our breath as we walked outside in the near-darkness.

I've always loved fall; it seemed filled with the promise of new things happening, the excitement of sports and upcoming holidays. I found myself thinking about activities I could do with Ethan and Olivia, ways to share more with them, improve our relationship. I knew there was a lot to do and it was a process, but the moments they let down their guard and acted more like kids and less like little soldiers gave me hope.

It also seemed as if the Fall Fest and our almost-kiss were an unconscious turning point for the dynamic between Ellie and me. There wasn't anything explicit or direct said between us, but our conversations always had a flirtatious edge when no one else was around. Every time we spoke, it was more banter and less business. Something about the way she was dressing now—all buttoned up and professional—turned me on even more than the breezy sundresses had. It was like a tempting package I couldn't wait to unwrap, and she occupied way more of my thoughts than I cared to admit.

It wasn't hard admitting to myself that I had it bad for the girl.

Sharing that with anyone else, of course, was another matter. Despite my growing admiration for her and obvious attraction, I worked hard to maintain a neutral outward appearance.

But it turned out one lesson I had to learn was that kids were far more observant than I realized. Here I thought they were completely entertained playing corn hole and chasing their new friends around the Fall Fest. But out of nowhere, Olivia casually grilled me about Ellie several days later, just when I thought I was safe.

"Dad?" Her voice was light, innocent, as she sat at the table and erased something from her math homework.

"Yes, honey?" I asked, not really paying attention. I was making my famous grilled cheese, and it was seconds from being done. A few seconds too long and the bread would turn to char. I used a spatula to peek under the pan-side and check doneness.

"Is Ellie your girlfriend?"

"What?" I whipped around, spatula in hand. "Why would you ask that?"

She shrugged a narrow shoulder casually, not raising her gaze to meet mine. "I dunno, she's nice. You like her."

My brain spun like wheels in mud, trying to find the right response for this scenario. I wasn't used to Olivia voluntarily engaging me in conversation, but I certainly didn't want to discourage it. This felt like progress. "I mean, I do like her, and I agree, she's nice. But she's also kind of my boss, honey."

"So?" Olivia raised her wide brown eyes to mine, questioning this idea in the innocent way only a child could.

"Well," I gestured artlessly with the spatula. "You're not supposed to date your boss."

"Isn't she younger than you? She looks younger than you."

Was that a nine-year-old insult?

"She is," I answered carefully. "Why do you ask?"

"If you're older, aren't you supposed to be the boss?"

"It doesn't always work like that, honey."

"Why?"

"Because sometimes people change jobs, like I did, and when you start someplace new, you don't always get to start as the boss."

"But you will be her boss one day, then? When you aren't new?"

"No... Ellie's daddy is the real boss. He owns the resort. But he's going to retire, and then Ellie will be the boss."

"So she's only the boss because her daddy owns it?"

"What? No, that's not what I said." I certainly didn't want her repeating *that* idea to anyone.

"Yes, it is. You said her daddy owns the resort and when he leaves, Ellie will be the boss."

A sharp, acrid scent reached my nose.

"Dammit, the grilled cheese!" I whipped around and scooped the sandwich out of the smoking pan, but it was already far too late. One side was perfect, the other side was black as pitch.

"I think it's burnt, Dad."

I slid the sandwich onto a plate and ran the pan under water to stop the smoke. It would be just my luck for the fire alarm to go off now, too.

"Yeah, I think you're right, honey."

Olivia appeared at my elbow and stroked my arm with a reassuring smile. "It's okay, Daddy. You can just make a new one."

A deep, bone-weary sigh escaped my lips. "Actually, I can't, Olivia. That was the last of the bread. But thank you."

"Oh." She glanced at the charcoal sandwich speculatively. "Well, can you take the burnt part off?"

My teeth were already on edge, but I knew she was just trying to be helpful. "I don't think that would work, honey. It's the whole sandwich."

"Just take off the burnt piece, then cut the other piece in half. Ethan only eats a half sandwich, anyway. As long as it's triangles, he won't notice. And you can share mine."

My heart swelled, and I swallowed down the sudden lump in my throat. When did she get so grown-up and smart?

"That is a *great* idea, Olivia. Come here." I drew her into a hug and squeezed her tightly. "Thank you."

She grinned and wrapped her little arms around my neck. "No problem, Daddy." She paused for a second. "But I should probably finish my home-work," she added, a little out of breath.

"Of course, honey." I planted a kiss on the top of her head, then released her. "Go ahead." I turned and started dissecting the sandwich, then checked on the tomato soup.

She waited until she was safely settled back into her seat to add, "Even if Ellie is your boss, she should be your girlfriend. I like her."

I was still mystified about the reasoning behind this conversation, but I also didn't want to shut her down. "Thanks for the vote, kiddo. I'll think about it."

"She likes you."

Even though I knew it was coming from a nine-year-old, I desperately wanted it to be true. "What makes you say that?"

A smirk stretched across Olivia's cheeks and she sat up straighter. "She watched you a lot at Fall Fest when you weren't looking. She smiled at you a lot."

"She did?"

"Uh-huh." Her gaze dropped to the paper in front of her again.

It felt like there was a driver behind this conversation that I was still not seeing. "Livvie, why do you want Ellie to be my girlfriend?" I asked in a light tone.

She didn't look up from her homework when she answered casually, "Because she's nice, and she took us horseback riding."

That's what this was all about. The bubble of excitement in my chest deflated in a way that only the innocent commentary of a child could manage.

"Ahh, so you think I should date Ellie so you can go ride horses again?"

"Yup." She wrote the answer to a math problem carefully on the sheet without glancing my way.

That's my kid.

THE NEXT DAY, all that kept spinning through my mind were Olivia's words. *"She watched you a lot when you weren't looking. She smiled at you a lot."*

But did that actually mean anything? Ellie smiled a lot in general. She smiled at everyone. It was part of why she was so damn charming—Ellie never met an enemy, just a friend she didn't know yet.

Obviously, she was smiling more at me now than she had the first couple of weeks we worked together, but that didn't really signify anything since she was clearly pissed at the situation then. So just because she was more comfortable with my presence now didn't mean there was any interest attached.

But what if there was? In the military, there's a very strict chain of command. Definitive rules on who you can date, and what happens if the person you want to date is in the no-fly zone.

The boss is definitely in the no-fly zone.

But technically, Ellie wasn't my boss. JJ was. And if I stayed on, it was just as likely that I would be in a different department. More than likely, if Ellie wanted to date me, too.

However, Aspen Ridge was run by people who were all basically family. Would any of them really be fine with me dating Ellie?

Just thinking about it was enough to tie my stomach up in knots.

It was baffling. There was no way this would work. I had to put her out of my mind and just hold out until I got out of this office. With any luck, in a couple of months I'd be working in a completely different building and I wouldn't have to catch the tantalizing scent of her perfume wafting down the hall and drawing me into lurid fantasies.

Like a total coward, I stayed in my office all day, avoiding the temptation of stopping by Ellie's for fear of doing something I shouldn't. It was bad enough I'd agreed to help with this trivia night. Suddenly the idea of sitting in a pub, having cocktails around an untold number of other employees, was almost terrifying. It dredged up the memories of the night we met—the memories I only allowed myself to mull over when I was in bed alone—and heat crept up my neck when I remembered running my hand up her silky thigh...

"Hey, you alright?" Ellie's voice, along with a light tap at my open door, nearly made me jump out of my seat.

"What? Yeah, I'm fine. I'm great. How are you?" Flustered, I manically shuffled papers on my desk and wiggled the mouse on the computer, trying to look busy. One errant thought about her thighs and kissing sent the blood rushing to my lower half, and now I was in an extremely awkward situation. I tucked myself even tighter under the desk.

Ellie's eyes narrowed in disbelief. "You look a little worked up. Is everything okay?"

"Yep, nope, everything is good. Did you need something?" A sweat broke out along my back, and guilt swirled in my stomach. Somehow, I didn't think she would find it flattering that I was sitting in my office thinking about her and sprouting wood.

Her expression turned confused. "No, you just usually stop by my office in the morning and I haven't seen you all day. I'm about to go visit the staff at the Peak 9 condos and stop in to make sure everything in Seasons is set up for tonight. Would you like to come?"

What, stand up so you could see the tent I was pitching beneath the desk? "Not today, but thanks for the invite. I need to wrap up some stuff here before the end of day." I flashed her a wide, desperate smile, that I hoped passed for confident.

"Okay, suit yourself." Ellie shrugged, then switched topics. "You got the slides ready for tonight, though, right?"

"Yep, it's right here and ready to go." I held up a thumb drive. "I'll meet you down there. Seven, right?"

"Yeah. I'm looking forward to it. Trivia nights are usually pretty popular. It'll be nice to have company this time." She gave me a warm smile that made my heart thud in my chest.

Nervous energy was still racing through my veins. I couldn't imagine spending an entire evening with her like this. In a darkened room with alcohol? There was no way I'd be able to behave myself. Best to set myself an escape plan early. "Yeah, sounds good. I probably won't stay too late, though. I've got a lot to do tomorrow, so I should do an early night."

Disappointment crossed Ellie's face, darkening her sky-blue eyes. "Wait, what? It's Friday night, old man. Live a little. I promise it'll be fun."

"I really shouldn't stay out too late—" I could feel the sweat dotting my upper lip.

"What are you, sixty? You sound like my dad."

"Hey your dad is very spry for sixty, so if early bedtimes do it for him-"

"Stop right there. I don't want to know what 'does it' for my dad."

I couldn't help laughing, the tension easing in my body. Ellie always got around my defenses. "Fine, you win. I can hardly have you comparing me to your dad. But I'm making no promises!"

"Deal." She smiled wickedly. "I might just make a rebel out of you yet, Captain Stuffed Shirt."

"Come on, I'm not even wearing a button-down." I pointed to the branded polo shirt. "See?"

"Yeah, you know what *I* see? Ironed creases on

the sleeves, you nerd. You can't help yourself, can you?"

"I hardly think that's a flaw. Neatness of appearance is right up there with cleanliness, and they say cleanliness is next to godliness."

"Oh, so now you think you're a god? Your ego knows no bounds."

I laughed again. "Alright, fine, I give up. I'll see you at seven, Ellie."

She beamed in response. "I'll see you then. Oh, you know we bill this occasion as 'bar casual,' right? No need to bust out the formal wear."

"Ha ha, you're hilarious. I'll see if I can rustle up some overalls."

"Perfect, I'll dig out my daisy dukes."

My brain temporarily short-circuited with an image of Ellie in extremely tiny shorts, but I recovered quickly. "Well, don't go all out on my behalf. Regular cut-offs will do."

"Noted." She smirked. "Later."

Heaven help me. As she retreated from my office, I mentally filed the daisy duke image of her away for another, more private time.

Tonight I had to be on my best behavior, or I would lose it completely.

AFTER RUSHING home to change into jeans and a t-shirt, I picked up Ethan and Olivia from after school and delivered them to my parents for the weekend.

Guilt swamped my chest when I considered I was dumping my kids off in order to hang out at a bar. I tried to remind myself that they were ecstatic to spend another weekend with their grandparents, and my folks were hardly less enthused. Ethan barely shouted out 'goodbye' before he ran straight into the garage to see what his grandpa was up to at his workbench.

Olivia, as always, was a bit more perceptive. "Are you okay, Daddy?" She peered up at me as I walked her to the front door.

"I'm fine, Livvie."

You're acting weird. Why'd you change clothes?"

"Because I have a work thing tonight."

"With Ellie?"

"Maybe."

She grinned. We'd reached the steps, and she bounded up to the top and spun around to face me. "Ask her about the horses."

My answering smile came easily. "You got it, kiddo."

"Thanks, Daddy." She wrapped her little arms around my neck and pulled me closer for a hug.

I held her tightly and breathed her in. She smelled like apple shampoo, and my heart swelled, sudden emotion rising like a wave in my chest.

"I love you, Livvie. And I'm so proud of you. Did you know that?"

She pulled back and nodded. "I know."

Just then, Ethan raced out of the garage and charged up the porch steps. Not to be outdone, he dove into my chest for a hug, too.

I squeezed both of them together, my eyes flooding with emotion that also inexplicably blocked my throat. I rubbed their little backs and dropped my cheek on top of their heads for just a moment. As much as I wished I could make this last forever, I knew I had to let them go. I seared it into my memory, then leaned back and dropped a kiss on both of their foreheads.

"I love you guys. Have fun with Gramma and Grandpa, and listen to them! I'll see you Sunday."

"Love you, Daddy." Olivia turned and headed for the entrance.

"Love you more!" Ethan shouted before tearing off into the house, cutting Livvie off at the doorway.

A fond chuckle rose in my chest, and I pulled in a deep breath, tilting my head back to draw the threatening tears back into my eyes. These little moments proved I was doing the right thing. Every day they seemed to shine a little brighter, to open up to me a little more, and each time felt like a massive win.

I knew I should pop in and say hi to my folks, but a glance at my watch sent me back to my car at double time—I was running dangerously close to being late.

Fortunately, I made it through town to Peak 9 in record time and walked in to Seasons exactly at seven.

"My my, you are punctual, I'll give you that." Ellie was at the end of a gleaming mahogany bar, connecting her laptop to the projector wiring. The device itself was suspended from the ceiling in the center of the room, and already playing a mirror image of her desktop on the screen on the far wall.

Ellie had changed clothes as well, and just the sight of her sent my pulse racing. She wore a black tank top and a pair of worn-in jeans that hugged her figure in a sinful way for such a casual outfit. My mouth watered, and I swallowed down the nerves.

Oblivious to my ogling, she asked, "Have you always been like that, or is it a military thing?"

It took me a second to realize she was talking about the punctuality. I shoved my hands in my pockets, walking slowly to her position in what I hoped was a casual stroll. "Truthfully? I was always late for *everything* in high school. So I can definitely say it's the military that made me this way. They kind of instill an automatic panic response at the idea of being late that just never goes away."

She laughed. "Well, I'm glad I never joined. I don't think I'd be well-suited to that life. Do you have the thumb drive?"

"Yes, right here, sorry." I pulled the small cylinder from my pocket and handed it to her.

She removed the cap and installed the device on her laptop, tapping open the slideshow.

Eighties synth pop music poured from invisible speakers, and the animation I'd spent the week programming zoomed forward to present the first question.

"Wow, Jake, this is outstanding! I was expecting some white slides with black text, maybe an occasional image. I've never seen a slideshow like this."

A small blossom of gratification unfurled in my chest, but I tried not to look too pleased with myself. "Hey, I told you I'm a PowerPoint Ranger. It's a skill."

"It definitely is." She clicked through several slides, watching the images and text zoom around as the sound cycled through several tracks. "Is it all like this? All hundred questions?"

"You bet. I don't do anything by half-measures."

"Well, I have to admit, I'm impressed. This will certainly be the fanciest trivia night we've ever had." She grinned up at me and my chest squeeze.

"Thanks, I'll make sure and let my CO know that certification translated to the civilian world."

"CO?"

I cringed; I still hadn't figured out how to stop using the military lingo. "Sorry, Commanding Officer. And there aren't actually certificates for this stuff. It's just a common joke that we get awards for strange things and that the skills don't translate over to civilian life."

Mercifully, Ellie laughed. "No, I get it. I'm sure there are lots of skills like that where there's no civilian equivalent. But I'd say this is a useful skill. I'm glad I asked you to do it. I couldn't have done anything like this."

The heat crept up to the tips of my ears, and I knew I was blushing furiously, but I had no control over it. Thankfully, the pub was semi-dark. "Well, thanks. Do you need help setting anything else up?"

We set out a stack of answer sheets and pens on the bar, close to the door. But after that, there was nothing left to set up and twenty long minutes until the event started, leaving me and Ellie essentially alone in the dim pub.

As if sensing my discomfort, Ellie said, "Why don't we get a drink? We'll have to camp out down here for the evening anyway, since I have to stay plugged into the system."

"Well, that's horribly archaic," I teased. "You don't have Wi-Fi in here? One star for this resort, that's completely unacceptable."

Ellie chuckled, then flagged down the bartender so we could get a couple of beers. "You know, you're not far off. People actually do review like that. And we do, actually, have free Wi-Fi in here. It's just the projector isn't Wi-Fi enabled—it's not exactly a priority. I think I'm the only one who uses it, and only for trivia nights. In our conference rooms we have electronic white boards, USB ports, all the modern amenities."

"I was just teasing. I think this resort is very well-appointed."

"I know, but the reality is customers can be harsh. That's part of why I started this whole 'employee satisfaction' program. The employees worked hard, and aside from a paycheck, there was little else for them to be excited about. When you add in overly critical and sometimes just downright mean guests, a lot of them would rather quit and find something easier. So I made it my mission to make Aspen Ridge a more fun place to work, and as an unexpected result, it's actually created a better experience for the guests, too." Our beers arrived, and she took a long swig.

I sipped my own, my brain mulling over her words for a moment before I spoke. "You know, my only work experience prior to this was the military. It's not the same as a civilian job at all. You sign a contract, and they basically own you for the length of it. I went where they told me, when they told me, and worked as long as they told me doing whatever they ordered me to do. I couldn't just quit because I had a lousy day—you literally go to jail for that. So my mindset is different, I guess, when it comes to work."

Ellie nodded. "That's reasonable, and I'd say it's

pretty clear in how you approach things. I don't think you do half-measures."

Pleased, I smiled and settled further into my chair.

"But that said, it's not as bad as it sounds. There are programs on every base where they try to provide entertainment and community for everyone stationed there. We had festivals and street fairs and low-cost excursions to local attractions outside of base, too.

"So I guess what I'm saying is, I get what you're trying to do, and I admire it. It makes a difference; a job can either be a place you go to collect pay, or it can be like a family. The military is like a family no one on the outside can really understand, and I see how you're making that happen here." I summed up, suddenly nervous again. I set my beer down and wiped the condensation on my jeans.

Ellie's answering smile was breathtaking. "Thank you, Jake. That really means a lot. My dad and the VPs have kind of treated it like a pet project that keeps me busy and doesn't do any harm, so they leave me alone. But he's always claimed that Aspen Ridge is a family—I think he didn't realize that we lost that feeling in all the expansion. Suddenly we had more employees than he ever met in person, and the people at the lower tiers weren't getting the same family experience. I thought this was a good way to improve that." She reached over and placed a palm on my knee. Heat radiated from the spot, and I went completely still for fear of doing something odd and embarrassing myself. "I'm glad you see it from my perspective."

"Yeah, of course. I mean, I've witnessed how popular these events are first hand." I grabbed my beer bottle again, trying to cool my sweaty palm. "See?" I gestured to the door, where groups of people were filing in, chatting happily and picking up their answer sheets before choosing a table. "You're definitely making a difference for them, and they obviously appreciate it."

Before I even knew what happened, Ellie leaned forward and kissed me. Her scent filled my nose, and I froze completely when her lips pressed lightly to mine. It was over lightning fast, so quickly I could almost convince myself it didn't happen. But it did, and the surge of heat running through my body remained.

Ellie hopped out of her seat and started greeting people by name, then got to work running the slide show. I stayed by her side, and we chatted lightly through the evening. Ellie accepted compliments on the slides and finally announced the winning team before everyone went home. Neither of us said a word about the kiss.

But the lingering feeling of her mouth, and the

taste of her lips, clung to me for the rest of the night. Ellie had kissed me, and I was so surprised I sat completely still. I didn't even kiss her back. In fact, the night we met, she had kissed me first, too.

And the one time I almost made a move, I backed out. She had to think I was either too timid, or just not interested. Both of which were untrue.

I had to make sure she knew how I felt before we left, or it would congeal into a giant ball of awkward over the weekend and I'd miss my chance entirely. Sweat slicked my palms as I waited for the last few employees to leave. Ellie was wandering among the tables, picking up pens and helping the bartender clear glasses.

Resolved, I rushed over to help and Ellie beamed at me in response. I followed her to the bar with a handful of glasses, and we carried on tidying up.

Suddenly, the perfect idea popped into my head. "Hey Ellie, do you have any plans next weekend?"

She tucked a loose strand of hair behind her ear and scooped up a half-full mug. "Um, I'm not sure, but I don't think so. Why?"

My heart sped up to double time, but I spat the words out. "I'm taking Ethan and Olivia into town for the Aspen Ridge Oktoberfest, and I was wondering if you'd like to come? They've been asking about you since the Fall Fest."

She glanced up in surprise. "They have? That's sweet. Yeah, Oktoberfest is a pretty big event around here. The town actually throws a lot of celebrations. It feels like there's always something going on."

"So... would you like to go with us?" I wiped my sweaty palms on my jeans.

"Sure, that would be fun. My friend Tessa owns the Aspen Ridge Brewery, they always have a booth with these great bratwurst. And there's another place that does giant soft pretzels. Ethan will love them."

Emotion over her thinking of my kids warred for control with the gratification that she had accepted my proposal. Sure, it wasn't a proper 'date' date, but she was agreeing to hang out with me, and my kids, outside of work. That meant something for sure. "Great, we can just meet you there, if you like?"

"Yeah, let's talk about it next week. It'll be a good time." She carried the remaining glasses to the bar and packed up her laptop bag.

We waved goodnight to the bartender, and I followed her outside, my heart pounding. The thought that I needed to proactively kiss her, so she knew how I felt, beat like a drum in my mind. But I couldn't figure out how to make it happen.

"Tonight was fun," she commented as we stepped outside.

The temperature had noticeably dropped, and goosebumps rose on my bare arms in response. I felt as if my body were on fire.

"Yeah, it was," I agreed. "And good job with the

questions. I got some wrong, and I had to type all the answers for the slide show."

She laughed, and my heart thumped again in response. I honestly had no idea why, but Ellie thought I was funny. And I loved the way she laughed, her head tilted back and her eyes sparkling in genuine amusement. Ellie never did things by half measures, she was fully in, whatever it was.

Acting on some powerful instinct I didn't know I possessed, I reached out and cupped the back of her head, pulling her mouth to mine.

This time I didn't freeze; my lips moved against hers with determination, and after a second, a sigh escaped Ellie's throat and she kissed me back. Her lips were eager, as if she'd just been waiting for me to make this move, and when her tongue slid along my lower lip, I chased it enthusiastically. The memory of how right it felt to kiss Ellie that very first night—the sparks flying around us like a meteor shower—surged back in my brain. This was so right; and it had always been right.

Ellie's body pressed against mine, and I wrapped my free hand around her waist, feeling the heat of her skin beneath her thin camisole. I don't know how long we kissed. The taste of peppermint on her tongue, the warm amber vanilla fragrance of her filling my senses.

I was dragged back to reality when Ellie shivered violently against my body. My hand slid along her arm, finding her skin chilly and covered with goosebumps.

I pulled back slowly, rubbing my hands along her arms. "Are you cold?"

"Y-yeah," she admitted, a slight tremor in her voice as she huddled close.

My body was an inferno from the rush of blood, so I definitely couldn't relate, but I knew the right thing to do. I wrapped my arms around her shoulders, resting my chin on her head as I pulled her in tight. "Okay, let's get you warm. Where'd you park?"

She pointed, and it was as natural as breathing to slide my fingers between hers and guide her to her car.

Suddenly bashful, she fumbled her keys and glanced up at me shyly. I waited for her to get inside and get her Jeep running, heat blasting immediately from the vents, before I leaned in to the door frame.

"Drive safe, okay?" She nodded, and I leaned in to press one more soft kiss to her lips before I let her drive off.

When I pulled back, Ellie's eyes were closed, a dreamy expression on her face as her lips chased mine.

Finding me gone, her eyes fluttered open, and she smiled. "Goodnight, Jake."

"Goodnight, Ellie. If you think of it, shoot me a message and let me know you get home safe."

"You got it, Captain Wright," she grinned, and I stepped aside so I could close the door.

With a little flirtatious wave, she drove off, and I watched until her taillights had disappeared into the trees.

CHAPTER 10
ELLIE

"Oh my god, I *knew* it!"

Tessa and I were out to brunch at Rocky Side Up, and she was practically swooning over her eggs Benedict. "It's about time, El. I *freaking* called it. I hope you remember that. I better be the maid of honor at your wedding," she added sternly, before taking a swig of her mimosa.

"You're ridiculous," I laughed, scooping a bite of my omelet. I'd hardly eaten anything, too busy relaying every detail of last night's epic smooching to my best friend. The melted cheese was already congealing. "It was one kiss. We're hardly headed for the altar."

Tessa scoffed. "You say that now, but I see the look in your eyes. You've got it *bad*. Besides, this isn't your average play boy. He's a commitment kind of man, El. He's got *kids*, he's not trying to mess around. You know it's a big deal for a guy to invite you to hang out with his kids, right? How long was he in the military for?" Tessa jumped topics like a bunny rabbit with ADHD, especially when she was excited.

I swallowed my eggs and washed them down with coffee. "I mean, I met Olivia and Ethan at the Fall Fest, and it's just an invitation to hang out at Oktoberfest in town. All of Aspen Ridge will be there. We'd probably bump into each other even if he hadn't invited me. And as for your other question, I'm not sure. Over fifteen years, I think."

"Do you know how long he was with his ex wife?"

"I'm not sure, but it was a long time. I think they might have been high school sweethearts."

"See?" Tessa said meaningfully, waving her fork at me. "He doesn't play around."

"He's on the rebound," I scoffed. "I doubt he's looking to get serious anytime soon." Despite my words, I couldn't help recalling the look in Jake's eyes last night. There was something so solid there. So sure, and steady, and *real* in that gaze. For a moment I'd felt absolutely grounded, the world spinning around us while the two of us were firmly planted together.

"I'm telling you," Tessa shrugged. "Commitment guys don't do rebound."

"Well, regardless, there's no rush. Right now I've still got to do whatever it takes to make my dad satisfied, so he'll step down and let me take over as CEO. He would not be cool with us dating while we're in the same part of the company, you know that. But once he's gone, and we transfer Jake out—did I tell you my dad decided to put him with James, over at mountain ops?—there could be something there."

Tessa grinned like the Cheshire cat. "Yeah, uh-huh. Keep telling yourself that you're not going to jump him before that happens."

"Tessa!" I admonished, then lowered my voice when I realized the tables nearby were glancing at us in annoyance. "I have to behave. Aren't you listening? Dad wants me to be this 'prim and proper professional' woman. I'd hardly convince him of that if I'm hooking up with Jake."

"Oh, come on, your dad loves Jake. You told me yourself."

It was true, Dad was constantly singing Jake's praises whenever I was within earshot. At first I'd was annoyed, seeing as how he'd brought Jake in to 'shape me up.' But I realized he just held Jake in high regard. Jake didn't seem to curry favor or anything, just was an outstanding employee who worked hard. My dad valued that.

My chest warmed as I thought about it. "You're right, he does. He's lined up a pretty sweet job for Jake with James too, who also, incidentally, really likes him."

"See? He fits right into the family." Tessa leaned back triumphantly, pushing away her empty plate and signaling the server for another mimosa. "He's perfect."

"Tessa, you know it's not that easy. I have a lot of work to do with Aspen Ridge, and once my dad leaves, I'll have even more. I don't have time to date, let alone take on a whole family."

She sighed. "I hear you, but can you just give it a chance? You don't have to marry the guy, but at least don't freeze him out. Go out, have lots of dirty sex, get your groove on."

"Tessa!"

"Hey, if the guy was married for over ten years, he knows how to keep a woman satisfied. That's all I'm saying."

"He is a fantastic kisser," I admitted, the smile creeping across my face at the memory.

"See! I'm telling you, all signs point to bang."

"Okay, but even if I wanted to—and I'm not admitting I do!—you said yourself he's a commitment guy, with the kids and all. I don't know if I'm ready for the total family experience. I have a lot on my plate and we've barely kissed a few times."

"I'm not saying you have to marry the guy,"—I

shot her a look, and she recanted—"I was joking about being a bridesmaid, El, you know that. But that doesn't mean you can't test out the hot rod and see if you like how it drives."

"Fair," I agreed. "And he said the kids are at his parents' all weekend."

"Holy shit, El, he gave you an in!"

I nearly spit out my coffee, trying not to laugh. "Why do you make me sound like a criminal?"

"He told you he doesn't have kids all weekend? That's a freaking invite, my dear. Guaranteed."

"No, you're a lunatic. It wasn't like that. He was just saying he planned to have a quiet weekend since his kids were with his parents."

"Jesus, woman, are you blind? He was telling you he had no plans, and no kids, all weekend. Was this before or after he kissed you?"

"Well... it was before he kissed me, but after I kissed him."

"WHAT!" she shrieked, and I slid down in my seat in embarrassment as half the restaurant glanced our way. "Wait a second. You didn't tell me you kissed him first!"

"It wasn't a big deal," I hissed. "He was telling me about his life in the military and how he liked what I was doing with the employee programs, and I just kind of leaned over and kissed him. It was just a peck on the lips."

The smirk on Tessa's face was smug. "You little

liar. You played this whole thing off like you didn't know how he felt and he surprised you, and then you finally admit you kissed him first. Well, the ball is definitely in your court now."

"Wait, what? Why is the ball in my court?"

"You kissed him first." She ticked off her points on her fingers. "Then he told you he was kid-free and without plans all weekend. Then he planted one hell of a smooch on you, escorted you to your car, and sent you home all glowy and weak in the knees. Did you text him when you got home?"

"I did."

"And how did he respond?"

"He thanked me for letting him know and said 'sweet dreams.'"

"Ha! See? Gate's wide open, babe. He's waiting for you to run through."

"*How* do you conclude that?"

"If he had said something like 'have a great weekend' that's him assuming, or implying, that he won't see you again until Monday. But he only said 'sweet dreams', which leaves it open for the entire weekend." Tessa retrieved her fresh mimosa from the table and took a long, triumphant sip. "Ball is in your court, and if you want to get a little somethin' somethin', all you gotta do is ask."

I set down my coffee and picked up the mimosa I'd been ignoring in favor of caffeine. It'd sat long enough for condensation to collect on the outside, and the cold droplets ran down my fingers while I sipped. It *had* been a while since I'd gotten some action, and I couldn't recall being this excited about a guy since Zach and I first started dating. The last couple of years of on-again, off-again felt more tedious than fun. "You really think so?" I asked finally.

"Girl, I know so. You guys want to keep it on the DL around your dad? That's your business. But I guarantee if you text him and invite him out, he'll be up for it."

"Maybe, but we've got plans tonight. I'm not going to blow you off for a guy. Ride or die, remember?"

"Honey, you know I'm living vicariously through you with all of this. But you don't have to cancel. Why don't you just invite him to come with us?"

I lowered my chin and leveled a disbelieving stare her way. "To karaoke? Come on, most guys hate karaoke."

"Not all, and trust me, you have an in on this one. Didn't you say he loves eighties movies?"

"Yeah, so?"

"Girl, did you even look at the Underground's calendar?"

"No." I shrugged. "They have karaoke every second Saturday of the month, and we go every time. Why would I bother?"

Tessa shook her head at me, then whipped out

her phone, tapping a few times before turning it to face me.

This karaoke night, inexplicably, had a theme. A garish, neon-colored graphic proclaimed tonight's event dedicated to eighties music.

"Tessa, you are an evil genius. If I didn't know any better, I'd say you orchestrated this."

She put her phone away and settled back in her seat with a smug grin. "It's perfect. You have to admit, you couldn't have planned it better yourself. Even if he doesn't want to sing—which would be lame, let's be clear—he's still going to have fun. And then you two have a chance for a little mm-mm." She shimmied her shoulders and gave me a meaningful look.

"Okay, I'll invite him, but I'm not doing it to have sex. It's too soon, Tessa."

She reached across the table to clink her champagne glass with mine, and after we both took our sips, she smiled. "Famous last words, my friend."

WITH TESSA'S GUIDANCE, I crafted the perfect text invite for Jake to join us. I tried to make it as nonchalant and obligation-free as I could, but under the influence of several mimosas, Tessa was an almost unstoppable force. Even so, Jake agreed to meet us for karaoke.

Suddenly, our fun girl's night had turned into an evening I had to prepare for, and fortunately Tessa sobered up quickly enough to help me. I settled on a short floral dress with thigh-high boots and a soft, oversized sweater that hung off one shoulder. I had planned on jeans and a t-shirt for girl's night—ordinarily I wasn't trying to look hot for bottom-basement karaoke. But Tessa insisted I had to go all in, and she had certainly dated a lot more than I had, so I took her advice. She, however, stuck with jeans.

I'd been purposefully vague about what time to arrive, since I didn't want it to sound too formal, so I wasn't sure what time Jake would show. Tessa and I usually slid in a few minutes before the karaoke started because it didn't draw a large crowd and drinks were cheaper next door at Sarah's Corner. So, we had a couple steadying rounds of rum and coke before we slipped over to the Aspen Underground.

True to its name, the Underground was actually downstairs from the street level, although not technically underground since there was an outdoor landing. Flyers were taped all over the entry way advertising the specially themed karaoke night, and to my absolute shock the place was packed.

A guy with a mullet and a red, white, and blue sweatband was singing 'Don't Stop Believing' and the audience was singing along.

In dismay, I glanced around and realized all the tables were full, suddenly regretting my high-heeled boots. Damn Tessa; if not for her, I'd be in comfy flats right now. I didn't see Jake among the crowd, either.

We made our way to the bar and flagged down Max. "Quite a crowd here tonight!" I shouted over the enthusiastic roar of the audience. "What gives?"

"It's the costume contest," he shouted back, already fixing our usual drinks. "There's a big prize. It brought people out of the woodwork."

Tessa and I exchanged a glance, then dug out our phones to pull up the flyer.

Sure enough, below the large colorful letters proclaiming '80's Karaoke', there was a lot more information detailing the contest and how to win. Apparently, the winner had to not only be in costume but also sing an eighties song in order to be entered.

"How did we miss that?" I asked, and Tessa just shrugged. "Okay, well you don't get to shame me for not knowing it was eighties night when you apparently didn't read the flyer, either!"

Max slid over our drinks and we opened our tab, then stood together by the bar, staring out at the crowd.

"So, where do you want to go?" Tessa asked. The singer finished his song and slipped off the stage, and Andy the MC took the mic to announce the next singer.

"I dunno. I guess we could just hang here for a minute and see if something opens up?"

Tessa glanced at the door doubtfully, where more people were pouring in every minute. I scanned the crowd for a table and spotted someone in a giant windbreaker with a huge mustache waving in our direction. He didn't look familiar; must have seen someone coming through the door behind us.

Tessa nudged me. "Should we go up and put our names in for a song? From the looks of this crowd, it could be a while before we get called up."

"Yeah, that's probably smart. Do you know what you want to sing?"

Tessa rolled her eyes. "Come on, like you have to ask."

Careful not to spill our drinks, we slipped between the tables. My phone buzzed in my purse, but I ignored it while we filled out our song request. My phone began buzzing more insistently, indicating a call, so I set down my drink and fished it out.

It was Jake. He must be running late. I canceled the call and opened up a message, planning to text him and tell him it's too loud to answer the phone, but then I saw he had texted me. When I read his message, I glanced up in shock, then erupted in laughter.

"What did I miss?" Tessa was at my elbow, having turned in the slip, and eager to be in the know.

"Over there," I pointed to the guy with the wind-breaker and mustache, "that's Jake. I didn't recognize him, but he got a table."

Tessa leaned back, a disgusted expression on her face. "When did he have time to grow a mustache?" she commented with distaste. Tessa hated mustaches.

"He didn't. He's obviously dressed up for the contest. Come on."

We wove through the crowd and made our way to Jake, who had incredibly hoarded a table and chairs for the three of us. He hopped down from his stool to hug me in greeting, immediately sending me into another peal of laughter.

Besides the neon-blue, extravagantly oversized wind breaker, Jake had on the tiniest blue shorts I'd ever seen on a man—dangerously close to revealing something that should never be seen in public—complete with white sneakers and crew socks pulled up his calves.

"Wait, you need the full effect," he grinned beneath the Magnum PI-style mustache. Tessa claimed her seat while I waited, and Jake fished out a pair of oversized, mirrored aviator sunglasses. After placing them on his head, he did a few deep knee bends and lunges, preening for the surrounding crowd, who were enjoying the show entirely too much.

"Alright you win best in show," I laughed. "You remember Tessa?"

"Of course, nice to see you again," Jake held out his hand for a shake.

"Likewise," she answered, then looked back and forth between us expectantly.

I raised a brow. "What?" A new singer was on the stage, and we had to shout over her to be heard.

"You guys should sing something!"

"Oh no, I don't do duets."

"You sing with me."

"That's different. We sing together." Wanting to steer the conversation away from this track, I turned to Jake. "Okay, you gotta tell me where you got this outfit. It's... something."

Jake grinned, but the way his fake mustache made his upper lip disappear distracted me. "It was my dad's!"

I burst out laughing. "No way! Does he wear it now?"

"Nah, he'd never fit these shorts now, he's just kind of a hoarder. But I remembered seeing a photo of him from his Navy days. I always thought it was from Top Gun—like I thought my dad was in that movie when I was a kid. So when you invited me and I checked out the event, it inspired me. I asked him about it and he said he kept the outfit, along with a bunch of his old navy stuff."

"I'm assuming the mustache wasn't a hand-me-down?"

"Nah, that I had for another reason." He drew off the sunglasses and waggled his eyebrows.

It grew too loud to talk, and we waited for the applause to die down, only for the MC to announce, "next up is Captain Wright!"

Jake slid the glasses back on his face. "Looks like it's showtime, ladies."

He hopped off his stool, took a swig of beer, and strode to the front to the swelling applause as people got a look at his outfit.

The MC gestured to Jake when he climbed on the stage, prompting a round of hoots from the crowd. "Is this your typical look, or are you entering our contest?"

Jake leaned over the mic to answer. "Uh, that would be an affirmative on the contest, sir."

"Alright well, your song's cued up, Captain Wright. Good luck!"

Jake took the microphone and did a couple of lunges for good measure, to the groans and cheers of the crowd.

To his credit, he hit the lyrics right out of the gate, but I couldn't stop laughing when I realized he'd taken the Top Gun theme all the way. By the time he reached the chorus, the entire bar was signing along with, 'You've lost that lovin' feeling'. I roared, and Jake worked the crowd; they loved it.

Tessa punched me lightly on the shoulder, casting a sly grin my way. "Okay, I really like him."

"Well, that's high praise coming from you," I teased. "Was it the mustache that did it, or the shorts?"

"Oh, the crew socks. Definitely the socks. But," she shrugged, a mischievous gleam in her eye, "the shorts are illuminating. Definitely define his, um, best assets."

Heat rose to my cheeks as my eyes drifted to the spot she was complimenting. "You're not wrong," I agreed, leaning in to not be overheard. "From what I felt when we made out, he's packing heat."

"Is that a fifty-cal in his pocket or is he just happy to see you?"

My laughter turned into snorts, which made me laugh even harder.

"I mean, I've heard of a moose knuckle before, but that thing looks like a mammoth-"

"Tessa, stop, I can't breathe," I wheezed.

"Is he part donkey? Because I've heard-"

"TESSA!" I gasped, practically choking from laughter.

She rolled her eyes. "Oh fine, you ruin all my fun. I'm gonna go prowl, see if I can ruin some tourist's night by getting him all hot and bothered and then sending him back to his vacation rental alone."

"Fine, just don't actually go home with one! Oh, and listen for our song!" I shouted after her.

She made an acknowledging hand gesture as she walked away, and seconds later, the crowd roared with applause as Jake finished his song and took a bow.

The grin on his face stretched from ear-to-ear when he returned to the table and took his seat.

"Well I must say, well done, Captain Wright," I complimented, clinking my glass to his bottle.

"Thank you, thank you. That was a rush. It's been ages since I sang karaoke."

"You did great. Do you think the costume helped?"

"Yeah, it definitely made a difference. It's kind of like getting into character." He slipped the glasses off his face and tucked them into a pocket. "Speaking of, it doesn't look like you're in a costume."

"No, I'm not. We didn't realize there was a contest, if you can believe it. Tessa and I come here pretty much every month, and it's usually dead. I think we do it out of habit more than anything."

"If it makes a difference, I think you look great either way."

Warmth spread across my cheeks. "Thank you."

"So where did Tessa go? I didn't scare her off, did I?"

"Nah, she's hunting."

His head tilted. "Hunting, like hunting with a gun?"

"No," I laughed. "It's sort of a long story, but I'll

try to keep it brief. A while back, Tessa met a guy, and even though she knew he was only in town for the week, she was really into him. She thought they had something, and she was all invested in the idea of a long-distance relationship. Like she was ready to go all in."

"After a week?"

I shrugged. "I know. She can be impulsive like that. Anyway, they have a great week. He promises to keep in touch, and does a little at first, but just gradually replies less. Then she gets a message from someone explaining that they were the guy's fiancé and to stop texting him."

"Ouch!"

"Yeah. So she told her what that guy had done while he was here, claiming he was single and thinking of moving to Aspen Ridge in order to hook up on his boy's trip. After that, Tessa has taken it as her personal mission to get back at guys like that."

"Woah, she tracks down their girlfriends and everything?"

"Nah, she's more clever now, and she doesn't really want to get involved. She mostly flirts and strings them along—so they don't try it with anyone else, you understand—and then ghosts them on their last night in town. It's kind of diabolical, but also kind of hilarious."

"Remind me never to get on her bad side."

"Will do, but just so you know, she already said she likes you."

"It was the mustache, wasn't it? Ladies love the 'stach."

Laughter bubbled out of me. "No, definitely not the 'stach. But take the compliment, she doesn't like many people."

"Well, thanks, I think."

"You're welcome."

Our conversation piddled out, and we focused on our drinks. The current singer was a woman in a hot pink, ruffled dress with black fishnets on her arms, belting out a Pat Benatar song, and she was fantastic. When the applause for her died down, Andy announced, "Now it's time for some of our regulars. Let's get Ellie and Tessa up here!"

"That's me!" Tessa shouted, sprinting for the stage with her hands up. I followed, suddenly self-conscious that I wasn't in costume. Tessa had stolen some guy's baseball cap, and with her faded KISS t-shirt and ripped grey jeans, she almost looked like she was in costume.

"Let's kill this," she flipped the cap backwards on her head and bumped my hip with hers, handing me a second mic.

I don't know why, but sudden nerves wriggled in my belly. I was used to this place being dead when we sang.

A loud whistle caught my attention, and I

glanced through the bright stage lights to see Jake with his fingers in his mouth. The whistle ended, and he waved, cheering us on.

The music started, and I dropped right in.

Tessa and I alternated the lyrics like we usually did, singing the Joan Jett tune in the style of the Beastie Boys, but singing together on the chorus. The crowd cheered, and even though we knew we weren't winning any contest, we still had fun.

After our bow, Tessa followed me back to the table.

"Great job. You guys were outstanding!" Jake greeted us with high fives.

"Thanks, but I don't think we really compare to your *performance*," Tessa said with an edge. "I mean, I think you've really got it in the *pocket* with that one."

"Tessa," I warned, but she just gave me a sly grin.

"I gotta go. I've got a live one. He's already invited me back to his hot tub." She rubbed her hands together like a cartoon villain.

"Wait, you're not actually going, are you?"

"Hell no. I'm going to make him take two more shots, so his buddies have to drive him home. Then I'm going to tell him to pick up non-latex condoms at the market across town because I have sensitive lady bits. And *then* promise I'm going to meet him but never show, and act like I fell asleep. You know how I do this, Ellie. A little faith?"

"Okay, just let me know you get home safe, crazy. Oh wait, I rode with you. Can you drop me at home before you start your diabolical plan?"

Tessa's grin curled like the Cheshire Cat's. "Oh, I'm sure Captain Mooseknuckle can give you a ride."

Jake choked on his beer.

"Tessa!" How was it possible to be so embarrassed you wanted to melt through the floor, but also laughing hysterically? That was one of Tessa's unique gifts.

"I can give you a ride, Ellie," Jake offered, recovering from nearly drowning in beer but clearly blushing profusely.

"See? All good." Tessa pulled me in for a hug. "You're welcome. I love you. Wear a rubber. You don't know where that thing's been."

"I hate you," I replied, still laughing. "Enjoy fucking up someone else's night."

"Oh, definitely will!"

And in a flash, she was gone.

"She's... something else," Jake commented vaguely, a note of shock in his voice.

"Yeah, she is. She must really like you. She never acts like herself around strangers."

"I'll take the compliment?" he replied in a confused tone.

"She's like a cat. An old, surly house cat, that wants nothing to do with people most of the time. Most people she'll just ignore. But if she likes you, that's when she'll come out and play. Just know sometimes she'll dig her claws in you while she does it. But that's how she shows love."

"Surly house cat; got it."

"So..." I glanced at my empty glass. "Should we get another round?"

"I'd better switch to water for a while. I may have had a couple of shots to get the courage up to sing, and since I'm driving precious cargo, I need to be extra sober for the ride home." His eyes were warm and admiring when they held mine.

"Are you drunk now?" I asked, confused. He didn't seem drunk.

"No, I just don't want to drink any more and tip over the edge."

"Well then, why don't we just leave? It's really loud in here."

"So early? I'm okay to hang out a while, if you want to."

"Oh, do you want to stay for the contest to see if you won?"

"No, I don't care. It was just for laughs. I just didn't expect the night to end so quickly."

And that is when I caught up, my heart beginning to race. "Well... why don't we go to my place? It's quieter and we could have another drink or switch to tea or something, if you prefer." I tried to present it like I wasn't just inviting him back to my place for sex, but I still wasn't sure which way I wanted to go.

"Sure, okay," he agreed, suddenly nervous.

I gathered my purse and stopped by the bar to pay my tab, but Max informed me Tessa's 'new friend' had already paid our tab, and handed back my card.

We were still laughing when we made it onto the sidewalk.

"She really has it in for that guy, doesn't she? My truck's just over here," Jake gestured up the street.

"Yeah, she's something else. I kind of agree with her, however. They bring it on themselves, being dirtbags."

"But how does she know they're dirtbags? They could actually be single guys just looking for a fun weekend."

I glanced up at him suspiciously and he paled. "Not that that's something I'd do, but I mean, if that's what both people want..."

"She has her methods, but I think she targets the ones that feed her the most bullshit."

Jake held the door to an extended-cab pickup open and I climbed in, buckling my seat while he walked around to the other side.

He waited until he was pulling away to comment, "Is it me, or is it sad that it's so easy for her to find those guys?"

"I agree, it's sad. She considers it a service that

she does for the younger women in town, keeping them from ending up in the same spot she did."

"I suppose that was kind of crushing."

"Yeah. It's been a few years, and she hasn't seen anyone seriously since."

Conversation lagged as I gave him directions to my condo. My body hummed with nervous energy, but our conversation had seemed to stay completely PG. I didn't know what was on his mind, but all I seemed to be able to think about was picking up where we left off last night.

When we made it to my place and stepped inside, Jake let out a low whistle.

"I'm glad we came to your place first. I'd be embarrassed for you to see the box I live in."

"I don't believe that for a second," I snorted. "You iron your polo shirts, Jake. You've got to keep a tidy house." Changing subjects, I asked, "Do you want a drink?"

"Sure, whatever you're having." He stuck his hands in the pockets of his windbreaker. "And yes, I'm neat, but you have to remember I have two small kids. It's like a tornado sweeps through every hour they're at home. It's impossible to keep up."

"Somehow I doubt that." I fixed a pair of rum and cokes and passed him a glass. "Come on, I'll give you the tour."

It was one big open space, decorated with ivory marble in the kitchen, pale wood cabinets and floors, the same stone on the fireplace, and neutral-colored furniture. I flicked the switch on the fireplace and led him down the hall, pointing out the bathroom, the guest room, and the master in the back before we returned to the living room and settled on the couch.

"You see? Not big at all."

"It's not huge, but it's spacious. The open floor plan and the high ceilings are part of it, I'm sure." He gestured at the floor-to-ceiling windows that faced the mountain. "That, too."

"Yeah, I know what you mean. But it's not a lot of floor space—I don't need much. I love a fireplace, and a view. I mean, this is why we live here, right?"

"That's true. And when you own the place, I guess you can afford the view. All I have a view of is my neighbor's backyard."

I felt a flicker of embarrassment. "I'm not trying to show off," I murmured.

"Oh, no, that's not what I meant. And believe me, I'm happy with my house. I can't tell you how nice it is to be in a real neighborhood that's not on a military base. And we're right around the corner from my parents, which is the main reason I bought where I did. I'm not judging you."

The tension in my chest eased. "Okay, thank you." My eyes turned to the fire, and I took a sip of my drink. Jake copied the movement. Somehow we'd drifted away from the sexual promise of the evening and now it was rapidly growing awkward. Even so, my body was absolutely thrumming with the desire to straddle his lap and unzip that windbreaker. I was considering making a move when he spoke.

"Ellie?" Jake's voice sounded resigned.

"Hm?"

He paused. "Um, I should probably go." He stood, taking another sip of his drink, and walked to the kitchen to leave the glass in the sink.

I followed, confused. "Is something wrong? It's still early."

He shoved his hands back in his jacket pockets and sighed. "No, I just..." he searched for words for a moment, then laughed. "I just feel ridiculous. I'm in this outfit with these tiny shorts and I don't feel remotely manly right now. It seems like I should make a move, but then I don't really know if you want me to, and I'm just thrown off by the whole thing. I think the best option is for me to go home, put my tiny shorts away, and try again by asking you out on a proper date-"

Before he could even finish his sentence, I'd set my glass down and marched straight up to him, determined. If he didn't know what I wanted, I needed to show him.

Reaching up, I grasped the collar of the windbreaker and tugged him down to kiss me. The cold sweetness of his mouth was cool and refreshing on my tongue, and his arms circled around my body as he kissed me back with enthusiasm.

When I pulled back, his lips followed, searching for mine.

My voice was a low purr when I spoke. "This outfit is hilarious, and I love that you wore it. But if you're uncomfortable, you know what you should do?"

"No," he shook his head, confused.

"You should take it off."

A MISCHIEVOUS GRIN took residence on his face as Jake turned us, pressing my back to the kitchen island while we continued kissing. I reached for the zipper and tugged it down, exposing a white tank top with a faded blue US Navy logo stretched across his wide chest. The zipper got stuck at the waistband, and after a moment, he stepped back to just pull the entire thing over his head.

It was my first chance to run my hands over his body with very little coverage, and it did not disappoint. My fingertips explored the mountains and valleys of the muscles on his arms and shoulders, his skin hot to the touch.

Our kisses grew more desperate, his teeth tugging at my lip and our tongues twirling madly in a seemingly pre-determined rhythm. Jake's hands, solid and hot on my skin, slid up my body. One gripped me under my sweater and the other cupped my neck, pressing gently while his thumb stroked downward below my chin. The heat built between us, a myriad of sensations pinging my brain all at once, leaving me overwhelmed and drowning, yet desperate for more.

As if reading my thoughts, Jake gripped my hips with both hands and lifted me onto the island. His hands continue upward, dragging my sweater over my head and exposing more of my skin to his touch. He wasted no time settling himself between my thighs, and they locked around his body, squeezing him closer. Pressure was rapidly building below my belly button. It had been so long since I had a man's body between my legs, and my nerves were alive with anticipation.

Repeating the move that had nearly sent me over the edge the first time we kissed, Jake laced his fingers into my hair and gripped it firmly, drawing my head back and forcing a startled gasp from my lips. His mouth, hot even against my now-scorching skin, trailed down my neck and across my exposed chest. His free hand rose to stroke a thumb over my nipple through the thin fabric of my dress while his tongue dipped into the crease between my breasts. My hands rested on the cool countertop, supporting my weight as I arched further to give him more access.

Tension coiled even tighter in my belly, and I used my legs to draw him in, tightening until I felt his body brush against me. A low moan poured from my lips, and Jake's hand dropped from my breast to the back of my hips, tugging me forward to press even harder against him.

My moan turned to a gasp, and a rumbling growl rose from Jake's throat. He held me in place, kissing every inch of my exposed skin, and I wriggled, enjoying the sensation but also trying to convey that I wanted to move on.

"Jake," I whispered.

His head rose, and he cradled the back of my skull, bringing my face back to his to reclaim me with delicious kisses. My arms wrapped around his body, and I dragged my nails down the hard bulges of his back, all the way until I was gripping his ass through those tiny shorts, pulling him even tighter against me. I had no shame; I ground my body against him, reveling in the sensation of all of his hardness against all of my softness.

As much as I was enjoying myself, I was definitely ready to keep the show moving.

"Jake," I tried again, pulling my lips from his and kissing down his neck. "Maybe we should move to the bedroom."

And just like that, he froze. His entire body went rigid, and he might even have ceased breathing for all I could tell.

I straightened, trying to catch his eye. "Jake?"

Abruptly, he stepped back, out of the circle of my legs. "We... I should go. It's late." Conflicted, he leaned in to press a quick kiss to my lips, then bent down to grab his jacket.

"Jake, wait a minute. What's going on?" I grabbed his arm, stopped him from retreating.

He pulled in a deep breath before he answered. "It shouldn't be like this. You deserve better than this."

"I... what do you mean? I was having a delightful time before you stopped suddenly."

"No, I mean we should have a proper date, where I'm not in these stupid tiny shorts mauling you like an animal in your kitchen."

I smiled coyly. "I happened to enjoy being mauled by an animal in my kitchen." I tried to tug him back to me, but he remained firm. "Did I do something wrong?"

His eyes finally held mine, complete sincerity in their depths. "God no, Ellie. I mean it when I say you deserve better. I'm not just after sex. I don't want you to think that."

"Of course I don't think that, Jake. I just consider sex a perk of dating."

That drew a tiny half smile from him. He sidled back between my knees and wrapped his hands around my waist. "Well, it can't be dating if we don't actually go on a *date*. And I want to date you, Ellie.

Maybe it's old-fashioned, but please go with me on this. Let me wine and dine you, and when we make love for the first time, it will be candlelight and romance and... fireworks. I want to give you the full 80s movie package." His voice dropped as he nuzzled the side of my head.

"So no mauling?" I couldn't help the note of disappointment in my voice.

Jake chuckled, wrapping his arms around my body and pressing a few slow kisses to my head, his breath warm on my hair. "Not tonight. But if that's what you want, we can arrange it for another time. Anything you want, it's yours. Just all in due time."

I heaved a sigh. "Alright, if you insist. But you'd better find a boombox for when that bucket list item comes up."

He arched back with a laugh. "Yes ma'am. Anything for Ellie Tremont."

CHAPTER II
JAKE

"Dad, look at what I made!"

"Dad, Gramma and I made your favorite cookies. Come try one!"

The twin shouts of excitement overlapped as soon as I stepped through my parent's door, and the kids came running up to me for hugs.

"Hi guys, I missed you too," I chuckled. And I had —I realized that every time they were gone, the house felt empty. I'd never experienced that in Alabama, even after Cheryl left. I'd been so overwhelmed with everything I had to do, I barely had the brainpower to keep it all together. Every moment alone was like a second for me to catch my breath. Now we seemed to have settled into a flow, and while I enjoyed adult time—especially time like last night—I was genuinely looking forward to having them home again.

I let them pull me through the house so Ethan could show me the model car he had built with my dad's help. Olivia held a chocolate chip cookie with walnuts under my nose until I gave in and took a bite.

And just like when they were little, and I returned from a deployment, the pair of them clambered on my lap, each claiming a leg, and leaned against me. Despite being quite a bit bigger, they were content to share space. I wrapped my arms around both their middles and squeezed them close, planting a kiss on the back of each head.

My heart thudded in my chest, a tingling feeling prickling my eyes. For the first time in—I wasn't sure how long—my life felt like it was headed in the right direction. Everything, miraculously, was going well. The kids were happy. I enjoyed my job, and I was sort of seeing an incredible woman who brought out a side of myself I hadn't seen in ages. I lived just a few blocks from my parents, and we were heading into my favorite season: fall. Everything at this moment was right.

"Meatloaf will be ready in five minutes, guys. Why don't you two go wash up?" My mom beamed at Ethan and Olivia, and just like that, the moment was over. They hopped off my lap and raced for the bathroom. We could hear them fighting over who got to wash their hands first.

Mom gazed affectionately after them, smiling to herself as they negotiated.

"I got to the sink first!"

"Yeah, but I have the soap! You can't wash your hands without the soap, Ethan."

"That's not fair. You're not allowed to take the soap off the sink. It's against the rules!"

"Who said?"

"Guys," I called after them, laughing. "Olivia, give Ethan the soap, he was there first. Ethan, why don't you move over and make room for your sister? It's big enough for you both to wash at the same time."

The arguing stopped, and after a few moments, both emerged with damp splotches on their shirts.

We sat down to dinner, and after Mom took the kids into the living room to watch a movie while Dad and I cleaned up.

"You're in a good mood," he commented, handing me a soapy plate to rinse and dry. Despite retirement, my parents still didn't believe in dishwashers, apparently.

"I am, actually."

"Did you have a good weekend?"

"I did. I missed the kids, though."

"Well, that's to be expected. But I hope you got out and had some fun. How was the costume thing?"

"Yeah, I did. I helped Ellie with a trivia night thing Friday, and last night was actually a karaoke/costume contest with an 80s theme. Hence the outfit. Thanks again, by the way."

Dad's placid expression shifted into one of surprise. "Karaoke? Not something I would have pegged you for, son."

"Hey, I've been known to belt a tune once or twice. It was a good time."

"I'm glad you had fun. And you went with Ellie? Who is Ellie? The kids have been talking about her a lot."

"Isabelle Tremont. She prefers Ellie."

"I see. Isn't she your boss? And also the woman you're supposed to be training?"

It almost felt like I was having this conversation with Olivia. "No, she's not my boss, technically. I work for JJ Tremont, her dad."

"But isn't she in line to take over as CEO? That sounds sort of like a conflict of interest."

"Why? Are you saying it's against her interest to date me?" I didn't mean my tone to come out as harsh as it did.

"No, I'm not saying that at all, son. I'm just saying that there has to be complications for her, dating an employee. What does her father say?"

I squirmed internally. "He doesn't know, yet. It's really new, we're keeping it low-key for now."

"Ah." It was one syllable, but it felt like a mountain of reproach. Dad focused on the plate he was scrubbing, and I searched for an explanation.

"You don't understand. We met before either of us knew who the other was. And we cooled it as soon as we realized, but... honestly, she's just amazing, Dad. She's smart and funny, and I feel like a different person with her."

"A different person, how?" He handed me another plate, and I dutifully rinsed and resumed wiping.

"I dunno, exactly. It's like she brings something out of me, something I forgot was there. I've gotten so bogged down in responsibility I think I forgot how to have fun, if that makes sense? I mean, yeah, we'd have barbecues with friends and take the kids on vacations, but those were never really fun for me. It was always an itinerary, getting the kids from point A to point B, checking things off an endless list of 'childhood experiences' we didn't want them to miss out on.

"Honestly, Cheryl did most of it and I just did what she told me. And then when we broke up, I had to take on both roles—being 'Dad' and 'Mom'—and I didn't have time to even think about how I wanted my life to change, too. I was just holding on tight and rowing as hard as I could, trying to keep the ship on course. But Ellie," I sighed, unable to voice what I felt. "With Ellie it feels like... like a breath of fresh air. Like she makes me want to loosen up, allow the wind to take the sails for a minute so I can stop rowing, if that makes any sense at all."

I set the plate down on the dry stack and reached for the next one, but Dad had stopped washing, and now he turned the water off and turned to face me.

"Divorce is hard, son. Thankfully, your mother and I never went through it, but friends of ours have. I can't tell you how proud we are that you've stepped up and are trying to do right by our grandkids."

He grabbed the cloth from my hands and dried his. For some reason, in this moment, the details in his face stood out to me. His neatly cut greying hair, the deep creases at the corners of his eyes. Everyone has always said how much I look like my dad, and as if it snuck up on me, I suddenly realized he'd grown older while I wasn't paying attention.

Dad dropped a hand on my shoulder, and my throat grew thick. His eyes were still bright, and they held me firmly now.

"We're so grateful you're here, and we both think you've made all the right decisions for Ethan and Olivia. You have a support network here, and a job that allows you to be home with them. As proud as we are of your service, we know that the military life is hard on children. We toughed it out when you were growing up and you did just fine. But as a single-parent household, it's just a lot for those kids to navigate. While I know how hard it was to give up your career when you were so close to retirement,

I'm very proud of you, son. I want you to know that."

The emotion in his voice pricked at the back of my eyes, forming a catch in my throat. I loved my dad, but he was not an emotional man. I'd always modeled my behavior on him as the stoic provider for the family. This show of emotion caught me completely off-guard.

"However," he continued, "now that you're here, you need to stay the course. JJ Tremont is a good man, but he has strong opinions about how Aspen Ridge should run, and who his daughter should date."

He handed me back the towel and turned the water on, reaching for the next plate.

"I know, and we're very aware of the issues, Dad. It's not anything, yet."

"Well, I'm glad to hear that. You and Cheryl... well, you'll forgive me for saying it, but you were never a good fit. Your mother and I did the best we could—we wanted you to be happy, and Cheryl was who you chose—but that attraction to someone so different from you is what led you to this point in the first place. So it concerns me to think you might be headed down the same path."

"Dad, I-"

He cut me off. "I know Ellie is not Cheryl, and I know you say it's nothing serious yet. But I know my son, and I've seen this look before. Once you get your mind set on something, you see it through to the end. So I will not try to dissuade you, but I want you to remember what went wrong between you and Cheryl, so you can be sure not to repeat those mistakes. Most importantly, you need to keep Olivia and Ethan your focus. What they need most from you right now is stability, and you can't let this relationship get in the way of securing your position here. They have to come first right now."

My retort lodged in my throat. Even though the gentle reprimand stung, he was right, of course. I'd barely landed here, gotten my feet under me, and I was already thinking about chasing after Ellie despite the consequences.

"You're right, Dad," I sighed. "Thank you for bringing it up. I will take things slowly and keep my focus on the kids."

"I know you'll do the right thing, son. You always do."

We finished up the dishes and I eventually got the kids home and tucked in bed. For a long time after, I lay awake, thinking over my dad's words.

In just a few short weeks, I was already witnessing the change in Ethan and Olivia. They were clearly happier here, even more relaxed around me. They chattered happily on the drive home, and bedtime was now sleepy smiles and kisses instead of dutiful 'good night, Dad's. Everything I had hoped for with the move here was coming true. Ethan had less trouble controlling his temper, and Olivia was acting more like a joyful nine-year-old than a battle-hardened soldier. She had been talking animatedly about an upcoming choir performance at her school, excitement glittering in her eyes.

And my position at Aspen Ridge was precarious. I needed to solidify my place here if I wanted to see my kids continue to come out of their shells. JJ promised me a few months, and based on my perfor-mance, the potential to be placed in a more perma-nent position. But that was no guarantee, and I had no idea how that would change if he found out I was dating with his daughter.

Something told me it wouldn't be good.

CHAPTER 12
ELLIE

"Oh, shit."

"What?" Tessa looked up from her huevos rancheros in surprise.

We just finished dishing about our week, and I'd pulled out my phone to text Jake about Oktoberfest today. Only to discover a reminder for an event I'd completely forgotten about.

"I can't hang out with Jake and his kids today. I have to be at Snowshoe for the golf tournament."

Tessa's face dropped. "Oh, shit."

"Yeah."

"Can't you cancel? You hate golf anyway."

"I can't. My dad and I committed to it months ago. He'd definitely be pissed if I pulled out last minute to hang out with Jake at Oktoberfest."

"You don't think he'd understand?"

I leveled a glare at Tessa. "Are you kidding? You know how my dad is about these big charity events, and he doesn't know we're dating. No, he would not understand at all." I flung my head back in frustration. "Ugh, this sucks. Jake told me about a dozen times this week how excited his kids are to see me."

"Ouch. Blowing off a guy is one thing, but ditching the kids is rough. They take that shit personally."

I glanced suspiciously at Tessa. "You know, this whole time you've been giving me a lot of advice about guys with kids, and I don't recall you ever dating one. Is there something you're not telling me?"

Tessa's eyes widened, and she batted her lashes innocently. "Me? No. I just watch a lot of romcoms."

"Tessa..." I held her gaze and waited.

My best friend could never be a spy. She cracked under the lightest pressure. "Okay, fine. I was seeing a guy who had kids for a while over the summer. I didn't say anything because it never became a thing. He was super careful about keeping me separate from his kids and while at first I understood, it bothered me. When I said something, he admitted he didn't see us working out long term, and that was why he didn't introduce me to his kids. So, it ended after a couple of months."

"Damn, Tessa, why didn't you say anything? You know I'm always here for you. I don't judge."

"It's not that. I liked him and I didn't want to jinx it until it became a thing, and it never did. So, no point." She took a long swig of her mimosa. "Trust me, I'm fine."

"I just wish you'd told me. I feel like a terrible friend. I didn't even know you went through that."

"It's all good. It clearly wasn't meant to be. You, however... what are you going to do about Jake?"

"I have to rip the bandaid off. There's no easy way to do it. I'll text him."

I took a steadying sip of mimosa, then shot the message off.

> Hey Jake, I'm so sorry to do this, but I completely forgot I have a charity golf thing today with my dad.

> Oh, no problem. What time? Maybe we can meet up after?

> The tee off is at 3, and there's a dinner after. I don't think I'll be able to. Could we meet up tomorrow? Oktoberfest is all weekend

> Ethan and Olivia are already excited to head down today, I can't push them off to tomorrow. And 2 days of festival is a bit much

> I understand. Maybe we could do something else?

Maybe. Olivia has asked about the horses

> Great! I can schedule another trail ride for us tomorrow, my treat

Ok, sounds good. We'll see you tomorrow

> Ok, have fun! Get a pretzel for me!

You got it.

"... Well?" Tessa had watched me texting furiously, but now she was out of mimosa and clearly overly curious.

"We're going to take the kids on a trail ride tomorrow instead. Just a sec." I shot off a text to the stable master, Rachel, and reserved three horses. "Okay, that's done."

"So, how'd he take it?"

I shrugged. "Good. He didn't seem super upset."

"It's hard to read emotion over text."

"Well, he didn't say he was upset."

"Do people normally *say* those sorts of things?"

A flicker of worry wormed through my chest. "He said he understood, and that the kids were excited.

But he said Olivia brought up the horses, so I think they'll be happy about that."

"Yeah, it was a good save. Kids love horses."

"See? Nothing to worry about."

DAD PICKED me up for the charity event at two, and the entire drive to Snowshoe he reminisced about the years I dated Zach, how he was looking forward to seeing him. Guilt unfurled like a flower in my chest, each comment from my dad like a petal that pressed against my lungs and made it harder for me to breathe.

It was clear that—despite all of my assurances we were done—he still expected Zach and me to eventually get back together. I'd never told him about Zach's goals to absorb Aspen Ridge under the Snowshoe Ridge Resort(s) banner—he would have felt completely betrayed. I figured as long as it never came to pass, it wasn't worth mentioning. Zach and I went our separate ways and Dad would forget all about it, no problem.

We hadn't talked about it much lately, with all the focus on the coaching me to take over. So I didn't quite realize he was still holding this candle for our former relationship until now.

"It's been ages since we've seen Zachary," he repeated for the fifth time as we turned off the highway. "You should bring him around more often, Izzy. He hasn't seen all the improvements we've made since last season."

"We're not dating anymore, Dad," I reminded him with a bit of an edge to my tone. I'd already said it several times in the twenty-minute drive.

"I know, honey, but I know how you two are. You separate but you always come back to each other. You've been like that since high school."

"It's been over a decade since high school. Aside from events like this, I haven't seen Zach in a year."

"Well, unlike *some* people, Zach keeps in touch." He pulled into a reserved spot in front of the golf club and opened his door. "Perhaps you're just not giving him a chance to explain."

I hopped out of the Yukon and followed him around to the back. "Dad, there's nothing to explain. We've grown up, we're different people who want different things. It's nothing terrible, it just didn't work out."

"We'll see," he smiled knowingly and pulled out my golf bag. "Here you go." He handed me the green and white bag and I slung it over my shoulder. It was practically brand new; I only golfed with my dad at these sorts of events. He ensured we had everything branded with Aspen Ridge logos and colors, like our matching forest green polo shirts.

"Hey, great to see you guys!" Zach's voice, warm and familiar, reached my ears.

I looked up to see him approaching us from the clubhouse, wearing white pants with a baby blue Snowshoe-branded polo and a matching cap. He was tall and lean, sporting the same sparkling blue eyes and all-American smile I fell for in the first place. My heart gave a little lurch as a wave of nostalgia hit me.

"Hey there, sport!" My dad greeted him with a half-hug, and I waited for the male bonding to finish.

"Hi Ellie. Great to see you." Zach's smile turned sweeter, and I let him pull me in for a hug.

"Hey Zach. How've you been?"

"I can't complain. We've been busy here getting things in motion for the season. We built a new luxury condo complex over by Aspen Creek and added a footpath into the village. It's already half booked for this winter."

"That's great Zach. I'm happy for you."

"Wait 'til I tell you about our improvements." Dad threw an arm around Zach's shoulders and steered him toward the sign-in table. They chatted happily while we checked in and got the keys to our carts. I waited impatiently for the torturous awkwardness to be over. Once we teed off, I wouldn't have to see Zach again until the dinner.

"We're paired up with Zach and Brian," Dad announced gleefully, but I could easily read through his feigned surprise.

"Dad, it's supposed to be random, so we get to know a new business owner in the area. That's the whole point. They always pair the bigger resorts with smaller businesses."

"Well, I may have pulled a few strings." He winked at Zach, who grinned back, obviously in on this plot.

"That goes completely against the spirit of this event." I knew I sounded like a petulant child, but I had not expected to be spending the entire day with my ex.

"Oh, come on honey, it's just about raising money for charity. It doesn't really matter who we're paired up with. I just thought it would be nice to catch up with our old friends. Why don't you two share a cart, and I'll ride with Brian. We have a lot to talk about."

I may be blonde, but I knew a plot when I saw one. This entire charity event had turned into a setup that everyone was in on except for me. I hoped I wouldn't be fielding pressure from Zach about his merger idea all day.

As if on cue, Brian drove up in a golf cart sporting both his and Zach's clubs, in matching Snowshoe-branded bags, naturally. Brian was good-looking for an older man. Zach was practically a younger, carbon-copy of his father, down to the lean build and blue eyes.

"Ellie, so good to see you. It's been ages!" I

couldn't help the warm rush of feelings as I hugged Brian; he'd always treated me like family.

"Nice to see you too, Brian. I hope you old-timers are ready to get your butts handed to you."

"Pah, why are you trash-talking us? We're on the same team, Izzy." Dad greeted Brian, then set about swapping his clubs for Zach's.

"I'm not trash-talking, just trying to remind you of reality. Zach and I don't live on the fairway like you two."

"You may be surprised," Brian grinned. "Zach's been working on his game a lot this summer."

I turned to my ex, stunned. "Seriously? I thought you hated golf, like me."

He had the grace to look sheepish. "Well, what can I say? A lot of deals get made on the course. You have to go where the money goes, Ellie."

If I'd been surprised at his plans to absorb Aspen Ridge, I was now utterly shocked. "Who are you, and what have you done with Zach?"

The three men guffawed, and I stewed internally. They were all in on it, all three of them. Previously, it was Zach and me against the dads, but now I was alone, since Zach had obviously switched teams.

After grabbing both our bags, Zach scooped up the cart keys. "Come on, we're parked over here." We agreed to meet our fathers for tee off, and I followed him with my arms crossed to the cart parking.

Zach left me nothing to do but claim my seat, so I sat and waited in silence while he stowed our gear.

When we were driving slowly toward the first tee, he spoke.

"It really is nice to see you again, Ellie. You look good."

"Thanks," I replied stiffly. "It's been awhile."

"Yeah, it has. I miss you, you know. You don't call anymore."

"I told you I had nothing more to say after our last meeting."

"Ellie, it doesn't have to be like that."

"I don't know how you think it could be, Zach. We kind of have opposing goals. I want to run my family's historical business as the independent, billion-dollar, world class resort it is. You want to absorb it and turn it into a carbon copy of Colorado Disney world," I gestured around the extravagant golf course.

"It's not like that, Ellie. With our investors we could expand your growth by two-hundred percent, and no one wants to erase Aspen Ridge's charm. It makes more sense to ensure that each resort maintains its own unique feeling, so our portfolio offers something different at each location."

"Your *portfolio*," I spat. "We're an independent resort and I plan on keeping it that way."

"Okay, I hear you. We don't have to talk about this today, Ellie. Clearly it's not an idea you're interested in right now, so let's just table it, okay? Can we have a fun day for charity, like we used to?"

I eyed him dubiously. "I dunno, Zach, can we? This used to be a joke for us, the two worst players on the mountain. We whacked balls all over the place, had a few beers, celebrated our abysmal golf game. Apparently, you aren't in my league anymore."

We were approaching the first tee-off where our dads were waiting, and Zach slowed the cart to a crawl. When he met my gaze, his eyes were bright with mischief. "What if we could? How about I promise not to try too hard, and you... just do whatever you want. Let's just have fun."

"Are you sure your dad isn't counting on you to win? He seemed pretty proud of his baby boy back there."

"Whatever. I'll blame it on your bad influence." He nudged me with his shoulder. "What do you say: Allies?"

I thought for a moment, then grinned. "Alright, it's a deal. Let's see who can lose the most balls."

Zach tipped his head back and roared. "I did just get a fresh new case, Snowshoe-branded, of course. Dad will be pissed if I lose them. You're on!"

By the third hole, we were laughing maniacally, like rebellious teenagers. Brian had a few choice words for Zach about his abysmal score, but I didn't miss the pleased smile on my dad's face as he watched us.

And I had fun. It was nice having my friend back. We'd grown up under the same pressure, the same expectations. The average person off the street didn't understand what it was like, growing up the 'owner' of a billion-dollar resort. There was an expectation to not only take over but expand the business; to take care of the people who lived there and worked for you, who depended on your family for their livelihood.

Zach and I had a lot in common, and while I'd never consent to letting his company absorb Aspen Ridge, I definitely still wanted him in my life.

Jake sent me a few photos of his family at Oktoberfest, including a photo of with them all with Tessa, and Ethan with a pretzel as big as his head. The kid's entire face was lit up, his eyes as round as saucers. It cracked me up, and a twinge of remorse squeezed my chest. I really wished I had gone with them, experienced their excitement for the first time. I responded with a few photos of my own, including one of my dad and Brian poking through a swampy area, looking for the ball I lost. I told him how much I was looking forward to our ride tomorrow.

When the game was over, there were local media everywhere taking photos of the awards and the dinner after. Even though they were unhappy, our fathers accepted our 'biggest losers' award with grace, and Zach and I mugged for the cameras.

CHAPTER 13
JAKE

"I wish Ellie was here, Dad. You should send her a picture of that guy's hat."

Obligingly, I lifted my phone and snapped a photo, but I didn't send it. It'd been like this all day, the kids bringing Ellie up every other minute, demanding I send her pictures so she didn't miss out.

I knew Olivia was pushing for us to get together, but I'd assumed it was more horse-based than sincere affection.

Clearly, I'd missed something. It was actually Ethan, more than Olivia, who brought her up today, and his demands for the photos. He'd been pretty upset when I let them know Ellie wouldn't be meeting us, but the promised horseback ride smoothed things over immediately. Ethan declared his intent to 'help' Ellie again, and Olivia watched me with eyes that were far too knowing for a nine year-old.

Oktoberfest was fun with the kids, but I couldn't help sharing their sentiment that it would be more fun with Ellie. Something in her brought out a side of me I didn't know existed. Like the guy who dressed up in tiny shorts and a fake mustache for an eighties costume contest, just to make her laugh. I hadn't done something like that since my enlisted days, but when I looked at the bar's website, I assumed Ellie was dressing up, too. I didn't want her to keep seeing me as a 'stuffed shirt', so I went all in. It was fun, and later that night was even more fun. Even though Dad brought me back to earth with his little chat, and we were cautious at work, it felt like I'd been floating for the last week.

This minor disappointment brought my feet solidly back to the ground. Ellie had a lot of obligations with Aspen Ridge, and that sometimes included nights and weekends. I knew that. I also knew that there was plenty about Ellie's life before I arrived I *didn't* know.

After I got the kids home and in bed, exhausted from their day of festival excitement, I sat on my couch and ignored the tv. Surely, if there was a charity golf game going on, there'd be some news about it, right? Maybe I could just get a glimpse of what she was up to. There was no harm in it.

I pulled up a browser on my phone and searched 'Aspen Ridge golf' to discover the only golf course within two hours was at Snowshoe Ridge Resort. So I searched 'Snowshoe Ridge charity golf' and started scrolling through the results.

Sure enough, there were plenty of articles to choose from. Clicking on the first one, I found a cache of photos, along with a short write-up of the event. Ellie hadn't lied. It was a charity golf tournament played by local business owners to raise money for a housing subsidy program. I flipped through the photos until I found one that made my heart drop to my stomach.

In it Ellie and JJ stood on a stage with two men, obviously father and son. The two older men held up a small trophy with a gold-plated golf ball on top, and Ellie and the younger man leaned into each other, their bodies pressed close, smiling happily at the camera. I scrutinized the guy; he was tall, good-looking, and held Ellie possessively against his side. The caption read, *"Isabelle and James Tremont, Jr., owners of Aspen Ridge Resort, and Zachary and Brian Grafton, owners of Snowshoe Ridge Resort, celebrate their 'Biggest Loser' win at this year's Snowshoe Charity Golf Tournament. The prize is awarded to the team with the worst score of the game."*

These were clearly people Ellie and JJ knew very

well. Probably worked with on more than one occasion, given that they were in the same business. Their clear familiarity in the picture made it easy for my brain to jump to all sorts of conclusions. In fact, now that I thought about it, I'd heard JJ mention the Graftons once or twice. I was pretty sure he'd talked about golfing with Brian, mentioned his son. I just hadn't picked up on any sort of relationship between the son and Ellie. Was there something there?

I scrolled through the rest of the photos, but aside from one showing them all at the same hole together, there was nothing else of Ellie. I clicked through the rest of the articles, but found nothing from this year.

Heart pounding, I started digging through older articles. It looked like they both played at last year's tournament, but they hadn't been on the same team, so there were no photos of them together.

I knew what I was about to do would only hurt myself, but I had to know.

Tapping on the search bar, I entered 'Isabelle Tremont Zachary Grafton' and hit search.

A host of entries popped up, including some dating from Ellie's time in high school. A photo of a young Ellie in a puffy dress with a tiara on her head, her arm linked through the arm of a young Zach, who sported a tuxedo. *"Aspen Ridge's Prom Queen, Isabelle Trenton, with her date, Zachary Grafton."*

Clearly, small towns had nothing better to report

on than local high school news. There were tons of articles about Ellie like she was local royalty, and I finally landed on one that cleared up any doubts. It was a photo of Ellie in a cheerleading uniform, 'AR' on her chest and ribbons in her hair. She stood next to the tall, imposing figure of young Zach in a football uniform with the letters 'SR' on the front. *"Despite supporting the opposing team, Isabelle Tremont said she's rooting for boyfriend, quarterback Zachary Grafton, to lead his team, the Snowshoe Ridge Grizzlies, to victory."* Ellie stood tucked into Zach's side in nearly the same position as the photo from earlier today.

With a hint of worry swirling in my stomach, I closed the window and set my phone down. Surely she wouldn't be seeing me if there was something going on with that guy.

I needed to give Ellie the chance to tell me for herself before I jumped to conclusions. There could be a lot of reasons she hadn't told me yet.

WE ARRIVED at the stables with plenty of time before our ride was due to begin, and the kids were practically bouncing out of the windows with excitement. As soon as I parked, they flew out of their seats, not even closing the doors before they rushed up to Ellie, who stood outside, smiling.

"Oof, hey guys! I missed you too." She laughed, ruffling their hair affectionately. "Ethan, are you going to be my big helper again today?"

"Yup," he replied, puffing his chest. "I'll keep you safe, I promise."

"Well, that is a relief, thank you. Olivia, I have Rosy all saddled up for you. I bet she's excited to see you again."

Olivia stared at her dubiously. "Are you sure? Can horses really get excited?"

Ellie crouched down, so she was closer to their height. "Oh, you bet. Want to know a sure-fire way to make a horse excited to see you?"

"Yeah!" they said in unison.

Ellie pulled two small apples out of the bag at her feet. "Here, you each take one and give it to the horses. Hold it like this, on a flat hand," she demonstrated, "or they might accidentally mistake your fingers for food. Rachel is inside. She'll help you."

The kids took the apples and turned to me for permission with twin expressions of excitement. "Go on, but remember what she said about how to hold them!" I shouted as they ran off down the trail to the barn.

Ellie stood, dusting off her jeans. She wore a flannel shirt and had her hair in a braid today, looking every bit the low-key, casual woods woman. "Hey, I'm sorry about yesterday. I totally forgot I'd signed up for that tournament with my dad. I hope they still had fun."

"They did, but they missed you. We all did."

Ellie's gaze dropped, a sweet smile crossing her face. Instead of responding, she turned and started down the path. I matched pace at her side.

"How was the tournament? Did you win?"

She barked a laugh. "Me? No way. I'm the worst golfer, so bad even my team couldn't make up for me. I sent you those photos of them looking for my lost ball. That wasn't proof enough?"

"For all I know, you hit just that one off course for the photo op. Maybe you did it because you didn't want me to feel bad. I have no idea."

"Well, suffice it to say, I am *genuinely* that bad. Golf is not my sport at all."

"Who was on your team? Were they upset that you lost?"

"It was my dad and some family friends, the Graftons. They own Snowshoe Ridge, the resort one town over. We've been friends since I was a kid."

"Just friends?" Even though I kept my tone light, I knew Ellie could tell what I was up to.

She stopped walking and sighed, then turned to face me. "Zach and I used to date, but we're just friends now."

"Okay. I was just surprised to find out you were hanging out with your ex on my own instead of hearing it from you."

"I know, and I'm sorry, okay? I didn't want to have this conversation over text. Zach and I were highschool sweethearts, and throughout college. We broke up when I left to get my MBA and when I came back, we tried to rekindle it, but it just wasn't there. We don't want the same things. It... just ran its course, I guess. I haven't seen him as anything more than a friend in over a year."

I nodded, accepting her answer despite the sliver of worry that lived in my gut.

Even so, it still felt important to tell her how I felt. "Look, I know we're not anywhere close to something serious yet. But before we can get there, we have to be on the same page with what we want. And I still don't know enough to say that we are."

"You're right," she agreed. "This is all pretty new to me, too. I have a lot of balls up in the air, not the least of which is taking over Aspen Ridge. My dad would not be happy to find out there's something going on between us—he's got some pretty old-school ideas about getting involved with employees."

I couldn't help but bristle at the words. It wasn't fair; I knew that as the boss's daughter, she had every reason to see me as an employee... but I'd imagined us more like co-workers. On a similar foot-ing, at least. Calling me an employee was akin to saying we were nowhere near the same level.

"...But," she added, setting a small hand on my

bicep and drawing my gaze to her face, "I like you, Jake. I have since that first night. I know we had our disagreements at first, but I feel like we've just been growing closer together. I don't know for sure where it's going right now, but I know I want to keep going and see where we end up."

My heart thudded in my chest, pleasure curling through my body to hear her say it. "Me too," I admitted with a sigh. "I like you. Obviously, my kids love you. I've never seen them take to someone so fast. And I know it's complicated with JJ. I don't want to make things harder for you. I just... if we're going to do this, let's do it together. Okay?"

"Yessir, Captain Wright," she teased with a coy smile. "There's a lot I still don't know about you. Seems like we have some sharing to do soon."

My lips curled into a smile of their own volition. "Seems like we do. But we'd better catch up to those kids or they'll tear the barn down before we can stop them. Complete heathens, I'm warning you."

"Nah, I don't buy it." Ellie shook her head. "They're great kids, and even if they weren't, Rachel would put them in their place. She spends all day domesticating animals. She can definitely keep them from any major destruction."

We shared a laugh and finished our walk to the barn.

"How was your weekend, JJ?"

We were sitting in his office, going over the list of requirements. I'd boiled it down from his original, nebulous ideas of how Ellie needed to 'improve' in order to take over. Over all, he seemed rather pleased with her progress, and we'd moved on to other topics.

"Oh, it was fine. The usual. Izzy and I had that golf tournament, you know."

"Yeah, she mentioned it. She said she was the reason your team lost."

JJ chuckled. "That she was. My girl, hopeless at golf. Well, maybe Zach can teach her a thing or two before next year."

Even though I knew who he was referring to, I feigned ignorance. "Zach?"

"Zach Grafton, his father owns Snowshoe Ridge Resort. He and Ellie started dating in high school."

"Ah, I see. So they're still close?"

"Well, I haven't heard her mention him in a while, so I think they had a falling out. I pulled a few strings to get us on the same team for the tournament. Seemed to work out. They were thick as thieves by the time we were done." He leaned back in his seat with a satisfied air.

"That was generous of you," I commented carefully. "To take an interest in their falling out."

"Well, we always knew they would end up together. Even when Isabelle broke it off—she broke up with him before her MBA program, if you believe it—I knew they'd get back together. They always seem to find their way back to each other."

"I'm sure it helps that you're there to lend a hand," I hinted, as calmly as I was able.

"A father does what he can to ensure his baby girl's happiness," he winked smugly.

"And you think she's happy with him?"

"I mean, I know they've had their disagreements. But yeah, I think they make each other happy. They grew up in the same circumstance, children destined to inherit ski resorts from their parents. It has a lot of moving parts, this job. No one understands that better than Zach, and she needs someone who can be her partner. That's hard to find around here."

"A shared history definitely helps," I agreed. "But high school romances don't always work out. My ex wife was my high school sweetheart."

"Ah, well, I'm sorry to hear that. I met my Rebecca in college, and she had plans to go to New York or some fool thing. But instead she came here to help me run Aspen Ridge. Best decision she ever made, I'd say."

"Does Ellie look like her mom? Aside from the blue eyes, of course. She obviously got those from you."

JJ's expression dropped. "My Rebecca passed away a couple of years back."

"I'm sorry, I forgot. Ellie told me that."

"It's okay. But yes, Izzy is the spitting image of her mother at her age. She had blue eyes too, but they were more aquamarine. Bright, like the stones." His expression turned wistful and his voice softened. "She's definitely where Izzy gets her heart from. Sweetest woman I ever met. Always wanted to do more."

"That definitely sounds like Ellie," I agreed. "She really cares a lot about the employees. It's admirable that she's so invested in their happiness."

Abruptly, JJ's tone turned gruff. "Yes, well, there has to be a balance. The business has to run, has to make money, in order to provide for the employees. This whole place was basically a one-horse abandoned mining town when my father and Roger Blackwell founded Aspen Ridge Resort. The entire area built up around the resort, and they depend on the tourists the resort attracts for their livelihood. It's a heavy weight, you know. Ellie bears it well, but I know she feels it. We've never held back from impressing upon her how important this business is to the community."

"I'm sure she's well aware."

"But that's why I have to know she can handle it," he insisted. "I can't leave her with more responsibility than she can bear. She has to be up to the challenge before I drop the entire thing on her shoulders."

I paused for a moment, thinking. "Sir, permission to speak freely?"

JJ waved his hand at me dismissively. "Get out of here with that 'sir' business. Shoot."

"I know you feel you carry the weight of the entire town on your shoulders. But wouldn't you agree that when Ellie takes over as CEO, it's not exactly the same thing? She'll still have you on the board, helping her. She'll have James and your other co-owners to lean on. She may become the head of Lodging, but it seems to me the responsibility is distributed pretty well. She has a lot of support."

He thought it over for a moment. "Well, maybe you're right," he finally admitted.

I continued. "I know you've been seeing this transition as you effectively handing over the keys and walking out the door, but it doesn't seem to me it will really be like that. And I think Ellie is lucky that she'll be able to take over—perhaps make a few mistakes, as most people do—but still have the support you've built up around her. The question really comes down to when you're ready to hand over the reins and let her drive."

JJ was silent for a long moment, thinking. "You're not wrong, Jake. It's hard to let go and allow my daughter to steer the ship I've run for so long. It was hard enough when it was just a car, but now I'm looking at handing over this entire resort and leaving it in her hands. It's not that I don't think she's capable, of course she is. But this place has been like my third child, maybe even my second wife. Maybe more, since I grew up here, knowing I'd run it some day. I was a lot like Isabelle, you know. I had a mountain of ideas of how I wanted to change things, make it better, grow the business. Robert and I both did—we had so many plans, some of them great and some of them absolutely crazy. But at any rate, Aspen Ridge has been in my blood since I was born. I've done everything I can and now I'm faced with the reality that I have to let go. It's a lot to walk away from."

I didn't really know how to reply to JJ's story, so I decided to share my own. "JJ, did you know that in order to retire from the military, the requirement is twenty years?"

He nodded slowly. "Yeah, I knew it was something like that."

"Do you know how many years I had in?" When he shook his head, I continued. "Fifteen. I was five years away from earning a full retirement when I walked away."

JJ let out a low whistle. "Ouch. Why did you do it? They didn't kick you out, did they? Surely you could have held out five more years."

I shrugged. "I probably could have. I could make anything work, if it was only me in the equation. But this decision wasn't about me; it was about my kids. If I stayed in the Air Force five more years, Olivia would be fourteen by the time I got out, and Ethan twelve. They would have gone through their childhood without their mom and barely having their dad. My obligation to the military would have eaten up their childhood, and by the time I got out, it would have been too late to fix it. So I gave up what I had planned for my life and went in search of something better for all of us. That landed me here, in Aspen Ridge. And now my life is very different—it's not what I thought I wanted—but it's so much better. My kids are happier. I finally get to be home with them every night, and I know I made the right move for them. So even though it wasn't what I thought I wanted, I know it was the right choice."

JJ's blue eyes were trained on my face, and they narrowed slightly toward the end of my speech. "I see what you're doing, Jake. I'm not senile yet. You think I am hesitant to let Izzy take over because I'm more concerned about what I want than what's right for her or Aspen Ridge."

"I think you sometimes have a rigid way of thinking, and *Ellie* thinks differently than you do. I agreed with you that some of her choices weren't in the best interest of the company, and we've been working on those. But I also agree with her that the way things have always been done doesn't need to be the way going forward. I think you should give her the chance to show you she can lead in her own way, and be just as successful as you have been."

JJ thought over my words for a long minute. "You've given me a lot to think about, Jake. You're a real straight shooter. I've always liked that about you. A man doesn't like to be told how to manage his own kids—I'm sure you understand that—but I appreciate your perspective. I'll think about it some more."

CHAPTER 14
ELLIE

I was just packing up, planning to head to Peak 7 to visit the housekeepers, when Jake's phone number popped up on the caller ID. He'd left early for some family thing.

"Hey, what's up stranger?" It wasn't like most guys to call. There was something old school about it that made me smile.

"Hi Ellie," a small, feminine voice replied.

Surprise rippled through me. "Oh, er, is this Olivia?"

"Yes."

"Hi Olivia. Why are you calling me? Is your daddy there?"

"Yeah, he's here."

"Is he okay?"

"He's fine."

"Okay... so why are you calling?"

"I asked my dad if I could call you. He said yes."

"Okay, what can I do for you?"

"Will you come to my choir concert?"

That was a surprise. "I'd love to! Thank you for inviting me. When is it?"

"It's tonight. We're going to get pizza first. Do you want to come?"

"Oh, um, sure. Can I talk to your daddy real quick, Olivia?"

"Okay."

There was a muffled noise as the phone swapped hands, then Jake's voice. "Hey, sorry about the ambush. She just brought it up now, and honestly, I was so thrilled that she wanted to ask you. I didn't know how to say no." He chuckled. "So, there you have it. If you can't make it, we understand, it was a last-minute invite." His voice took on a clear, almost-commanding tone, and I could picture him looking down at Olivia's hopeful little face, trying to convey his message.

"Well, I don't have any plans, so I can come. If you really want me to," I added, not sure whether or not to be flattered.

"Of course we do. Like she said, we're going to Tony's for pizza first, then heading to the school from there. If you'd like to join us? We're meeting my folks too," he added as an afterthought, like it might be a deterrent.

"Okay, yeah, I'm in the office. What time are we meeting at Tony's?"

"Five, we don't do late dinners when bedtime is eight."

"I got it. I'll meet you there. I'm still in my work clothes. Hope that's okay."

"Whatever you have on is fine," he replied, then added in a whisper, "thanks for doing this. I think she's nervous about singing in front of people, and suddenly it was very important to ask you to come."

"Well, tell Olivia I feel very special that she invited me. I'll see you soon!"

"Okay, see you."

My heart was pounding, although I wasn't sure why. Olivia's sweet invite to her choir concert was definitely unexpected, and I was flattered that she wanted me to go.

Of course, then I realized what made me nervous. I was about to meet Jake's parents for the first time. I hadn't met a guy's parents since Zach and I started dating in high school. I dated a bit while getting my MBA, but nothing serious enough to necessitate meeting each other's parents. This all came on rather suddenly.

I drew in a deep breath to slow my racing heart. I just had to remember it was just Olivia being Olivia. She probably didn't have anyone else to invite, and knowing all the other kid's moms would be there, she probably wanted to have a stand-in of sorts.

Woah, did I just consider myself a stand-in for Olivia's mom? Where the hell did that come from?

Before I could let my nerves get to me, I shoved those thoughts aside. A little girl was counting on me, and there was nowhere I'd rather be.

I did a quick check in at Peak 7, then made my way into town with plenty of time to find parking and meet up at Tony's. It did not surprise me to see Jake, with Ethan and Olivia, already waiting outside.

"Ellie!" The kids cheered as soon as they spotted me and fenced me in with hugs.

"Hey guys, it's good to see you too. I dunno about you, but I'm *starving*. Are you ready for some pizza?"

"Yeah!" they replied in unison.

"Good, Tony's is my favorite. What kind of pizza do you like?"

"Pepperoni," Ethan answered first.

"Sausage and peppers," Olivia replied.

"And what about you, Jake?" I glanced up to meet his gaze, which watched us with obvious affection. "What do you take on your pizza pie?"

"I like Hawaiian, but I usually end up eating whatever is left of theirs," he confessed, grinning.

"Well, we can fix that. I think between the two of us we can put away a whole Hawaiian pizza, don't you?"

"I'm up for the challenge, if you are."

"You're on."

"Hey kids!" A shout from behind Jake drew their attention away, and in an instant they were both tearing down the sidewalk toward an older couple. Obviously Jake's parents.

My fingers shook with nerves, but Jake wrapped his hand around mine and tugged me forward. "Mom, Dad, this is-"

"Ellie!" Ethan shouted excitedly. "Ellie's here!"

"Yes, I see that," the older gentleman said with a laugh, then turned his gaze to me. "Ellie, lovely to meet you. I'm Malcom, and this is my wife, Violet." He stepped forward to shake my hand, and his wife did the same.

"It's very nice to meet you both." Somehow I kept my voice steady, despite my nerves.

"Come on Grandpa, Ellie is *starving*. We have to go inside. Let's go!" Ethan grabbed his hand and tugged him toward the door.

Laughing, he held the door open for the little boy, and the rest of us followed inside. Once we had a table and placed our order, the kids ran off to play video games with the pile of quarters Malcom provided.

"So, you're Isabelle Tremont, of Aspen Ridge, right?" he asked conversationally.

"Yeah, but I prefer Ellie. Isabelle always felt way too fancy to me."

The older man chuckled. "Pretty much since he could speak, Jake refused to answer to Jacob. He said it wasn't his 'real name' at some point. Despite what it said on his birth certificate. But what can you do? Kids have minds of their own." His gaze traveled affectionately to Jake.

"That I understand, although I wish my dad was as understanding as you are. He's called me Izzy since I was a little girl, despite my refusing to answer to it since I was eleven."

"That's a long time to hold on to a nickname you don't like."

"Tell me about it. He says he's an old dog who can't learn new tricks. I tell him he's just stubborn. Either way, I don't think he's gonna change soon."

"Well, it's always good to acknowledge the situation as it is," he agreed. "So, how is Jake working out for you?"

Jake, who'd been taking a sip of his iced tea, choked, spewing the drink back in his cup. "What?"

Malcom continued earnestly. "It's always good to get a feel for how you're doing at a new job, son. If you don't ask, you miss an opportunity to get an answer and improve."

Oh, the job, right. "Nothing to worry about, Mr. Wright. Jake is doing a great job. He fits right in."

"Malcom, please. I'm glad to hear that. I knew it would be a difficult transition for him out of the military, but we're so grateful to have the chance to see him more." His voice cracked with emotion, and Violet took her husband's hand where it sat on the table. He smiled at her in appreciation, then his gaze strayed to his son. "We've barely seen him a half dozen times since he joined the Air Force. So despite everything that's happened, this is quite the blessing to us."

"I can imagine it's nice to have time with your grandkids, too."

Violet answered. "Absolutely. These past few weeks have been the best we've had in a dozen years. We feel very fortunate to know we're looking at lots of time with them going forward."

Just then, the pizzas arrived, and the kids materialized out of nowhere to claim their share.

We ate in silence interspersed with happy family banter, and I soaked it up with a smile. I hadn't had a meal like this since James and I were still in school. I had occasional meals with him and his kids now, but it was usually on more formal occasions. It was fun, sitting around a casual meal and just enjoying the noisy company of a family.

By the time we made it to the school, Ethan was yawning and Olivia was a bundle of nerves. As soon as I joined them in the parking lot, she slipped her little hand into mine and clung to it as we approached the doors.

"Are you nervous?" I asked her gently.

She nodded, as if afraid to use her voice to speak.

"What scares you the most?"

"Being in front of all those people, singing bad, and then everyone makes fun of me." She answered immediately, as if this scenario was already clear as day in her mind.

"Okay, then let me give you a bit of advice." I crouched down so I could look her straight in the eye. "If you're nervous at first, just move your mouth to the words, but don't make any noise. That way, it *looks* like you're singing, but no one will know you're not *actually* singing. Then, when you feel a little more confident, you can sing in a tiny baby voice, and as you get more confident, you can sing as loud as you're supposed to. Does that sound like a plan?"

She nodded again with wide eyes, then threw her little arms around my neck. "I'm glad you're here."

"There's nowhere I'd rather be. I'm so happy you invited me," I answered. "If you're really nervous, you can look at me, okay?"

"Okay."

I stood, and she clasped my hand again, not releasing it until we made it into the school auditorium. When her teacher came to collect her, I gave her one more swift hug. "You'll be great. It's okay to be nervous, Olivia. Just remember that everyone else is nervous too, and everyone in the audience watching is super proud of you."

"Are you proud of me?"

"You know I am. Go on, you'll do great!"

She flashed me a wide smile, then trotted off in the direction her teacher pointed.

We sat through the whole concert, and I held my gaze on Olivia the entire concert. She smiled and gave me the 'thumb's up' when she took the stage. I couldn't tell if she actually sang or not, but I saw her eyes rarely strayed from mine, and she smiled the entire time.

AT ETHAN and Olivia's insistence, I returned to their home for hot cocoa after the concert. Jake's parents excused themselves pretty quickly, and then before I could leave, the kids insisted I help tuck them in to bed.

My heart swelled—I adored kids, but I had never experienced this before. It felt warm and sweet, to read them a story, pull the covers up to their little chins, and kiss their foreheads goodnight. We left their rooms lit with spinning stars from clever little lamps, and the sounds of ocean waves.

"It helps them fall asleep anywhere," Jake explained. "You can't always guarantee silence, but if they're trained to a certain sound, you can practically put them to bed in a war zone."

And he was right; when we checked on them a few minutes later, they were both out cold.

Jake eased their doors closed, and we returned to the living room and our cocoa.

He turned off the overhead lights, leaving just a floor lamp to complement the fire. His fireplace was gas, too, and it put off a warm glow that settled over me like a blanket.

"I love your house," I complimented him, leaning back on the couch. "It's very cozy."

Jake, seated so close our thighs were touching, laughed. "Isn't that rich people speak for 'small?'"

I swatted his arm. "No, I'm not being condescending. I mean it. It feels... comfortable here. Sometimes I feel like my place is kind of cold. The tall ceilings are pretty during the day, but at night it feels like an endless cave. And my house looks like a showroom, with next to no evidence that I live there outside of my bedroom."

"It is a little devoid of your sunny personality," he agreed. "Why is that?"

I shrugged, taking another sip of my cocoa. "Honestly? I rarely hang out there. Usually I'm out doing something at the resort, or in town, or if I'm just hanging out, it's at Tessa's house. She's got this whole modern, cozy cabin thing down pat. I guess I never bothered because I'm never there."

"I suppose," Jake started slowly, "if I were alone, and I didn't have a family, my place might look a lot like yours. Nice, neat, every surface clean. I imagine it's hard to make someplace feel like home when it's just you. Since I have Ethan and Olivia, it's super important to me for them to feel like they have a home."

"And you've done a great job," I insisted. "This place is very inviting."

"You know what else is inviting?" He asked in a low voice that made my breath hitch. "Your mouth." He took my mug gently and set it down on the coffee table, then leaned in closer, his eyes glossy in the semi-darkness.

My heart rate rose and my tongue ran across my lower lip, anticipating.

This time, when he kissed me, it was gentle, delicate. Every move was slow and deliberate, from the feather-soft stroke of his fingers over my cheek to the way his tongue parted my lips with the lightest pressure.

I drew in a shuddering breath and melted beneath him as he pressed me into the pillows. I felt light-headed, the way it feels when you take too many deep breaths too rapidly, like I had pulled in slightly too much oxygen. His fingers continued to trace light patterns across my cheek, over my hair, across my ear, always delicate. Like I was something precious. It sent shivers down my spine, an aching desire for more clenching my belly.

His lips slid away, and he pressed his cheek to mine, his breath warm on my ear. "Come," he said simply, then stood, gripping my hands and pulling me upright.

My pulse absolutely raced as we walked slowly down the hallway, past the kid's rooms, to the master at the very back of the house. I trailed behind him, one hand hooked gently in his warm fingers. When we reached his room, his bedside lamps were already on, set low enough to maintain the mood.

We passed through the doorway and he closed the door behind us, quietly turning the lock on the doorknob with a low click that made my heart pump even faster. He hadn't gotten out of the kitchen in my place, and now we were in the bedroom. This felt different.

Jake crossed to the low dresser and flicked the switch on a butane lighter, touching it to the wicks of a few jarred candles before setting it back down again. He carried one to each of the nightstands, leaving the others on the dresser, before returning to where I stood, waiting.

I was still in my work clothes, a demure, high-necked dress with a blazer. I'd left my boots by the door, so my bare feet sunk into the plush carpet. Jake had on a fitted sweater and jeans, and I'd worked all night to avoid ogling him openly in front of his kids and parents.

But now I was free to enjoy the view, although some instinct told me to follow his lead instead of taking charge. He had the sleeves pushed up to his elbows, his muscular forearms accentuated by the play of light against the deep shadows.

He stood before me for a moment, drinking me in, then he reached out and hooked a finger into the front of my blazer, popping the button out of its hole. A sigh escaped my lips, and with impressively gentle hands, he pushed the garment off my shoulders, allowing it to fall freely to the floor.

Now he moved in, running the backs of his fingers up my arms, his body close enough that I could feel the heat of him. His breath stirred the hairs on my forehead, and I continued listening to that strange inner voice telling me not to make a move yet. My limbs practically shook with anticipation. The last time we'd been tearing each other's clothes off, but he stopped me because he wanted our first time to be more romantic. He had the candles, but I wasn't really sure what all encompassed his ideas about romance.

I certainly didn't want to scare him off again.

His hands reached my shoulders, trailing up my neck before they cupped my face and pulled me in for a kiss. A slow, languid kiss where his mouth was patient and soft on mine.

When my hands rose and settled on his waist, he pulled back and spun me around gently so my back was to him. I realized the sound of ocean waves I was hearing wasn't coming from either of the kids' rooms, but from a sound machine resting on his dresser.

"You're so beautiful, Ellie," he whispered with reverence. Gently, Jake gathered my hair and pushed it over my shoulder, then tugged the zipper on the back of my dress down until it reached the bottom of my hips. Cool air washed over my back, causing a ripple of goosebumps to rise on my skin. His warm hands soon followed, spreading across my shoulders and pressing the dress forward, so it too fell to my feet.

Every simple, deliberate touch heightened my awareness, elevating each tiny sensation that zinged across my body. His warm breath on my skin became an inferno. The gentle stroke of his fingertips left a trail of goosebumps in their wake, my body shivering at the intimacy of the touch.

Jake's hot lips pressed kisses to the back of my neck, traveling down my shoulder as his hands gripped my waist, fingers splayed across my stomach. My breath came in rapid little pants, and I wasn't sure what to do with my hands. He was behind me. There was nothing easy for me to touch.

When his fingers rose to stroke my breasts delicately over my bra, I celebrated the small win that I'd actually worn something sexy today. The matched set of dark blue lace was a little on the risque side for my normal everyday wear, but it always made me feel sexy.

"Your skin is like silk, Ellie. I love touching you."

Of course, the feeling was now heightened by ten, with Jake kissing at my neck and pinching my peaked nipples through the thin fabric. One hand trailed down my quivering belly, lightly tracing over the lace band and stroking at the damp spot between my thighs. My belly clenched, and another sigh escaped my lips. The tension in my body was like a taut wire, and I didn't know how much of this slow, deliberate teasing I could bear.

Without waiting for further guidance, I turned in the circle of his arms and dragged his head down to meet my desperate lips. He responded better to my eager kisses, and his hands slid down my back, landing on the curve of my ass and giving it a firm squeeze.

A groan rumbled in his throat. Clearly, his patience was wearing thin as well. I tugged at the sweater, then finding his shirt tucked into his jeans, I tugged that out until my fingers found bare, silky flesh over rock hard muscle. His stomach flexed, and my hands searched further until I found his nipples and returned the favor he'd given me a moment ago. His breath hissed as it passed his lips.

Then I decided this barrier needed to be gone, and I tugged until he took the hint and removed it completely.

Now when I pressed against him, there was nothing but a scrap of fabric between our feverish skin. I could feel the rapid beat of his heart, the sweet, woodsy scent of his cologne filling my senses, the sounds of the ocean our background music.

With a swift move, he bent down and swept my legs out from underneath me. He carried me to the bed and deposited me gently on the dark comforter like I weighed nothing at all.

My heart rate picked up, and I started squirming in anticipation, trying to pull him down on top of me.

Jake wasn't having it. With one hand, he reached behind me, unhooking my bra and pulling it lightly down my arms. His dark eyes drank me in, resting on my taut nipples with his lower lip pulled between his teeth. Finally, he leaned down to kiss me, then immediately began working his way down my chest. With his eyes firmly locked on mine, he pulled first one nipple, then the other, into his mouth. I gasped at the sensation, first the heat, then the wetness, then the gentle graze of his teeth.

"Jake," his name poured out of me like a plea, and my fingers threaded into his hair, gripping it desperately. I felt the gentle stroke of his fingers between my legs again, and I could scarcely keep myself from shoving his face down there in search of release.

But as it turned out, he didn't need my help.

Jake dragged his nose across the flesh of my belly, pressing my legs wide with his hands and planting a light kiss to the spot I wanted so desperately for him to touch. He inhaled deeply.

"You smell like heaven, Ellie," he purred, hooking his fingers into the lace band and pulling it down my legs until I was completely exposed. With gentle strokes, he worked his fingers up the soft flesh of my thighs, until I was shaking, positively quivering in desperation for release.

I gazed down at him as he settled between my legs. His eyes locked on mine while he wrapped his arms around my hips. When the heat of his mouth finally met my aching flesh, I released a low moan and my hips rose of their own volition, searching for more pressure.

Jake groaned, the reverberation sending electric tingles through my body, and tightened his grip on my hips more firmly, locking me in place.

His movements become more forceful, hungry, as he worked the spot guaranteed to make me see stars.

I wasn't sure if it was the slow, deliberate way he led me down this path tonight that wound me up so tightly, or the repeated encounters over the last several weeks that never reached a pinnacle. But it seemed he brought me to fireworks far faster than I would have thought. My body shuddered, a desperate plea of, "Oh, god, Jake!" pouring from my lips as I clenched his hair between my fingers and light burst behind my eyelids. The ocean waves faded from my ears; all I knew in that moment were the ripples of pleasure still coursing through my body, and the languid strokes of Jake's tongue as he slowly extracted every last drop of pleasure from me.

But instead of a sleepy, dreamy haze, my body felt as though it was immediately revving up for round two.

I tugged at his hair. "Jake." I curled forward to slip my hands under his arms, pulling with all my weight. He obliged, crawling up and pressing the length of his body against me. My lips found his again, and my fingers traveled down to his pants lightning fast, popping the button and tugging at the zipper. I slipped my hand inside, gripping him through his shorts, and he groaned.

"I want you, Jake," I whispered in his ear. "I want you," I repeated, peppering kisses along his jaw. That seemed to spur him to action, and he pulled back to tug his remaining clothing off and settle his body against me, completely free of barriers now.

Jake propped his head up on one hand, his eyes impossible to read, even now. "Are you sure you want this, Ellie? I'm happy to wait, there's no rush for me. This has already been far more than I would have asked for."

I reached a hand between us and slipped it around him, watching as his eyes fluttered closed in response. "I'm sure, Jake. I want you as close to me as two people can get."

"But you deserve-"

I cut him off with a finger to his lips. "You said I deserve candlelight. We have candles. You said I deserved romance. This has all been quite romantic, in my opinion. You said I deserved fireworks, and I just saw them. Now all that's left is for you to see them with me."

I spread my legs wider and pressed against him, then pressed more kisses to his cheek, his jaw, finally enticing him to drop his lips to mine. At first slow and sweet, Jake rapidly increased the pressure of his mouth, the motion of his tongue, and the grip of his hands on my body. I rolled my hips, and just as he pressed against me, he paused and pulled back.

"Condom?"

"It's fine. I'm on the pill."

"Are you *sure*?" Now I could tell he was toying with me, the smirk on his face a dead giveaway.

"Jake!" I slapped his shoulder. "I swear if you don't follow through this time, I'm going to consider you the biggest tease-"

I lost my words as he moved forward, the pressure both a release and the start of an even bigger crescendo all in one. Jake claimed my mouth, kissing me gently while he moved with slowly increasing speed. My legs wrapped around his hips, my body rising and falling, lifting to meet him.

"Ellie, I really care about you," he breathed, slowing to gaze at me with adoration.

"I know, Jake." I kissed the tip of his nose. "I care about you, too."

And as if we had some unspoken code, all pretense of 'romantic love-making' fled from the room. My nails dug into his back, and he pushed deeper, harder, faster. His hands wrapped around my shoulders and held me, his kisses deep and claiming. I tightened my legs around him, meeting him for every powerful stroke. We raced toward the end together, and when we found an even higher peak than I'd reached before, the starbursts of light were all the brighter, with our hearts pounding as one.

AFTER WE RESTED and shared warm, languid kisses, I got dressed and headed home, figuring it wasn't good for the kids to wake up and find me there. Jake walked me to my car in just his flannel pajama pants and bare feet, despite the cold. I clung to the heat of his bare chest while he kissed me goodbye, his hand once again tangled in my hair. I drove home in a moony haze, his scent on my body bringing back flashes of the night's pleasure.

But after I got home and showered, I discovered a kernel of anxiety in my chest that I couldn't quite shake. I felt it growing larger as I prepared for bed, and I ran over the possible causes in my mind.

There was no impending event this week that wasn't meticulously planned, and I actually felt pretty good about where I sat with my dad. Tracing back to when I last felt completely at ease, I realized the anxious feeling began with Olivia's phone call, inviting me to her concert.

Surely that wasn't the issue; I loved Olivia, and Ethan. They were great kids, and I was flattered she wanted me to come. The whole evening had been a delightful surprise, even meeting Jake's parents. They were a sweet couple, obviously fond of their son and grandkids, and loving toward each other. So what could be the source of my anxiety?

Then realization hit me like a hammer: it was them, all of them. The whole scenario, where I'd suddenly become a surrogate mom to kids I barely knew.

As much as I liked Jake and adored his kids, there was no way I was ready to take on an entire family. I still had a lot of things to check off my list! And I promised Mom I would never set aside my plans for a man... I practically swore it on her deathbed. You don't just ignore a promise like that.

I moved to the kitchen, fishing a bottle of rosé from the fridge and pouring myself a glass. Realizing what I was stressed about had the opposite effect from normal; now, instead of easing my anxiety, it was adding to it. Adrenaline surged through my body and I couldn't stand still, pacing back and forth in my gleaming modern kitchen. I tried to slow my heart down, deep breaths interspersed with shaky sips of wine. Sweat pooled under my arms,

It's fine. I'm stressing myself out over nothing. Jake can't possibly expect me to plop into his life and take over the role of mother. He knows how important running Aspen Ridge is to me, and we aren't even technically a thing yet. I'm psyching myself out.

I refilled my glass and returned to my seat on the sofa, heart gradually slowing.

Of course Jake wasn't expecting anything. He was very clear, even with Olivia, that he had no expectations. We could definitely take this slow. There was no need for rushing things. We weren't even dating, officially, for crying out loud. At the very least, we needed to keep it cool until he was moved over to Jame's supervision, and then we could see where things went. I had plenty of time before any sort of clock started ticking.

Besides, I still wasn't sure I even wanted kids of my own. I loved being an auntie to every child I met, but my first focus had always been Aspen Ridge... I always figured the rest would come later, or not. But the employees always needed me, and the town. That was more than enough for any one person to take care of. If I wasn't sure I wanted kids of my own, what did that mean for step kids?

Jake had to know how important it was to show Dad I was focused on the business. He already thought I was flaky and getting tangled up with a guy with two kids was especially messy. It wasn't as if I could run off for PTA meetings in the middle of the day, or choir practice.

Jesus, why was my brain traveling so far down this road?

We. Aren't. Even. Dating.

Perhaps the best plan was to cool things off with Jake, just a little, so I didn't feel so much pressure. Focus on the business, on meeting Dad's expectations, keep having fun with Jake, but keep it light. Surely Jake would understand.

Except I had no idea how to do that.

"Izzy, don't forget that you have the Rocky Mountain Boys and Girls' Club Gala tonight." Dad popped his head into my office. He was clearly on his way out the door, and from the looks of it, heading for the golf club.

"Wait, what do you mean 'I' have the gala? I thought we were going together?"

"Eh, something came up." I didn't miss the way his blue eyes shifted guiltily. "Besides, this is more of a young people thing, anyway. And you should get used to attending these things on your own. It's your opportunity to appear as the head of Aspen Ridge."

"I'm not, really, you know that. There're several 'heads', including James, Dad."

"Yes, well, Mountain Ops just doesn't present as well as Lodging, honey. Everyone knows where the money is made in this business, and it's on feeding and housing our guests."

"But the mountain is the reason we have guests in the first place," I argued back. "If anything, James should attend with me. And Robert. Is he going?"

"Robert and I have an important meeting with a member of the board. He's got a potential investor that he wants to bring in, so we're going to hear him out."

"You mean you're going golfing with your cronies."

"Don't act so offended, Izzy. You do things your way, I do them mine. It's worked for my entire career. I hardly see the point in changing now."

"Yeah, well, I don't recall you blowing off big, newsworthy events for the golf club a decade ago."

A huge grin spread across his face. "That, my darling, is the benefit of having such an able-bodied Assistant CEO. You go, have fun, enjoy the party in the gymnasium or whatever. Take a friend! I'll see you tomorrow. Let me know how the food is!" He tapped twice on my doorframe and departed, whistling on his way out.

Great. Not only an event I had to get dressed up

for, which I really didn't feel like after a long week of work, but now I had to attend alone.

For the drive home and the entire time I spent getting ready, I debated calling Jake. We'd paid for two plates, and I knew Jake had a suit or two at the ready. He could probably take Ethan and Olivia to Malcom and Violet's, and escort me to this party.

But even though it seemed like something a dating couple should do, I couldn't bring myself to make the call. For one, it would definitely bring our little tryst to light. I could probably explain it away to Dad, since he told me to take a friend, but how would it look to other people?

More importantly, how would it look to Jake? I knew without a doubt if I asked him, he would go as long as it was within his power. There was never a doubt in my mind about that. But would he enjoy it, or would he be uncomfortable the entire time?

The more I thought about it, the more my resolve hardened. I didn't need to bring him into this. It was too soon. He had so much going on in his life, and I didn't want to throw him to the wolves.

Especially considering that I knew who our tablemates would be.

I drove to the venue in my UGGs. Dad wasn't wrong. The event was in the community center, and while they usually decorated it beautifully, there was no need to be uncomfortable for the drive. I liked to dress up as much as the next girl, but there was a time-limit to how long one could wear elegant heels.

Almost as if he was watching for me, Zach materialized out of thin air when I slammed the door shut and headed for the entrance. "Hi, Ellie. You look gorgeous, as always."

A pleased flush spread across my cheeks, and I leaned into his hug. "You too, Zach. Nice tux."

"What, this old thing?" He joked, then offered me his arm. "May I escort you inside?"

I accepted, then glanced around curiously. "Where are your parents?"

He rolled his eyes. "Key West, if you believe it. They claimed they forgot about the gala and double-booked themselves. I think my dad just did it to get out of buying the crafts from the auction."

A tiny part of me wondered if this was a scheme between him and my father, but I kept that suspicion to myself. "That's right, didn't your mom buy like half of the kids' art last year? What did she do with all of it?"

"I have no idea, but I've never seen it around the house," he snorted. "It wouldn't surprise me if it went straight into the dumpster."

"You're kidding right? She wouldn't do that. Those kids were super proud of their artwork."

"Yeah, my mom wouldn't, but my dad sure would. And you know what she's like, out of sight, out of mind. Dad figures he did his part by making the donation. That doesn't mean he has to keep it. Once we own it, it's ours to do what we like."

"I suppose. I still feel bad for the kids, though."

He shrugged. "All that matters is that they raise money for the program. You don't really come here because you enjoy dressing up and having weak cocktails in an old gymnasium, do you?"

"True, but still. She could have let other people win the bid if she didn't actually want it."

"Ah, but you forget the most important part: my mom loves winning."

"Fair enough." We passed through the entrance, posing for a few photos on the short red carpet they'd rolled out in the hallway. It was a strange juxtaposition, how they had this incredibly glitzy event but hosted it in the aged community center. I'd attended a few of these. I knew the point was for those of us with the money to see how it helped the community. Every year they talked about the new improvements they made to the facility, and trooped in groups of kids for a talent show-style performance. A long table displayed artwork made by the kids, and a silent auction ran all night. They announced winners at the end. My dad typically picked one item to make a single generous bid on, then stuck the item on a shelf in his office until he replaced it with one from the following year.

Struck with inspiration, I dragged Zach to the

auction table. "Come on, let's find my dad's new art piece."

"Are you serious?"

"Yeah, it's for charity, and he always bids on something. Just because he bailed, that doesn't mean the kids shouldn't get the money. He usually throws ten grand down on some random thing, so let's pick one for him. His fault for not being here to pick it himself."

Zach chuckled, but he was game. We walked the length of the table and he wrote a few modest bids on behalf of his mom. Finally, I found the winner.

"This is the one," I announced, grinning maniacally at Zach.

He eyed the sculpture dubiously. "Are you sure? I mean, there are some really interesting works of art here."

"Oh, yes, most definitely. I think it's a great conversation starter, wouldn't you agree? Dad loves when people ask him about his pieces."

"I mean, it's interesting. I'll give you that. But I'm not sure what a blue, headless barbie on skis, holding a giant golf ball, really says in terms of an artistic commentary."

"Maybe she's a modern take on the headless horseman?" I shrugged, writing 'JJ Tremont - $10,000' on the first bid line. "Or perhaps she's some kind of yeti, protesting the development of golf courses in the mountains?"

"Maybe she's the ghost of the ski resort, coming in to usher a new age of winter golf?" Zach suggested.

We amused ourselves with increasingly weird suggestions as we made our way to our table. Naturally, since the other seats were reserved for the parents who had ditched us, that left only Zach and me to claim our seats.

The party got underway, and time never seemed to drag. Zach and I settled back into the same comfortable banter we always had: lighthearted jokes about the ski business and tourism, ripping on our parents and their old-fashioned mentality, comparing ideas for the future of snow tourism. It reminded me just how much history I had with Zach, and drew a stark comparison to Jake, who—try as I might—I just couldn't picture navigating the same scenario with similar ease. Sure, he'd look good in a tux, and I had no doubts he'd be a perfect gentleman, but would he really enjoy it? Would he feel out of his depths among the glitterati of the ski world?

My thoughts swept back to his reaction upon seeing photos of Zach and me at the golf tournament, and a nugget of guilt lodged in my stomach. I knew the answer to my own question. He definitely wouldn't be as comfortable here as Zach was. We'd grown up with these events, the expectation to show up, give to the community, represent our brands to remind people how much good we brought in with our businesses. This was normal for us, in a way it could never be normal for Jake.

Even so, some part of me knew I'd rather Jake was here with me than Zach. Zach was comfortable in this setting, but I hadn't forgotten his plan to wipe Aspen Ridge off the map and replace it with Snow-shoe 2.0.

So as familiar as this was, there was no mistaking my thoughts on it; whatever happened with Jake, Zach would never be the answer.

"Ellie is so pretty," Olivia commented with a dreamy sigh from the couch. The kids were playing on their tablets while I made our Saturday morning tradition: blueberry pancakes.

"Yes, she is," I agreed, half-listening. Ethan's pancakes had to be perfect circles with exactly 13 blueberries, or he wouldn't eat them. That kind of precision required concentration, and I was nothing if not thorough.

"Look, Dad. Doesn't she look pretty? Like a princess." Olivia had come into the kitchen when I wasn't paying attention, and when I turned, she thrust her tablet in my face.

The kids went to the Boys and Girl's Club after school, and Olivia liked to browse their calendar to see what next week's activities would be. She had a page open to the site, and a photo pulled up of Ellie, wearing a sparkling dress and an even brighter smile, clutching the arm of Zachary Grafton.

"Very pretty," I agreed, trying to ignore the sick feeling in my stomach. "What is that from?" It had to be an old photo she just happened across while being nosey on the site. I drew in deep breaths and tried to slow my racing heart. I still had no real claim on Ellie, and despite my feelings, we hadn't discussed exclusivity.

"It's from the fundraiser last night. 'Isabelle Tremont and long-time beeyoo Zachary Grafton attended the annual fundraiser gala, along with seventy-five other business owners in the area,'" Olivia recited, reading carefully. "Dad, what's a bee-yoo?"

"Spell it for me?" A sinking feeling told me I already knew what the word was, but I had to ask.

"B-E-A-U, beeyoo."

"It's beau, honey. It's pronounced beau, like b-o-w."

"That's dumb. It doesn't look like that at all."

"Well, that's the English language for you," I murmured, flipping the pancakes.

"So what's it mean?"

"What?"

"What does beau mean?"

"Um..." oh god, there was no good way to explain

this. "I'm not sure, honey. We'll have to look it up later." Feigning ignorance was the chicken's way out, but it worked.

"You don't know what it means?" Olivia's tone was incredulous, and I kept my back to her penetrating stare so as not to give myself away. "You knew how to pronounce it, so you have to know what it means."

"Well, I remember seeing the word before, but lots of words have different meanings, you know that." Desperately, I flipped the script. "What do you think it means?"

She was quiet for a minute, thinking. I slid the pancakes from the pan and poured another set.

"I think it means friend. They look like friends."

"I think that's a good guess, honey. Why don't you go tell your brother to go potty and wash his hands? You too, breakfast is almost ready."

"Okay Dad." She trounced into the living room, and I sighed in relief.

It was bad enough not really knowing where I stood with Ellie. But having my kids so invested was harder than I thought it'd be. And now this?

If we were being more open with each other, why didn't she tell me she was going out with Zach last night?

After breakfast, I let them have another half hour of tablet time while I researched the event. Down into the rabbit hole of online gossip I went, landing upon a gallery full of photos from the gala. Sure enough, every photo of Ellie included Zach, down to the table where they sat, close together, surrounded by empty chairs.

Then, because I needed to hurt my own feelings further, I started reading the comments.

"Such a handsome couple!"

"So happy for these two."

"Are they engaged yet? They've been together forever."

"Yeah, I want to know when we're going to see a ring!"

The comments section was full of admiring comments from well-meaning community members, all of them stumping this relationship that Ellie insisted she wasn't in. But if that was the case, why was she there alone with Zach? Clearly, there was no 'family event' excuse for this one.

My mind dredged up the question my heart didn't want to ask: why hadn't she asked me to go?

My gaze drifted to my children, both of them completely enthralled with whatever they were playing on their tablets, and a sharp pain squeezed my chest.

Zach was younger, wealthy, with none of the baggage that I carried around. He and Ellie were on the same playing field, had grown up in the same environment. I wouldn't know what to do at a fancy gala; not a civilian one, anyway. I probably would have shown up in my mess dress and embarrassed her. Ellie was smart—she probably realized that.

Maybe they'd had this planned for a long time, or maybe the golf game rekindled their affection for each other.

I tapped back to the photo Olivia showed me, of the two of them in front of a B&GC branded banner, and zoomed in. Ellie wore a gold sparkling dress, and she leaned into Zach, just a little, as if she were relying on him. Her smile was wide and genuine, her eyes bright. Zach looked like a model with a casual smile and an all-American charm, despite the tuxedo. Together, they really looked like a perfect, happy couple.

The sick feeling in my stomach grew. Maybe it was too soon for me to be dating; maybe I wasn't cut out for this. Ellie insisted she had no romantic interest in Zach, but this didn't really look like 'friends.' Random people online seemed to know all about their relationship and expected them to end up married with 2.5 kids. Even her own dad was openly trying to get them back together. Was Ellie just in some kind of denial about where she was headed?

Because even I knew there was no way I could compete with that guy. I had a small military pension, two young kids, and a whole lot of baggage. I had nothing to offer the heiress to a billion-dollar ski resort.

I'd been fooling myself that this would work. I knew that now.

I also knew what I needed to do.

I STEWED over it all day Saturday, and eventually bit the bullet, asking Ellie to meet me for coffee on Sunday. I suggested we meet at Bear Paw Brew; it was the only coffee shop I knew by name, thanks to the Fall Fest. She seemed happy enough to meet up, and the confusing mass of feeling swirled in my gut even as I waited for her outside.

My heart lurched when she walked around the corner; the temperature had cooled, and Ellie was radiant with jeans and a fitted leather jacket. She had a soft knit hat on top of her tousled blonde hair, with pink cheeks and shining eyes. As soon as she spotted me, she unleashed that irresistible smile, and my heart rate sped to double-time when she walked up and kissed me in greeting. Guilt bubbled in my stomach, seeing her so happy and knowing what I had in store.

"Hi Jake!"

"Hey, Ellie. Good morning," I opened the door and gestured her through.

"Good morning is right. I'm glad you suggested meeting up. It's gorgeous out today and I probably wouldn't have dragged my butt out of bed for hours if you hadn't. Are the kids here?"

"No, they're at their grandparents' this morning."

She led us to the counter, and we placed our orders. "Do you want to sit, or should we walk? I feel kind of restless, if you're up for walking. For some reason, fall always gets me excited. Something about the change in seasons, the excitement for the holiday, ski season; maybe it ties back to school, however twisted that is. I was always excited for back to school." She rambled on happily, an excited energy that I wished I could share.

"Sure, we can walk," I shrugged like it was no big deal, but I was secretly relieved. My nerves were running overtime, and I was restless, too. Just for a different reason.

Once we claimed our coffees—she got a pumpkin spice latte, which was just so *Ellie* I almost laughed— we stepped outside into the crisp fall day. I sipped my plain black coffee while she rattled on about her upcoming plans for employee events. We wandered down the small town main street, past shops decorated with orange and yellow leaf garlands and other fall motifs. There were a few people out, but the summer crowd had clearly departed. In the distance, the mountain peaks were white-capped, snow already working its way toward us for the winter season.

"Is there something on your mind?" Ellie asked after a few minutes of non-committal 'mms' and 'mm-hmms' on my part.

My heart throbbed again—this was it. I had to do it. "Yeah, I wanted to talk to you about something."

"Okay, shoot." She took a sip of her drink and smiled, glancing at a shop window.

"I... I don't know how to do this without sounding ridiculous, so I'm just going to jump in. Olivia was on the Girl's and Boy's Club website yesterday, and she showed me photos of you... with Zach. On Friday."

Ellie's smile dropped. "Oh, god, the gala. I'm sorry, I should have told you about that."

"I just... I mean, you say you're not seeing the guy, but then you're sneaking off to these events with him and not telling me about it."

"Hey, there was no sneaking," her tone was sharp. "I told you I have to attend a lot of these things. It's part of my job. And I didn't go with him, we were just there."

My voice grew sharper in response. "Well, that's not what it *looked* like. I mean, I feel like an idiot because I didn't know anything about it, and then these photos of the two of you pop up and everyone's commenting about how you're the perfect couple and speculating about when there's going to be an engagement announcement." My hand tighten on the paper cup and I focused on not squeezing it too hard, lest I crush it and end up with coffee all over myself. "I just—if it was so innocent, I don't understand why you hid it from me. As far as the whole town is concerned, you and this Zach guy are a couple, and it feels like I'm kind of just your secret."

Ellie released a long, pained sigh. "Jake, I'm really sorry. You're right. I should have told you about the gala. I had tickets with my dad, and he bailed on me last minute."

She stopped walking and turned to face me, her blue eyes bright and sincere.

"I didn't *go* with Zach, okay? He just was there, and his parents ditched him as well. It did kind of feel like a parental setup, if I'm honest. They still think we're going to eventually get back together, and I don't know how to convince them otherwise. Obviously, that is something I've got to put a stop to."

Ellie reached out and placed a hand on my shoulder. My need for reassurance warred with my upset about the situation. I wanted to accept her explanation, to let go of the anxiety in my stomach.

"I didn't ask you to go because it would have been last minute, and I know how precious your time with Ethan and Olivia is. I didn't want you to feel pressured to come up with something to wear and deal with all the drama. I didn't think it would be fair to you, so I just sucked it up and went on my own. I was not expecting things to end up how they did."

I nodded, drawing in a deep sigh. "Okay, that makes sense." The pressure in my chest eased.

However, Ellie wasn't done. Her entire demeanor shifted, her eyes flashing as she pulled her hand away and set it on her hip. "But to be honest, I think it's kind of unfair of you to get this bent out of shape about it. We're not really anything yet; you *knew* we had to take this slow, keep things under wraps until you move to mountain ops. We haven't even discussed exclusivity, so even if I *were* dating Zach—which, to be clear, I most certainly am not—it's not really any of your business."

My teeth clenched the second she pointed out we hadn't agreed to exclusivity, and my jaw continued to work through her statement. "I know, and I agree. I just thought-"

But Ellie wasn't interested in letting me interrupt. "*I* thought we were playing it cool for a variety of reasons, including Olivia and Ethan. But if you want this to turn into something, understanding goes both ways. I have to accept that you need to prioritize what's best for your family, and you need to understand that I have to prioritize what's best for the resort. At least for now, until I have everything firmly in hand. You need to accept that there are a lot of obligations that come with my position here. It's not just a nine-to-five, Jake. Yes, I have to go to these silly events, because the community expects me to be there. And like it or not, Zach is a part of the community, and he's going to be at a lot of these things. It doesn't mean anything, it's just the reality of the world I live in."

I felt my blood pulsing in my temple, and I fought to keep from spitting out an angry retort when I replied.

"You're right, we didn't specifically agree to be exclusive. Call me old-fashioned, I just assumed it was implied. I know you have obligations to Aspen Ridge, and I have obligations to my family. I own my part in how my last relationship fell apart. But it also felt like my ex was more concerned about getting what she wanted out of life than fulfilling the promises she made to me or our children. To *me*, family is more important than anything else. But maybe we don't agree on everything, after all." The derisive laugh escaped my lips.

Ellie's body went completely rigid, her blue eyes turned to chips of ice as she asked, "What do you mean 'we don't agree?'"

I squared my stance and gestured. "This, Ellie. You're smart and beautiful, but you obviously care more about your business than you ever will about me or my kids. I was so distracted about how you made me feel, how my kids reacted to you, I didn't think it all the way through. I don't blame you; you haven't done anything wrong. You've always been clear about your priorities, and I just fooled myself into thinking we might have a place near the top. But I don't think I can do this; I don't want my kids to get attached to a woman whose first priority is work. They've been through too much. *I've* been through too much, and I can't make the same mistake again."

"So, this is all a mistake to you?" Her face was still angry, but her voice broke, just a little, near the end. My heart lurched once more, but I held firm.

"You don't agree? We're already hiding it from your father, which doesn't make me feel great. I have to be honest. How long will it be before we can tell him? And my kids need stability, people they can count on in their lives right now. I can't even count on you to tell me what you're doing from night to night. You have your obligations, and I have mine. I think it's better we just let this whole mess go before it becomes a real disaster. Besides, as you pointed out, we're not really anything, anyway." The last sentence was bitter, revealing more of my hurt than I intended.

Ellie jutted her chin out, nodding slowly. "Well, if that's how you feel, I guess there's not a lot more to say."

"That's how I feel."

"Got it." She glanced into the window we'd stopped by. "You know, there's something in here I want to look at. No need to wait for me, you can go on. Unless you have something more to add?"

I swallowed. "I think I've said enough."

"Okay, well, I guess I'll see you tomorrow then. Bye, Jake." She turned and walked through the door without a glance back. My eyes followed her for a few moments as she browsed the racks, never once looking back up at me. Finally, I released a sigh and turned, walking back toward the coffee shop, alone.

CHAPTER 16
ELLIE

I spent a couple hours wandering in and out of shops on Main Street. But try as I might, I couldn't distract myself from the jagged wound in my heart.

I thought Jake understood me. I thought he truly saw me for who I was, understood what was important to me. He said he admired my passion for Aspen Ridge.

It may not have been L-word worthy, but I thought we were moving in that direction. When he proposed coffee today, it felt like everything was lining up. I imagined us wandering around town, browsing in shops, slipping between buildings to steal kisses without being seen.

How had the entire thing turned on its head so quickly?

When I'd been in and out of more stores than I remembered and my head still wasn't clear, I texted Tessa for an emergency summit.

> SOS Jake and I just broke up

Oh shit

come over I've got two bottles of rose in the fridge

And a fresh bottle of vodka if you need it

> Be there in 20

I left the shop, not remembering anything I'd seen inside, and it took me a minute to gather my bearings. Apparently, I'd meandered my way back toward my Jeep without even realizing it. I hopped in and cranked up the heat, my brain running through the entire conversation with Jake again. I wondered if there was something else I could have said to change the trajectory of that conversation. But there wasn't. I was honest. I told him how I felt.

And I guess he did, too.

Sighing, I put the Jeep in gear and started heading for Tessa's.

While I lived in one of the new condos on Peak 9, just outside of downtown and convenient for work or skiing, Tessa preferred to live away from town.

She had a duplex about ten minutes up the mountain on the opposite side from the ski hill, the other half of which she rented out to vacationers in the winter. I wouldn't call her style shabby chic so much as 'lived-in mountain'. Clean, comfortable, and worn in just the right way. Her place was my home away from home, and the parking space to the right of her truck practically had my name on it.

Before I'd even put the Jeep in park and turned the key, Tessa was already standing in the doorway with a bottle of wine in one hand and vodka in the other. She clearly hadn't done much today, since her long dark hair was wild and she was wearing plaid pajama bottoms with a long-sleeved top that said 'Go away, I'm hibernating' inside the silhouette of a bear. It coordinated nicely with her slippers that were topped with fluffy bear heads.

"Pick your poison, babe. I have everything we need for bloody marys, or if you want mimosas, I have some OJ."

"Sparkly stuff, straight up," I cracked a weak smile, and she wrapped both arms around my shoulders for a hug, the bottles clinking together.

"You got it, babe."

I followed Tessa into her house, immediately warmed by the golden wood paneling and crackling fire in the grate. My place had a gas fireplace, which was clean and convenient, but Tessa always insisted a 'real' fire needed actual wood. And to be fair, she used that fireplace a lot. She even split her own wood out back, providing it for the duplex renters as well.

Tessa and I were both modern mountain women, just cut from very different cloth. My place was cool and sleek with homey mountain touches, and Tessa's was like a modern, cozy log cabin. All the latest and best of everything, but that distinctive mountain charm that was so integral to Aspen Ridge. I really wasn't sure which I liked better.

By the time I'd slipped off my boots and settled into the worn leather couch by the fire, Tessa was already headed my way with two large stemmed glasses of bubbling wine.

I raised an eyebrow. "Excuse me, ma'am, but that is not a proper pour for sparkling wine," I teased as I accepted the glass, filled to the brim.

"Pah," Tessa snorted, settling into the seat next to me and pulling a thick, furry blanket over our legs. "I know this is not a five-ounce pour kind of story and I don't want to get up every five seconds. It's my day off. Sue me. Besides, there are no rules in my house, you know that." She took a long sip from her glass and smacked her lips. "Ah, so good. I got the entire bottle into these two glasses. Whoever decided that sparkling wine should be served in those tiny test tubes was not a bartender."

A half-hearted chuckled escaped my lips. "Funny, I thought it was more about how long it takes the bubbles to run out, or the wine to warm up."

"Well then, I guess you'd better drink up, babe, so it doesn't get warm." Tessa clinked her glass to mine and we both took a sip, then she looked at me expectantly. "Alright, hit me with it."

Sighing, I launched into the story. Starting with the gala, then Jake's text, and then our falling out this morning. Tessa listened intently with wide eyes, sipping her rosé and occasionally muttering in sympathy. By the time I was finished, our glasses were more than half empty, and I was feeling somewhat warm and definitely more relaxed.

"So... that's it?" She asked, her head tilted. "Like, you're just done?"

I shrugged. "I guess so. What am I supposed to do, Tessa? He can't expect me to drop all my responsibilities and become a stay at home mom. Aspen Ridge is my life—the people who work there, hell the entire town depends on me. I'm still stuck in this limbo, trying to prove to my dad that I'm ready to take over. I have obligations, and to be honest it's not fair for Jake to act like a jealous boyfriend just because some photos surface of Zach and me at an event. I attend a lot of events, and the same people go to all of them. Zach and I have history. I can't change that." I took another sip.

"I mean, I could be wrong, but it sounds to me

like he was more upset that he found out after the fact. Maybe he doesn't handle surprises well."

"That's not my fault," I sniffed, defensive. "My dad was supposed to go with me. I didn't find out until the last minute that he was bailing. You know how it is. I have to roll with the punches on this stuff. And it's not fair of him to expect me to run everything past him when we aren't even officially dating. Weren't, weren't officially dating," I amended. "I never had this issue with Zach—he didn't take anything personally. Everything with us just worked so easily." I sighed again. "I dunno. Maybe I just don't know how relationships are supposed to work. With Zach, there was never drama or hurt feelings. He always treated me well, always understood when something came up."

Tessa snorted. "I think you're looking on the past with rosé-colored glasses, babe."

"What? No, I'm not."

"You and Zach didn't fight much, but I wouldn't say there was no drama or hurt feelings."

I leveled a glare at my best friend. "And you know my relationship better than I do? Please, enlighten me."

"Well, first off, if you're going to make this comparison, you need to acknowledge that Zach never had to contend with the same situation Jake is. Meaning there was no ex showing up that you didn't tell him about. I'd imagine Zach might have gotten jealous, too. Plus, everyone in this town—including your dear old dad—loves Zach and ships you two like crazy. You're practically local royalty, as far as the town is concerned."

I had to give her that one. "Fair," I sniffed.

"Second, there were plenty of hurt feelings with Zach, just never his."

"What? I don't know what you're talking about."

"Sure you do. Zach blew you off plenty for things resort-related. You guys would have plans, and then he'd text you last minute and say something came up and you'd act like you were fine because it was work, but you weren't fine. You just sucked it up because he used the work excuse, but I don't remember you blowing him off nearly as much."

My first instinct was to argue back that she was wrong, but then the memories crept in. One time I'd planned a romantic picnic on the mountain; Zach was supposed to meet me so we could watch the sunset and I'd had it all set out with candles and the whole nine yards. He texted me when he was already twenty minutes late that he got caught up with the investors and he wouldn't make it. I'd called Tessa on the verge of tears and she came instead. More of those moments, both big and small, came back to me as I thought it over.

"You're right," I admitted finally. "But like you said, I always understood. Work has to come first, when all those people are depending on you. So I understand when Zach has to deal with things that come up, and at least he would understand that on my end, too."

"Is that really true, though? If you're going to run a business, be the boss, I think it's where you choose to prioritize. My mom runs the restaurant and my dad runs the brewery and distribution for ARB; they both have big jobs and a lot of obligations. But they never blow each other off for work. They make a point to plan and spend time together. That's their first priority."

"Your parents have it all figured out," I agreed.

"Yeah, I mean, it's kind of sickening when you really think about it." She grimaced. "I couldn't stand to be around them when I was in high school. But now I get that it's how they made it work. Their business, their jobs, are a priority. But their relationship is the *first* priority. They built the brewery together. If they didn't have each other, it would never have worked out. As sickeningly sweet as they can sometimes be, they've always kept each other grounded. It's partially why I've never gotten serious with anyone; until I find something that compares to what my parents have, I just can't see myself investing the time into it. So I can say from firsthand experience, a relationship can work with two busy people as long as they prioritize each other. The business doesn't have to take first place to be successful."

"Right, and I'm sure Zach and I could have made it work back then. I just didn't know how to ask for what I wanted."

"Yeah, and that's why you broke up with him after college. Because he kept treating you like an afterthought, and you were tired of it."

"Ouch, way harsh Tessa." I straightened up and leaned away from her.

"Hey, I'm your friend and it's my job to remind you when you forget shit like this. Zach is always nice, but he did some shit that really hurt your feelings. Intentional or not, how you felt was always second to what he thought was important. I don't really see that changing. Besides, you're kind of glossing over the most important thing, so I'll be a good bestie and remind you: Zach wants to absorb Aspen Ridge."

An uncomfortable feeling squirmed in my gut. "I know I was really mad at him for proposing it, but that's just how he is... he's always looking at the next peak over, trying to plan his next leap."

Tessa raised an eyebrow. "Ellie, you know I like Zach, but he has always had a one-track mind. He will just keep pressuring you until you give in and give him what he wants. He's been like that since high school. Hell, I wouldn't be surprised if he had this planned before you two were even dating."

A shocked laugh poured from my throat, and I nearly spilled the rest of my wine. I gulped it down quickly—we don't abuse alcohol around these parts —and as soon as I finished it, Tessa hopped out of her seat to fetch the second bottle.

"Think about it though," she said eagerly, her eyes bright. Tessa always loved a good conspiracy. "You guys went to different high schools. It's not like you were in the same classes or anything." She popped the cork and started pouring a little sloppily, the wine foaming dangerously closed to the rim.

"Tessa, we saw each other practically every weekend at all the community events our parents dragged us to. We were the only people our age there."

"Yeah," she agreed, filling her own glass. "And you guys were just friends for years. Then suddenly, out of nowhere, he asked you out. No lead up or anything. Don't you remember? You thought it was weird, even back then."

I took a long sip. "I mean, yeah, but we were in high school. Guys were awkward in high school, or did you forget? The first guy I dated asked me out by shouting down the hallway that I was hot. Zach was an absolute gentleman by comparison."

"Maybe, but I still think it's suspicious. No, hear me out!" She insisted when I started to interrupt. "Zach's dad had Snowshoe Ridge up and running, and now he's looking for opportunities to expand. Your dad obviously wouldn't go for it, and there you are, bored at these community meetings, being a dutiful daughter. Everyone already knew your dad was grooming you to take over. So he thinks 'huh, I can't get my fingers on Aspen Ridge now, but maybe if the kids get together, when JJ steps down, Zach could pull it off.'"

"Ridiculous," I scoffed. "Brian knows we have a board too, and the Blackwells own just as much as we do. They'd never agree to it."

"Maybe, maybe not. Maybe they figured if they got you on board, you'd advocate on their behalf. Maybe they looked at your cousin Blaise, and Robert's daughter, Stella, and thought they'd have a good chance at convincing them to go for it. That would just leave James and Reece as the potential holdouts, and while it might take some time, I bet they thought they could wear you all down. Surely your board would see the value in a proposal with the number of zeroes the Graftons would attach to it."

"I think you're digging way too deep on this one. Zach didn't bring up merging the resorts until last year. I don't buy that they've been planning it since high school."

"Hey, I only tell it like I see it." She shrugged, taking another sip. "I just know how those guys are, and I wouldn't put it past them."

"Yeah, I know what you mean." Now that she'd brought it up, my warm fuzzy feelings for Zach withered and died. Tessa was right. I was definitely looking back on our relationship with rose-tinted glasses, and just thinking about Zach wanting to add Aspen Ridge to his 'portfolio' was enough to put ice in my veins where he was concerned. Whatever had been between us, there was no getting past that. If he had understood me as well as I thought, he'd never have proposed it in the first place.

Unless she was right, and it was all part of a plan from the very beginning.

"Ugh, Tessa, I think I'm having a mid-life crisis. Did you just ruin my first love? I'm starting to doubt that you're actually my friend at all."

Tessa reached out an arm and pulled me into her body, allowing my head to rest on her shoulder. "No babe, I didn't. I'm your first love. And besides, you never loved Zach."

"What? Yes, I did." I tried to sit up, but she pressed her hand to my head and kept me in place.

"Well, maybe it was like puppy love. With you two, it was always a business transaction between friends. I know you cared about him, but from my perspective your feelings for the guy were luke-warm, at best. There was a rush of excitement at the beginning and then you both kind of settled into being a middle-aged couple with all your fancy resort obligations. Besides, he never loved you like I do." She patted my head sloppily, her dark hair spilling over my face as she rested her cheek on my head.

"I think I could have loved Jake," I admitted in a whisper, my voice catching in my throat.

"Yeah," she agreed. "I know you didn't see it, but you were different with him than you ever were with Zach."

"Different how?"

"You were more... *you* with Jake. Like you are with me. It's hard to explain, but around Zach it was like you were a different version of yourself. I really thought you were on to something with Jake."

"Me too," my eyes prickled with tears. "But if we can't meet on the same page now, it's never going to work out long term. I guess it's good to end it before it ever got serious."

"Are you trying to say you don't have serious feelings for him?"

"It was barely the beginning of something, Tessa. I mean, yes I felt something, but we didn't even have a chance to get it off the ground before he stomped it out and walked the other way."

"Well, I'm not walking away, babe. I'm always here for you."

"What would I do without you? Too bad we can't get married," I joked.

"I mean, technically we could, but I'm not interested, babe, no offense. I'm still holding out hope that a Finnish lumberjack will move in next door and sweep me off my feet. Speaking of," she sat up suddenly. "Let's see what the market is doing."

"Ugh, Tessa, no. *No* Tinder."

"Oh, come on, it's fun. It's not like we're going to actually meet any of them. I just like to see how many dirt bags are out here acting single, trying to score some vacation booty."

"I really don't know why you bother. They're all dirt bags, whether or not they have girlfriends at home. If they're on vacation, they're not looking for anything long term."

"That's why the service I provide is unique. I string them along and keep promising to meet up so they don't have time to hook-line-and-sinker a young, innocent girl that's not hip to the game."

"You're diabolical."

"It's too easy," she snorted. "Ooh, got a live one. Michael here is in town for one week only, and he's definitely cropped a girl out of this photo. You can see the blonde hair and an arm around his waist. I'm swiping."

"Tessa! What if that's like his sister or some-thing? Maybe he's just a genuinely nice guy looking for love." Alcohol always softened up my cynical side, but had the opposite effect on Tessa.

"Fuck no, he's not. He listed the dates he's in town and even mentioned which condos he's staying in, *specifically* the hot tub. He's a dirtbag, guaranteed."

"Fine, happy hunting." I leaned back in my seat and focused on the long-stemmed glass in my hand.

"Ooh, we matched. Yep, he's desperate! And he's here with a group of friends. Okay, you're involved now. I'm telling him about you."

"Tessa! Don't you dare."

"Oh hush, I'm calling you Jackie. Don't get your panties in a twist. He thinks my name is Savannah, anyway."

"Fine, just don't send him any pictures."

"Babe, my photos on Tinder aren't even me. I stole some random girl's photos years ago. She's got an entire crew of friends. You're the blonde."

"Isn't that illegal?"

"Meh, who cares? It's harmless fun."

"Not to the girl whose identity you stole."

"She was up here for a ski trip like ten years ago. She's probably in Ohio, married, with two kids by now. Besides, it's not like I stole her credit card numbers. I'm just using her photos to con dirt bags on Tinder. It's a public service. I'm sure she'd approve."

I didn't have the energy to dissuade Tessa on a mission, so I just took another sip and stared at the fire while she laid her trap for the unfortunate Michael.

CHAPTER 17
JAKE

I spent most of the day sulking around the house, knowing eventually I had to go to my parents for dinner and pick up Olivia and Ethan. The good thing about me being home, alone and upset, is that I couldn't sit still. I cleaned and organized the entire house before I left, which included ironing things that had no business being ironed.

I refused to examine how pathetic that was, and focused on how smart Ethan would look at school with all of his tiny t-shirts and jeans neatly pressed.

When I could put it off no longer, I made the short drive to my parents. As always, I was greeted with the homey smells of a meal cooking, and the joyful noise of my kids playing. It still amazed me how much this was a departure from a couple months ago—I hoped I'd never get used to it. Mom had them in the living room playing Jenga, and they taunted each other mercilessly.

Mom watched them with an affectionate gaze. "Your father is in the garage, Jake. He was working on that old bike out there. Maybe he could use a hand."

Taking the hint, I turned and passed through the kitchen for the garage. Dad was muttering to himself as I walked in; he had an old motorcycle that he hadn't driven since I was in school, and he was up to his elbows in grease. I figured the potential for mess, let alone unexpected expletives, was probably why Ethan was inside instead of out here helping. I cleared my throat loudly, so he'd know I was here.

Dad glanced up at me with a crinkly-eyed smile. "Jake, glad to see you. Hand me that wrench over there, would you?"

"Sure thing, Dad." I passed him the requested tool and crouched down beside him. He slid under the bike where it rested on wooden blocks. "How's it going?"

"Oh, about as well as you'd expect. I'll never get this fool thing to work. I should just take it to the dump."

"I've heard that before."

"I mean it this time. I think I'm through. I can't

figure out what's wrong with it. I swear I've tried everything."

"I have faith in you. You can do it."

"Hmph."

We stayed in a comfortable silence for a few minutes, my dad cranking at some bolt he couldn't get loose. I waited, but he didn't ask for my help, so I didn't offer it.

"The kids talked about Ellie a lot today," he commented eventually.

I stiffened automatically. "Yeah, Olivia saw some pictures of her yesterday from a gala on Friday."

"Oh yeah? Did you go?"

"No." My voice was surly, despite my best attempt at neutrality.

"Why not?"

"Because she didn't ask me, Dad."

"I see. Did she go with someone else?"

"Well, if she's to be believed, she went alone. But her ex just *happened* to be there."

"Ahhh. That explains it."

"Explains what?"

"Explains why you look like a kicked puppy right now." He peered up at me from beneath his bike. "You two okay?"

"Not exactly," I admitted. "We broke up. Well, sort of. I guess we weren't technically a thing yet, so I can't really say we broke up. But we're not seeing each other anymore."

"And that was her idea, I take it."

"No, it was mine."

"Because of this other guy?"

"Partially."

"But you said she didn't go to the gala with him. He was just there."

"Right."

"So, what are you upset about?"

I sighed. "Because Aspen Ridge is her priority, not me or the kids. And I don't want to have them get more attached to her, only for her to walk away when she decides it's too much commitment."

"Ah. So she said she didn't want a commitment, then."

"No, she didn't say that, exactly. She said that the resort was her priority and I should understand that. But she runs off and goes to these things and doesn't tell me. And then the next day I see photos of her at some event I didn't know about with her ex, and everyone is calling them a couple."

"So she hurt your feelings because she didn't tell you. That's understandable."

Irritation crackled along my jaw. "It's not that it hurt my feelings. That makes me sound like a little kid in the schoolyard, Dad. It's more complicated than that. But if her priority is always going to be the resort, that means the kids and I will always come second, and I want more for them."

"Is that what she said, that the resort would always come first?"

"No, but she said that's how it is now, and she hasn't said anything to make me assume that's going to change. When she takes over as CEO, her responsibilities will only grow. If she can't find time in her life for us now, that's not going to get better."

There was a long pause as he finally worked the bolt free, then he sat up, wiping his blackened fingers on a rag. Finally, he lifted his gaze to mine. "It's funny you say that, son. I seem to remember that girl dropping everything and running to meet us for dinner and Olivia's choir concert. With no forewarning, just on a whim and a phone call."

Discomfort squirmed in my belly. "Well, yeah, she did. But that was once, and this was the second time she had some event that she went to, where her dad was trying to set her back up with her ex. You even told me that JJ has opinions about who his daughter dates. Clearly, he wants her to be with this Zach guy. And since when are you on her side?"

"Of course I'm on your side, Jake. I want you to be happy. And maybe JJ just thinks Zach makes her happy. But the real question is, does Ellie want to be with Zach?"

"She said she didn't, but she sure looked happy with him in those photos from Friday."

My dad sighed heavily. "Son, the first thing I learned from your mother was to listen to what she *said*, not make my own conclusions from what I saw. If Ellie said she didn't want to date Zach, why aren't you listening to her?"

That took me aback. "Well, she also said she has to prioritize Aspen Ridge. So where does that leave us?"

"Call me crazy, but did you ever consider that you could prioritize her for a while? Instead of the other way around?"

The shock waves kept on coming. "What do you mean?"

"Son, you grew up in a military family. When you had your own family, you had the same expectations: you wanted a wife who was at home, taking care of the kids, while you served your country. There's nothing wrong with that, except that you chose a woman who wanted more. I wish Cheryl the best, but I know you didn't hear her when she said she was unhappy. You just assumed she'd get over it. You gave her no choice but to leave."

Guilt swam in my chest. "I know. I've thought about that a lot. I'm just as responsible for our marriage ending as she is. I understand that."

"So, you should understand not to make the same mistake twice."

"I am! I cut it off with Ellie because I don't think she wants that role, either. What else am I supposed to do?"

Dad shook his head and chuckled. "How can you

get all the math right and still end up with the wrong answer?"

"You lost me."

"What if the solution isn't that Ellie is wrong for you? What if the solution is that you're the one who needs to change, not her?"

A snort pushed its way out of my nose. "I can't exactly get rid of my kids to make her life easier, Dad."

"I'm not talking about Ethan and Olivia, Jake. I'm talking about you."

"So what exactly do I need to change, in your opinion?" I tried to keep the sarcasm out of my tone, out of respect for my dad.

"You're not in the military anymore, son. You're not beholden to Uncle Sam for how you spend your days. Did you ever consider offering to be the support that Ellie needs as she takes over her family business? You work a nine-to-five now, a cushy job with benefits, weekends off, holidays, and time for your kids. What if you stopped expecting Ellie to fit herself into *your* life and tried to make your life fit hers better?"

"I want to support her, Dad, but I also have responsibilities to my kids. I will not put them last. Besides, she didn't invite me to attend those things. She said her dad canceled on her last minute and she didn't want to ask me because of Ethan and Olivia."

"Well then, it sounds like you need to let her

know that you're willing to step in when she needs you. If she's afraid to disrupt your schedule, it means she doesn't feel comfortable asking. So you should offer. Your mother and I are always here to help if something comes up." I deeply resented how reasonable he made all of this sound.

"I know that, I just..." I threw my hands up, unsure of how to voice what I was feeling.

"It's scary, son, I get it. Listen, when I retired, you'd better believe that your mother and I had several pleasant talks. She let me know in no uncertain terms that she'd lived by the expectations of my career, and now that it was ending, she expected things to change. She wanted me to take on more of the household duties, free her up to enjoy more of her retirement, too. I admit, I always imagined her life was so easy, hanging around at home, throwing in an occasional load of laundry and gossiping with her friends at the commissary. I didn't realize that she had served just as hard, and as long, as I had. She kept everything running at the house and I always came home to a hot meal. Retirement was for us both, not just me. I had to switch my mentality, and we had to find a new rhythm that suited both of us.

"I'm sorry Cheryl wasn't able to manage that change with you. I know how she walked away is why you're scared to give Ellie a chance, and I know I've commented about them being similar.

"But them being similar isn't the problem. The

problem is you having the same expectations in a wildly different scenario. If you don't care that much about Ellie, if letting her go is no skin off your back, then maybe it's for the best. But if it's gutting you, eating at you from the inside out, then perhaps it's time to figure out what you can do, on your end, to make it work for her."

My mom's voice calling from the kitchen interrupted us. "Dinner's ready!"

"I'd better get in and see if your mother needs any help." He winked, then reached a hand out. I stood and pulled him to his feet. But before we left the garage, he regarded me seriously. "It's all about balance, son. There is no right way to have a relationship, every one is different. And not everything has to be done the same way we did it in the past. Perhaps that is the real lesson you need to learn here."

Long after I was home, and the kids were in bed, my mind continued churning over my dad's words. It was hard not to see the similarities in Ellie's position with her father and the business, and her position with me.

Both of us were trying to tell her things had to be done in the way *we* wanted, and she was pushing back against us both, wanting to do it her own way.

Of course, my dad was right. Why would I pick a woman like Ellie, admire her for all her strength and courage, her ideas and motivation, and then tell her she wasn't good enough because she wouldn't give that all up for me?

Ellie hadn't asked me to give anything up, she'd just asked me to be patient and work through the problems we'd face together. She asked me to understand when things came up, to trust what she said.

And I'd told her to hit the road.

The more I thought about it, the sicker I felt. My dad was a hundred percent right: I was taking a perfectly wonderful opportunity to start over with a whole new life, a brand new outlook, a new trajectory, and I was still stuck in my rigid set of expectations. Everything had changed, except for me.

I was the problem, not Ellie.

It took far less time to come up with a plan than it had for me to understand the problem.

My decision made, I laid down and focused on getting some sleep. In a few short hours, I would lay it all out there. Ellie might accept, or she might not.

But I at least had to try.

CHAPTER 18
ELLIE

"All I'm saying, Izzy-"

"Dad, you know I'm not going to listen to a word you say when you keep calling me by that nickname." I shuffled some papers on my desk, throwing my annoyance into cleaning up my office. Dad had come in extra early this morning, catching me by surprise. He parked himself in my corner chair with the plants and spent the last half hour trying to convince me to give Zach another chance.

"Fine, Isabelle, Ellie, whatever you want me to call you. All I'm saying is, no one gets you more than Zach—you guys grew up together. There's a lot of history there. You shouldn't just throw it all away."

"Dad, I'm not throwing it away. We're not

teenagers anymore, and we want different things. I like Zach as a friend, but I'm not interested in dating him anymore. Done. Final. Can we please move on?"

"I'm not done, Izz-abelle. I know you're on a mission to take over Aspen Ridge, but this just isn't a job you can do on your own. You need someone at your side-"

"Dad, I have all the VPs, the managers, the entire team you've built here. I don't need to have a boyfriend in the wings to tell me how to do my job. Besides, Zach has his own resort to run. He has no interest in being a househusband."

"All the better," he insisted. "You and Zach would have each other to bounce ideas off of, compare notes, help each other. He's an excellent match for you, Isabelle. He's always been good for your temperament."

My teeth ground together as I bit back what I was tempted to say. I didn't want to, but I was dangerously close to telling my dad the truth about Zach, not to mention Brian. If he knew what they had planned, it would kill him; their friendship would never recover.

"It's not going to happen, Dad. Can we please just let this drop?"

"I just don't want you to spend the rest of your life alone, honey. This resort is important, but it can't be your entire life."

After all of his insisting that I had to focus and

really be serious about taking over as CEO, this felt a bit rich. "It's not, Dad. I have a life, and I kind of resent the implication that you think I don't."

"I didn't say that, honey, but going out to brunch and drinking with Tessa is hardly a life. And you won't meet someone if you never step foot off of property, either. At least not anyone that'll make a suitable partner for you."

At least there we agreed. Jake and I had everything to make a run of it, but I couldn't be what he wanted. My priority was this resort. If that meant I would never find a man who wanted to be with me long term, then I'd accept that.

I still didn't buy it yet, though. There had to be someone out there who wanted a *partner*, not just a wife.

"I'm sure I'll find someone, Dad. It's really not your business."

"But it is my business, that's what I'm saying. *This* business depends on you to have a sound foundation. Without that, everything could fall apart. And Zach-"

"Zach wants to take us over, completely," I finally spit it out, and relief washed through my body as I unloaded. "He doesn't want to be my partner, or my support, Dad. Zach told me his plans over a year ago; that's why we broke up for the last time."

"What? I don't understand."

"Zach had it all planned out; he wanted to

absorb Aspen Ridge under a 'portfolio' of resorts, under the Snowshoe Ridge brand. He wanted me to let him take over, become his good little wife who's at home baking pies while he's out on the golf course, making deals with his board of investors, just like his dad. He doesn't want me anywhere *near* the CEO office of Aspen Ridge, Dad. He wants to turn us into a subsidiary of them."

My dad's eyes grew wide with shock when I started speaking, then narrowed in anger. "You can't be serious. He should know better than to think we'd just roll over and let him take over. His father-"

"His father helped him craft up this plan, Dad." I sighed, suddenly bone-weary. Sharing the secret that had been weighing me down for a year should have been a relief, but now I just felt worn out. "They probably started planning it back when we were in high school, if you can believe Tessa. She thinks it's what they've always been after."

"I can't believe it." He whipped out his phone. "I'm going to call Brian right this instant. If he thinks-"

"Dad, it's not a problem. I've already told him no a dozen times. But that's why I'm never getting back together with him; do you understand now? We want different things, see things a different way. I'm never going to allow Aspen Ridge to fall under his conglomerate, and he's never going to be satisfied with just allowing me to run it as I see fit. His ambition is as tall as the Rockies, and I can't imagine being with someone who can't be happy for one minute with what he has. There's just no bringing us to the same table."

Sudden motion brought my gaze from my father's angry face to the doorway, where Jake appeared. Not in the polo or a button-down, but the full suit like his first week at Aspen Ridge that made my jaw drop. His face was cleanly shaved, not a hair out of place on his head, but his cheeks were flushed, his eyes determined. As soon as they met my gaze, they locked in place, and he stepped right up to my desk. My heart started racing before a single word left his lips.

"Ellie, I'm so sorry. I don't know what I was thinking. It was fucking stupid of me to say that you couldn't be the CEO of Aspen Ridge and have us too."

"Jake-" I tried to interrupt him, since he clearly didn't see my dad in the corner with the shrubbery.

However, he was determined to get it off his chest. "I know. It was more than stupid. It was misogynist and wrong and idiotic, and I'm really sorry. I knew I owed my kids a father who would be there for them, the way I hadn't been for their entire lives. I was worried I'd never develop the relationship I wanted with them.

"So I moved them here, thinking a new place, a new job, would help. I wanted to be close to family, really attempt to be the dad who was home for every dinner, who took them to festivals in town, did stuff they were interested in on the weekends."

My dad was sitting stock still in the corner chair, listening intently to every word. Even though my eyes darted over to him several times, Jake never looked away from my face. I felt torn between wanting to lose myself in this epic apology and end it quickly so I could get my dad out of here before Jake went too far.

"And I need this job—there's nothing else for me here, and without it we'll have to move again. So I was determined to keep my hands to myself and do whatever was needed to make this work. Including staying as far as I could from you, despite how I felt after that first night. Despite how I've felt every time I've kissed you, or how often I think about you in my bed."

I could see the color creeping up my dad's neck despite the potted palms, and my entire face had grown painfully hot. Even so, Jake wasn't ready to stop.

"But it just didn't work; everything about you is so right for me. And my kids—my god, they love you. You are the single-best thing that has ever happened to me, as far as they're concerned. I didn't even tell them what happened yesterday. I was too embarrassed to face their disappointment. I know Olivia would have laid into me and demanded I apologize," he chuckled, "and then I realized she would have been right.

"Because I do owe you an apology. Because... I love you, Ellie."

My heart lurched in surprise, moisture prickling at my eyes.

"I know it's terrible timing. I know there's a thousand reasons this is a terrible idea. I know your father won't approve, and I know I don't fit into your world of golf tournaments and fancy charity dinners. But I love you all the same.

"I love how you live your life fully, how you're genuinely, unapologetically you. I love how you haven't ever met a stranger, just a friend you don't know yet. I love how your head tips back when you laugh at my terrible attempts at humor, like you actually think I'm funny. I love how my kids are practically ready to tattoo your name on their arms; they really think the world of you.

"But most of all, I love how you make me feel. I made my entire life about the military. I didn't know who I was without duty and sacrifice. I lost myself completely in it. It was my entire identity. But you brought out a side of me that had been asleep for a long time. Because underneath the stuffed shirt was a guy who just wanted to be loved for the dork that he was, and you made me feel like you could love me, ironed polos and all.

"I know I fucked up. I know I'm an idiot who

pushed you away right when you were ready to open up to me, who judged you for wanting different things than I thought you should.

"But if you give me the chance, I promise I want to be the partner you need. You may have to teach me—I'm not above admitting I don't know how to be the supporting spouse—but for you, I'd happily give it a try. I don't care how many times I get it wrong, as long as you let me try again. Because you're perfect, just the way you are, and you're worth it."

The tears were already running down my cheeks, and I was too entranced to do anything about it. I hadn't glanced again at my father since Jake said he loved me. I was lost in his gaze completely, in the way sincerity burned in his eyes with every word he spoke, striking me in the heart over and over again.

It was so much to take in, but my heart was full to bursting with the need to respond. I stood on shaky legs. "Jake, I-"

My dad cleared his throat in the corner, and I saw the horror slide down Jake's face as his jaw went slack. Like a slow motion scene in a movie, he turned to look over his shoulder and finally saw my dad, sitting in the corner chair, his neck and face an alarming shade of crimson.

Immediately, Jake's posture stiffened, his entire body turning toward my dad with his hands folded over each other behind his back. "Sir, if you allow me to explain-" he began, but Dad cut him off, rising to his feet.

"Do you mean to tell me that this entire time, when you were supposed to be preparing her for leadership, you've been having an *affair* with my *daughter*?" His voice was dangerously low, threatening in the absolute calm manner with which he delivered his words.

"I wouldn't call it an affair, sir, as neither of us was in a relationship," Jake replied stiffly. "But we have been seeing each other."

"It's my fault, Dad," I spoke up, and his piercing gaze whipped to me. "Jake and I met at the end of season party, and he didn't know who I was. We sort of... hit it off, and he didn't know I was your daughter until we both came in on Monday."

Dad's eyes grew round with surprise. "You mean to tell me you've been lying to me this entire time?"

"Not exactly," I rushed to explain. "Once we found out, we kept it strictly professional. For a while. But then we started growing closer. I thought we could just hold off until he went to work for James, so you wouldn't have to worry about us working together. But," my voice softened, and my gaze strayed to Jake's profile. He continued to stare stiffly forward, his entire body rigid. "We couldn't help it, Dad. I met his kids, and they're wonderful. But Jake is so good for me. He feels... right. We fell in love."

Upon hearing that word, Jake lost all composure and turned to face me again, his eyes shining. "Really?" He whispered, as if afraid to ask the question out loud.

I nodded. "Really. I love you too, Jake. And I love Olivia and Ethan. They're amazing kids. Probably because they have such an amazing father. And if you meant what you said, about being willing to support me and what I need to do here, I think we have the start of a great thing."

"I meant every word," he said the words with reverence, like a prayer spoken at an altar. "I'll do whatever it takes, Ellie, to prove it to you. Whatever you need, I can be it."

A fresh wave of tears trickled down my cheeks.

My dad cleared his throat again, and our attention snapped back to him. "This is... certainly a lot to wrap my head around," he began. "I don't know how to feel about all of this secrecy. But, if my baby girl is happy," his gaze drifted to me, and that's when I noticed the softening of his expression. "All I've ever wanted was for you to be happy and cared for, Izzy. I thought Zach was the one to do that, but clearly I was mistaken. And Jake is a good man. I've always liked him. Maybe I don't like that he was running around behind my back with my daughter, but I understand the situation was... difficult."

His gaze returned to Jake, his expression hardening. "So, if you meant everything you said, you two have my blessing. We'll have to proceed with your transfer to Mountain Ops, since Ellie knows how I feel about people dating in-house. But I think you've done what I asked you here to do. So I see no reason to make things more difficult."

"I meant every word, Sir," Jake replied in a clear voice.

"Good," Dad replied firmly, then cracked a smile. "And stop calling me Sir, for chrissakes. It's JJ, son." He pulled Jake in for a hug and gave him a firm pat on the back. "Now breathe before we have to call you an ambulance. They take ten minutes to get here. You'll be dead before they arrive."

That made Jake laugh, and a smile spread across my cheeks.

"Now, I'm going back to my office before I get hit with one more bombshell today. I don't know if my heart can take it. Why don't you two go take a long coffee break, sort your stuff out—somewhere off-property, if you don't mind? Just come back before lunch. We've got a lot on the schedule today."

"I thought you wanted me in the board meeting today, Dad?"

"Bah, don't worry about it. You've got a lifetime of board meetings to attend, Ellie. I can handle one more on my own."

I stepped around my desk and pulled him into a hug. "Thanks, Dad. I love you."

I knew his emotions were getting the better of

him, because he cleared his throat several times and his voice got rough while he patted me awkwardly on the back. "I love you too, Isabelle. Now go on, I'll see you later."

I gave him one last smile before I grabbed my purse, slipped my hand into Jake's, and tugged him out of my office.

EPILOGUE

JAKE

"Okay, say cheese!" I held up my phone and waited.

"Cheeeeeeeeeeeeeeeeese!" The kids dutifully plastered on fake grins and repeated the phrase, posing oddly as if they were in pain.

I snapped a few photos, then decided that was the best I'd get and waved them loose. As if we shot them from a cannon, they streaked down the walkway, turning to yell at my parents to hurry.

"I'm coming, Ethan, just take it easy," my dad huffed as he descended the porch stairs on stiff legs.

"There'll still be plenty of candy to go around. Folks here go all out."

Ethan had already pulled his red and white mask over his face, so his reply was muffled.

Olivia was just as impatient, but she dealt with it better, twirling and waving her glowing scepter around as she waited for my mom to catch up.

"I like your costume, Jake." Mom beamed in my direction.

Olivia stared at me skeptically, pushing her blonde wig back to see better. "That's a costume? It doesn't look like a costume to me."

"It's from one of Gramma's favorite movies, Livvie. You haven't seen it. It's a grown up movie."

Olivia shrugged and claimed Mom's hand, tugging her after Ethan and my Dad who were already halfway to the next house.

"Hey, you don't happen to have any watermelons, do you?" Ellie's voice called out from behind me, and the smile spread across my cheeks before I even turned around.

"Sorry, fresh out. But if it's alright with you, I'm happy to escort you to the party." I turned, and my breath caught the second my eyes landed on her. She had the look nailed, right down to the baby pink dress and shoulder-length wig.

I let out a low whistle. "Well, aren't you a sight for sore eyes, beautiful?"

"I could say the same thing." Her eyes trailed over my body. "I don't think I've ever seen you in a leather jacket before."

I struck a pose. "Oh yeah, it's new. You like it?"

She strode right up to me and ran her hand up my chest. "Oh yeah. It's a good look, Captain Wright." The low sensual turn her voice took sent a lick of heat up my spine.

"Now, now, Baby, you need to behave yourself. There are children present." I gathered her hands and brought them to my lips. "Come on, I promised we'd watch them trick-or-treat for a bit before we left."

Ellie slid her fingers through mine and we walked up the sidewalk hand-in-hand. Ethan and Olivia had already finished with the neighbors and were streaking down the sidewalk with their first candy of the night when they spotted us.

Ethan paused, his head tilting to the side, and he pulled up his mask to be heard. "Ellie, what happened to your hair? Why aren't you guys dressed up? It's Halloweeeeeeeen!"

Ellie and I glanced at each other and chuckled. Obviously, the adult version of 'dressed up' and the kid version were quite different. If you weren't in a rayon costume replica of a princess or a superhero, you simply weren't dressed up in Ethan's world.

"Eh, I didn't feel like it," Ellie replied. "I just

wanted to see you guys have fun. Go on, we're coming!"

Ethan pulled his mask back down and tore off after his sister, who had only waved at Ellie before trying to get ahead of her brother. We trailed behind my parents, dutifully congratulating the kids on every conquest, while my mom glanced our way more than once with starry eyes.

Finally, we said our goodbyes and headed back to the house and our cars, driving them both over to my place before Ellie climbed in with me. Ethan and Olivia were staying with my parents tonight, so we'd have the place to ourselves.

After the night's festivities.

The Aspen Ridge Halloween party was an annual celebration for the resort; the last big employee appreciation event before they had to buckle down and get ready for winter. Ellie's family and their co-owners, the Blackwells, sponsored extravagant prizes for a costume contest that had become legendary. We'd spent the better part of two days decorating the event space along with Reece, Stella, James, and even Tessa at times. And, as always, I was so impressed with how much effort Ellie put into these events. She thought out every detail, made sure everything was perfect, for no other reason than that she cared.

It was just Ellie—she was always trying to

surprise and delight everyone, make them feel special.

Little did she know, I had my own surprise up my sleeve.

The party was an absolute success, of course. The costume contest took ages. There were so many people who had gone all out it was difficult to choose winners. Fortunately, Ellie had a variety of categories, so there wasn't just one winner—which was also very Ellie—and the resort was incredibly generous. Season passes, weekend stays in expensive condos, spa packages, even cash prizes. Everyone had a great time, and Ellie was absolutely glowing with happiness.

My heart beat like a drum, growing louder and louder as we worked through the contest. After she gave out the last prize, it was show time.

I darted up the stairs onto the stage before she could start her 'thank you' speech and wrapped my arms around her shoulders. I slipped the microphone from her hand. She looked confused, a little embarrassed, but she smiled at me all the same.

My hand trembled when I lifted the mic to my lips. "Hey guys, thanks so much for being here. I just want to take a moment to give props to this amazing woman. She's the reason for all of this, for every outstanding thing Aspen Ridge does for all of us. If you've had a great time tonight, make some noise for Ellie!"

The response of the crowd was deafening, and Ellie ducked her head for just a second before she looked up and waved back at them, blowing kisses.

It took a moment for the noise to die down again, and I waited... she deserved to hear every cheer of appreciation they wanted to give her.

When the wave of sound was over, I lifted the mic again. "Now, I know this isn't how it's usually done, but I have a little surprise of my own. So James, hit it!" I ran to the side and handed off the mic to Tessa, who shot me a thumbs up, just as the lights dimmed.

When I took my place beside Ellie, the first notes of the song began, and Ellie burst out laughing. A few whoops sounded from the crowd, apparently the three people who had seen the movie and under-stood what was going on.

"You didn't!" She grinned up at me in surprise.

"Oh yeah, I did. Now shhh, this is supposed to be serious."

"Jake, you don't really expect me to do the dance, do you? We've never practiced."

"Eh, who cares? None of them have even seen the movie, anyway. Let's just have fun."

The lights came on as the tempo picked up, and the crowd started cheering.

We had no idea what we were doing; clearly Ellie and I needed some serious dancing lessons.

But we made our way through. I even picked her up and twirled her once or twice, and we laughed our asses off the entire time. The crowd lost their minds, applauding us. It was everything I could have asked for. I didn't attempt the lift, of course, but I don't think Ellie minded.

It was goofy, and ridiculous, and hopefully video of that moment would never see the light of day.

But for me, there was nothing better than sharing it with Ellie. I'd done a lot of things in my life, some dangerous, some wild. But nothing had ever made me feel as alive as I did just holding Ellie's hand. It was as if there was a door she unlocked that I never realized was closed before me. And now, with Ellie by my side, I could see nothing but open doors for the rest of my life.

THE END

WOULD you like a sneak peek into Jake and Ellie's future?

Go to SashaPierceAuthor.com/thewronggirl to join Sasha's newsletter and receive your free download!

If you're ready to jump into the next story in Aspen Ridge, get The Wrong Place by Sasha Pierce.

Read on to get a preview of The Wrong Place.

THE WRONG PLACE - CHAPTER 1

STELLA

Tiny crystals of ice beat at my face relentlessly as I raced down the powdery slope, but I hardly felt them. Strapped into my board, music in my ears, and all of my focus on the obstacles in my path—there was nowhere else I felt this alive. And much to my parents' chagrin, there was nothing that held my focus in this way. I did alright in school, but I wasn't the straight-A student my brother was. My parents always complained that I just didn't apply myself, and they were right. I didn't *care* about grades... they had no bearing on the future I chose. The only thing I'd experienced in my life that felt right, that felt like I was *exactly* where I was meant to be, was on a snowboard. Raised in a family that owned a ski resort, I was literally born to be on the slopes. Out here, no one could stop me; it was like I had wings. I *flew*.

Even with the frosty air, I was sweating under all of my layers. Snowboarding was deceptively physical—even though it looks smooth and effortless to the casual observer, it requires constant control of the muscles and awareness of your surroundings. I was an athlete, and I trained like one. Blood sang through my veins as I prepared for the approaching jump, crouching down only to spring up at the right moment to catch air. I had just enough time to execute a perfect tail grab before I straightened my legs, taking the impact with my right leg before easing down on my leading edge. Perfect.

As I merged with the traffic on the lower black diamond, I eased off the speed and stretched my complaining quads, switching to my heel edge and coasting through the flat spot where other winter sports enthusiasts were dismounting the chair lift. And even though my legs were already aching, I turned my board to the trail on the right instead of the easier route to the left. I'd promised to meet my dad for lunch in town, so this was my last run for a couple of hours. Might as well make it count.

When I tipped over the edge, I picked up speed, heading straight for the patch of moguls, where a few skiers were carefully picking their way through the mini hills of snow. Moguls aren't for the faint of heart, but they're especially challenging for a snow-boarder—you have to make a series of sharp turns to navigate in the valleys between them, and it's easy to catch an edge and fly asshole over elbows the rest of the way down.

My eyes remained trained on the path in front of me, my body twisting as I navigated heel-toe-heel-toe-heel-toe. I carved through the moguls like a hot knife through butter. When I was nearly through, a body that was tumbling instead of carving flew down the hill to my right, forcing me to turn and break my speed. My music was so loud I didn't hear him coming, but that was kind of the point. Hearing people coming up behind me was distracting, so music helped me block them all out and focus.

I finished the moguls and drew a deep breath, then steered myself toward the person who had such a bumpy ride down the hill that he still hadn't moved. His board was strapped to his feet, and fortunately, he wore a helmet. However, he was also spread eagle on his back and I couldn't tell if he was conscious or not.

Dropping to my knees next to him, I yanked my ear buds out and shoved them in a pocket. This close, I could tell he was young, maybe twelve or thirteen.

"Hey bud, you okay?" His head turned slightly

my way and his jaw worked even though no sound came out, so he was at least conscious.

The boy drew in a slow, creaky breath, stretching his jaw wide like he was struggling to get more air in his lungs. The metallic flash of braces shone on his teeth, but I didn't spot any blood.

"That's good. Just focus on breathing. Looks like you hit hard enough to knock the air from your lungs... it hurts like hell, I know. Just keep working on in-out slowly, okay? I'm going to check to see if you did any major damage." I felt carefully along his arms and legs, paying close attention to his reaction. His breath was coming more regularly, and he didn't jerk away in pain when I touched him, so he appeared to be intact.

"Can you lift an arm for me?" The boy did as requested. "Great, now the other one." Once he obliged again, I instructed, "Okay, now I want you to move your board a bit so we know your legs are working. Just bend and flex to wiggle your toe edge." His board moved accordingly. "Excellent. Now I want to get a look at your eyes. Can you lift your goggles for me?" I demonstrated, sliding mine onto my helmet above my eyes. The boy reached up slowly and did the same, and when his gaze landed on my face, his brown eyes grew as big as saucers.

"Oh shit, you're Stella Blackwell!" His voice cracked when he spoke, but it was still deafeningly loud. Clearly, he was breathing fine now.

"Busted," I grinned. "What's your name?"

"Dylan. Man, my friends are NOT going to believe this! Can I get a picture with you?" His cheeks had been pale a moment ago, but now they were fiery red.

"Well, let's focus on sitting up first, Dylan. Sound good?"

He nodded and pushed himself into a sitting position.

"How do you feel?"

"Super embarrassed I wiped out in front of Stella-freaking-Blackwell," he admitted, his blush deepening.

"Well, don't worry about it. I used to wipe out all the time. Still do occasionally," I added with a wink. "But what I meant was, how does your head feel?"

"Oh, I'm fine," he answered quickly. "But seriously, there's no way my friends will *believe* I met you. I told them all I was going to Aspen Ridge for our family ski trip and I was going to see you—everyone knows you're getting ready for the trials here—and they all told me that was stupid and there was no *way* you'd be on the regular slopes with everyone else. But you are!" Dylan whipped off his gloves and dug into his jacket pocket. "Please, one photo? They won't believe it otherwise. I promise I'm your biggest fan! See?" He showed me the background on his phone, which was a glamorous shot from a campaign I did for Branton Snowboards last year.

Now it was my turn to blush. How could I say no? "I'm very flattered. Come on, let's get you up. You don't want to take a photo on the ground, do you?"

"Yes!" He crowed before a horrified look crossed his face. "I mean, no, I don't want the photo on the ground. Hold on." He popped up on his board and brushed the snow from his clothes, grinning maniacally.

Fortunately for Dylan, I'm so short that I barely had a few inches on him, despite being a fully grown adult. I positioned my board just behind his and asked, "May I?" Holding my hand out for the phone.

Dylan was so flustered by this point that he had a hard time unlocking it, but eventually we figured it out and I leaned in close to snap a few photos. The kid was grinning ear to ear, and it was impossible for me to ignore the tiny flame of gratification I felt. Sometimes, I needed to be reminded that there were people in the world who thought I was something special; who traveled here just hoping to get a *glimpse* of me. That I was good enough, and something I was passionate about mattered to other people. That even if my own family didn't, there were lots of other people out there who supported my dreams.

When I had taken a fair number of photos for

Dylan to choose from, I straightened and tried to hand back his phone. But before I had the chance to move away, he whipped his face toward me and planted a fat, sloppy kiss on my cheek.

I froze in absolute shock, staring at Dylan, who gave me an impish grin. Quick as lightning, he tucked away his phone and snatched up his gloves.

"I'm never washing my lips again!" He declared with gleaming eyes before taking off down the mountain at top speed. He waited until he was a few hundred feet away to yell, "I LOVE YOU STELLA!"

That broke me out of my shock with a giggle, but then he added, "I KISSED STELLA BLACKWELL!!" in a shout that echoed across the wide expanse of trail as he sped along toward the bottom.

I should have seen that one coming.

Sighing, I put my earbuds back in and adjusted my goggles. As embarrassing as it was to have a boy in the midst of puberty shouting across the mountain that he'd kissed me—not to mention potential repercussions from the implication that I was some kind of pedophile—his adoration was flattering all the same. Making a mental note to have Andrea, my social media manger, check later to see if Dylan posted anything about it. I caught speed and carved my way down the mountain, trying to hold on to that warm glow as I prepared to meet my dad for a lunch that was sure to be a lot less amusing than an encounter with a hormonal teenage boy.

SEBASTIAN

I CRUISED SLOWLY down Glacier Run, my eyes darting across the swarm of bodies to scan for anyone who might need help. It was the largest green at Aspen Ridge and was always full to bursting with people who could barely remain on their feet. It had taken me a couple of weeks to calm down and stop assuming everyone on the ground was in imminent danger. I was learning to recognize when it was a simple case of 'fell over their own crossed skis' versus 'probably broke something.' A lot of time, as ski patrol, we didn't witness the accident. But usually other people did, and when a large crowd gathered around an individual, it was typically a clue they had a nasty fall.

I paused at the intersection between Glacier and Black Bear to observe for a moment.

It felt odd to be back here. Right, but also wrong somehow. Aspen Ridge was the scene of my popularity as a teen, with a bunch of things like being best friends with Reece Blackwell buoying me up to legendary status; not to mention being homecoming king and having a squad of admirers before I graduated. It wasn't something I'd ever sought out, but I certainly enjoyed the attention at the time.

Now I was back and it felt like a failure, some-how, returning here six years later with very little to show.

While my mind was wandering, Gary, my team lead, pulled up beside me and drew in a deep, satis-fied breath.

"Another day in paradise," he observed mildly.

"Yeah," I agreed, shifting gears. It was a bluebird day, not a cloud in the sky, and the air temperature was almost too warm for so many layers of clothing.

"Are you getting settled in?"

"Yeah, I am. Reece hooked me up with an employee rental, so it's furnished and everything. I can't complain."

Gary scratched at his silver beard with a mitten and turned his knowing ice-blue eyes on me. "I meant adjusting to civilian life, the change of pace compared to the military."

"Oh. Yeah, it's okay. You might be surprised, but the Army wasn't all go-go-go all the time. There was actually a lot of sitting around doing nothing."

He chuckled. "Yeah, I remember that part; it was the same for the Marines. But it's still different in the civilian world. And given everything you went through in six years, I can imagine it's still a change, even if it's a welcome one."

Sweat beaded on the back of my neck, my throat

constricting. My mind short-circuited with flashes of explosions, overturned humvees disappearing into clouds of dust, deafening silence, pools of dark red everywhere... the smell of death filled my senses.

Blinking rapidly, I swallowed and clenched my fists, drawing in a deep breath of fresh mountain air and bringing myself back to the present. "Yeah, it's a change. But at least I can put my medic skills to use here. And it's nice to be home."

Gary's inscrutable eyes didn't miss a thing; he asked me that question on purpose to observe my reaction. While the ski patrol had been happy to welcome me to the team, Gary was the most cautious. It took a while, but I found out he'd retired from the Marines as a Gunny Sergeant. He didn't talk about it, but when he met my eyes, I knew he saw through my composed smile.

It's impossible to hide the truth from someone who's been there.

So I understood his caution now. He was watching for signs I wasn't as well as I claimed to be. Making innocent references to things I tried very hard not to think about. Testing me.

The silence stretched between us as I held his gaze, almost too long, before Gary replied. "Yeah, it's nice to call a place like this home."

"Definitely. I grew up here. It was the first place I thought of when my contract was over."

"Did you work for the resort back then?"

"Nah, I was far more intent on riding the snow than shoveling it back then. I mean, I worked here during the summer, of course, just so I could afford a season pass and some new gear."

"Of course. Are these your old skis?"

"Nah, I gave all of that stuff away before I left. I didn't think I'd be back here for a long time. It was strange to get back on these things, and I wouldn't know what to buy at this point. But Reece has more than he even knows what to do with, so he's letting me borrow some so I can figure out what I want for next season."

I flashed him my widest grin, but Gary still hadn't cracked a smile. He continued observing me with his shrewd 'ancient warrior' expression.

When he still didn't speak, I felt obliged to continue the conversation. "It seems like a good season so far."

Gary nodded slowly. "The snow has been good. Not too many major emergencies, and only a couple of snowstorms bad enough to shut us down for a day. Which reminds me, it looks like we have another coming in tomorrow afternoon. If it's as bad as they're saying, we'll have to shut down early and likely remain closed for a day or two. Are you feeling confident enough to hit the bowls tomorrow?"

I nodded. "Yeah, I'm pretty solid. I hit a few of the double blacks today and it was smooth. I haven't gotten into much deep powder though."

Gary sniffed. "Alright. I want you to run the bowls tomorrow morning, get a feel for them. I'll probably send you to do a sweep if we have to shut down early, make sure the mountain is clear before we close the lifts."

"I can do that, but why me?"

That drew a twitch of a smile from Gary's lips. "I dunno if you've noticed, kid, but you're at least two decades younger than most of the patrollers this year. Some of us aren't as springy or bendy as we used to be. Besides, anyone you find back there will probably be closer to your age than mine, and I don't feel like taking lip from snowboarding punks when I'm trying to look out for their safety. You can handle it, right?"

"Sure thing, not a problem."

"Good. We'll talk more about it in the morning meeting. For now, why don't you go over to Peak 8 and check in with Jeremy, see where he needs some help."

"Yes, sir."

"Bah, don't call me sir, kid. I work for a living."

"You got it, Gary." I pushed off and meandered slowly toward the lift before he could say anything else. Everyone in the military knew better than to call an enlisted Marine 'sir', and I'd done it just to annoy him. I was growing tired of feeling like a bomb he was waiting to go off.

Sure, I went through some shit I didn't want to

talk about with anyone, let alone an all-too-knowing retired Marine with wary eyes.

But I was fine. Some things just weren't worth dredging up repeatedly.

It was far better to let sleeping dogs lie.

Need to keep reading?
Dive into Stella and Sebastian's story with The Wrong Place!

ABOUT THE AUTHOR

*S*asha Pierce is a long-time fan of romance and adventure. She's traveled the world, and currently resides in the shadow of the Great Smoky Mountains with her daughter Tessa.

Aspen Ridge is based on one of Sasha's favorite places in the world, Breckenridge, Colorado.

COMING SOON

Aspen Ridge is a series of interconnected standalone that feature multiple relationships in the same breathtaking ski resort town. Expect at least three more novels set in Aspen Ridge with characters you already know and love. **The Wrong Place** is out now, and **The Wrong Nanny** is coming February 2025.

Join Sasha's newsletter at

sashapierceauthor.com/newsletter

to be the first to know more!